David Sperry is a pilot and ins
Honolulu. He and his family l
book, David has written several articles for aviation magazines and newspapers. He spends his scant free time enjoying life with his family, bicycling, and hiking the great outdoors.

THE POUAKAI

BY

DAVID SPERRY

Enjoy

The Pouakai

ISBN-13: 978-0-9923654-8-6

V1.0

IFWG Publishing
Melbourne, Australia
www.ifwgpublishing.com

To Lana, for her infinite patience and love, and to Suzanne, for teaching me the joy of words.

PART 1
NANUMEA

2.30PM

Outside the cockpit window, the cobalt blue Pacific Ocean sparkled, a mere seven miles below me. An endless series of swells pushed up by storms over the deserted islands of Kiribati, a hundred miles to our west, were etched with whitecaps like ribbons of fine lace. It gave the impression that the world was still normal.

I scanned the instrument panel of the worn Boeing 767 I was shepherding through the sky. So far, everything had held together. Our escorts, a pair of F-22 fighter jets and their KC-10 tanker, flew in formation a few miles on either side of us.

Brett Haldeman snored quietly in the co-pilot seat. His newborn baby girl had kept him up late last night, and the gentle rush of air around the cockpit lulled him to sleep shortly after takeoff. Relief pilot Jeff Lee sat on the jumpseat behind me, deep into a book of crosswords. He'd shown up for the flight bright-eyed and ready to go, even after being out clubbing until late last night. He'd been relaxed and dependable on my flights, so I didn't worry about him. Neither of them appeared bothered by the risks of this trip, but I was. I guess worry is the domain of the Captain, but I couldn't relax until we'd landed in Sydney. That would just be a temporary pause in the risk. We would fly home to Honolulu after a two-day layover.

I should have felt lucky. Most of my co-workers at the airline had been laid off when the tattered remains of the industry were nationalized. I should have been appreciative that my seniority and military background allowed me to keep this job, that I could still make a living as a pilot. The horrors of the past three years prevented me from feeling any gratitude, however. I was glad I could still fly for a living, yet I felt guilty that I was here, while so many friends were barely scraping by on government handouts. I couldn't find a way to enjoy the job.

6.45PM

The island's Chief picked his way across the sandy floor toward me, through the mass of people crammed into the shelter. An old pair of shorts and a deeply stained T-shirt were all he wore. He stopped in front of me, wiping a few beads of sweat from the dark brown skin of his forehead.

"Your friend is gone," he said quietly.

I nodded.

"You want this?" He handed me a dark rectangle; Brett's wallet. I stared at it for a moment, and then took it.

"Thanks."

"Your arm, better?"

It hurt, but the worst of the immediate post-crash pain was gone. "Yeah, I think so. Thanks."

The Chief nodded. "It was dislocated, but will heal."

"You've had medical training?"

He swept an arm toward the crowd around us in the decrepit Quonset hut. "No more than any of us. You learn survival skills when you live in place like this."

The shelter overflowed with several times the number of people it was designed to hold. Many of my crew and passengers had some sort of injury, major or minor. The salty, earthy smell of the shelter competed with the odor of broken and battered bodies packed inside. Lit with a few dim coconut-oil lamps, it gave me a twinge of claustrophobia. A handful of locals scurried about, tending to the most seriously wounded.

"We were really surprised to find you here," I said, "but we're grateful."

A smile crossed his weather-worn face.

"No more surprised than we were to have you drop in on us, Captain."

His smile faded, and he settled on the ground next to me, cross-legged. He extended a hand. "I am Chief Kalahamotu."

"Mark Boone." I returned the handshake. "Everyone calls me Boonie." I coughed. Pain shot down my ribs.

The chief waited for my coughing to subside. Then he asked quietly, "What is happening in the world, Captain Boonie?"

"How much do you know?"

"Our radio failed two and a half years ago. We have heard nothing since."

I closed my eyes and let out a long breath. Two and a half years. How would I tell him what had happened during that time? How would I describe the violence, death, and despair? And how would I explain that the entire world thought the Chief, and everyone like him, was dead?

2.35PM

"Palm Tree fifty-five, Hoku one," came the voice over the speaker from the lead escort fighter.

"This is Palm Tree fifty-five, go ahead," I said.

"We are moving to the tanker for refueling."

"Roger, we'll be watching."

I didn't envy those pilots, strapped into their fighters, with no room to stretch or stand up, for the ten-plus hours to Sydney.

The timing of this refueling sucked too. The weapons control radar on the number two fighter had died a couple of hours out of Honolulu, leaving just the lead ship with an operating unit. Radar was ineffective when they were hooked up to the tanker, leaving us blind. We had just crossed the equator, putting us right into the heart of the Roc's territory. It wouldn't take long to top off the fighters, but I'd feel better once they were full of fuel and back on station, sweeping the sky ahead of us for danger.

6.50pm

"We still don't know where the Rocs came from," I told the Chief. "The first reports came from Vanuatu, three years ago."

He nodded. "I heard from my cousin in Port Vila after they arrived that those things were dangerous but not deadly."

"That's true, until the Rocs started multiplying, and attacking in swarms."

"They came here later that year," His voice was barely above a whisper. "We did not know what to expect, but they came. Our cargo ship was sunk leaving Funafuti. After that, no more ships. A month later our generator ran out of fuel, and then the batteries died. We had no radio, no contact. We have not heard anything since."

I shook my head and took a deep breath. "They spread along the equator. From the central Pacific they moved east until they hit South America. They migrated westward too, around Indonesia, into the Indian Ocean and up against Africa. Experts thought that the Atlantic would remain clear, but they slowly worked northward until they got to the Red Sea. The UN, NATO, the US and Russia, China; we tried everything imaginable to stop them. The Sinai is a radioactive wasteland now, but it didn't help. They still kept coming. A year ago they made it into the Mediterranean, and from there they spread into the Atlantic. They hit the Caribbean and the Panama Canal six months ago, and joined up with the ones on the Pacific side. They're all the way around the world now."

"They're everywhere?" the Chief asked.

"In the equatorial oceans, yes. When they fly, they don't go more than ten miles inland, and the latest reports suggest that their range is increasing into cooler waters."

"When will they stop?"

"We don't know. They've encircled the Earth, and it's like a noose tightening to the point of strangling."

2.40PM

Jennifer had begged me not to do these trips, but I couldn't bring myself to stop. Fly north, she'd sobbed, fly to the mainland. Anywhere but across the equator. The money was too good though, and flying was the only thing I'd wanted to do as long as I could remember. I couldn't let those damn things stop me. For all the efforts of scientists and the military however, there didn't seem to be any way to stop the Rocs' spread.

I watched the tanker and fighters flying in formation, two miles to our left. The lead fighter was hooked up to the tanker, drinking in the precious fuel. I'd done that too, in the Air National Guard, before moving to the airlines. It's impossible to describe the joy of flying a machine like that, or even this worn-out airliner, to someone who didn't have a passion for flying. To be able to move so effortlessly through three dimensions, or to soar across oceans and time zones with ease and security; that was what I loved. Flying's ease and security had vanished when the Rocs showed up.

I ran my fingers through my hair, and glanced at the reflection in the sun visor. Too damn much gray up there, and just in the last few years too. I'd gone from a few strands to salt and pepper seemingly overnight. More salt than pepper now, really.

Maybe Jennifer was right. Maybe I should be thinking about moving on. I'd just turned fifty, but I'd been feeling a lot older lately. Josh and Kelly were both in college on the mainland. Even though the Rocs hadn't made it that far north yet, the economy of Hawaii had tanked because everyone was leaving. Nobody talked about them much in public, but it was assumed the Rocs would make it there eventually.

We could move far away from the ocean, Jen had suggested again last week, perhaps Colorado. They wouldn't get us there, she'd said, tears streaming down her face. If we did move, I would have to quit my job. With record unemployment, I probably wouldn't be working again. Especially not as a pilot. In a few years though, it really wouldn't matter where we were living. The world economy was listing like the Titanic, and it seemed that nothing could stop it from sinking. What lay beyond that was too scary to think about.

I glanced down at the nav screen. We were crossing five degrees south latitude. Another waypoint was coming up, and I had to make a position report. I brought up the data from the flight management computer, wrote it on the worksheet, and put on the headset to make the call. Just before I keyed the mike, I noticed a smudge above the horizon in front of us; a thin, grayish cloud that didn't match the sprinkling of cumulus buildups in the area. There were more of the same gray blobs below it, and off to our right too. Then the cloud moved slowly, shifting shape, and a knot tightened in my stomach. I couldn't see the individual dots in the cloud yet, but I knew what it was.

"Oh shit," I said, and took a deep breath. "Here we go."

6.55PM

"What else do you know about them?" the Chief asked. "What are they?"

"The latest guess is that the Rocs may be extraterrestrial," I replied.

The Chief frowned and shook his head. "Sorry, my English is not good. Extra, what?"

"It means they came from someplace other than Earth. From space."

The Chief looked at me, his expression unchanged. After several seconds, I added, "From the stars."

Both of the Chief's eyebrows rose slowly. He stood up and left without saying a word. I watched him go, and then shifted in my improvised seat to keep an eye on the survivors being tended to across the shelter. It seemed we'd been lucky, losing only five, but one of those had been Brett. I thumbed through his wallet and stopped when I came to a picture of his family. The snapshot had him holding his baby girl, with a big silly grin on his face. Looking at the photo, the brutal truth of his death hit hard. Pain welled up inside of me, and before I knew it, tears rolled down my cheeks.

2.45PM

"Hoku one, we've got trouble!" I said over the radio.

The fighter detached from the tanker and rolled left.

"Got 'em on the screen," he replied. The second fighter followed, and the tanker made a hard turn away from us, to separate the targets for the Rocs.

"Hoku, this is Reach," the tanker pilot said. "We've got trouble behind us too."

Dammit. There were Rocs behind us as well. Were they that intelligent, and able to plan a coordinated attack? It hadn't happened before, but maybe they were learning. Either that, or we'd just flown into the biggest flock of them ever seen.

"Jesus, that's a lot of them," said the second fighter pilot.

"Keep going forward," said the lead fighter pilot. "The ones behind us won't catch us unless we turn around. Reach, Palm Tree, stay close behind. We'll cut a trail for you."

The tanker rolled toward us, and pulled up in close formation alongside my plane. The fighters moved directly in front of us, ready to shoot their way through the gathering cloud. I still couldn't see the individual Rocs, but the cloud seemed to coalesce and darken ahead as the things moved into our path.

"How far?" I asked over the radio.

"Twenty two miles. Contact in just over three minutes. We'll wait until we're almost on them before we launch the missiles. Both of you guys stay close behind us."

"Roger," the tanker pilot replied.

"Roger," I echoed.

Brett and Jeff cleaned up around their seats, and strapped in. I made a short PA to the sixty passengers on the other side of the cockpit door, and gave them a rundown of the situation. I told everyone to put their baggage back where it belonged and strap in.

We sat in tense silence as the seconds ticked away. The plane couldn't fly much higher, and if we tried to descend, the Rocs could dive straight down and lose altitude more quickly than we could. Our only option was to go through them. If the fighters could clear a path for us, we'd be fine. As horrific as they were, the Rocs were still just some sort of animal, and couldn't fly nearly as fast as we could. If they placed themselves in our path and hit us though, the damage would be terrible.

"One minute to contact," the lead fighter said. "Thirty seconds to missiles."

We waited, as the seconds dragged on. The cloud became a mass of black dots, the Rocs gathering directly in our path.

"Fire."

Two streams of white smoke pulled away from the fighters, and seconds later blossomed in a flash of orange flame. As we closed in, the dots resolved into triangles, pin-wheeling toward the sea below.

"Fire," the lead fighter said again, and more missiles leapt ahead of us. Swarms of Rocs died, but they were still thick ahead of us. It was a cloud of them like I'd never seen before.

"Guns, fire."

Tracers leapt ahead of the fighters and still more Rocs fell earthward, but I couldn't see a clear path through the cloud yet. Then there were Rocs on either side of us as we flew through the path cut by the missiles and guns.

"Keep close," the tanker pilot radioed. "We don't want to—"

A sudden crash and scream burst across the radio. A white puff erupted from the nose of the tanker, as the plane wobbled in its flight path.

"We're hit! We're hit! Oh shit, my eyes…"

For the briefest moment I saw two of the elongated black triangles streaking toward the tanker and then a gut-wrenching blast of glass and metal fell back in the slipstream along the fuselage as the cockpit exploded. Shrapnel was sucked into the two wing mounted engines, and they blasted a sheet of flame and smoke out their exhaust. The crippled tanker's nose dropped as it rolled away from us. It made two lumbering spirals before the rudder and wingtips broke off. The tanker disappeared into a cloud, trailing smoke and fire.

"Fire, fire, fire!" the lead fighter ordered. "There's too many of them! Fire everything you've got!"

Multiple streaks launched from both fighters, and orange flame blossomed ahead. The tracers from their guns continued nonstop, trying to tear through the cloud of Rocs.

"Turn! Turn! Evasive—" The lead fighter broke up as several Rocs hit it. An instant later it exploded as the recently refilled fuel tanks came apart. Beyond the orange fireball was blue sky, with just a few more Rocs in our way.

"Keep going!" I shouted. "There's clear air ahead!"

"Roger," said the second fighter pilot.

Two black triangles streaked by, just feet to our left. I held my breath, but nothing happened. Our remaining fighter launched one more missile, and beyond its brief fireball was blue sky, and safety.

Two more black streaks went by on our right. *Slam.* Our airplane slewed violently left and right as the engine blew apart.

"Oh, shit!" said Brett.

The master warning light flashed red, and the alarm sounded. I clicked off the autopilot and the airplane rolled sharply right. I rolled us back level.

"Engine failure, right side," Brett yelled. "Keep the speed up, Boonie. Head downhill."

"You got that right." I wanted to put some distance between us and the Rocs.

I looked ahead and saw the fighter there, still in one piece. I didn't see any more Rocs, except for…

Three black triangles in close formation streaked by my window, and instantly another *slam* echoed through the plane, as we yawed violently.

"Dammit!" Jeff shouted. More red lights popped on, and most of the displays went dark as we lost the last generator.

"Dual engine failure. Run the checklist," I said.

Brett stared at the instruments, as if he couldn't understand what they were telling him.

"Brett! Checklist! Now!"

He grabbed the card and worked the items. I sucked in a deep breath, and tried to think, but the blue of the ocean below us seized my attention. We were going swimming.

7.30PM

The Chief came back to the shelter thirty minutes later. I sat in the same spot, trying to ignore the pain in my shoulder. Orange light from the sunset filtered through the blanket covering the opening to the shelter, casting a ruddy glow over the people inside. From outside came the sounds of wind in the coconut palms, and distant waves breaking over the reef.

"Why are they here? What do they want?" the Chief asked, squatting next to me.

I shook my head. "We really don't know why. We don't know what they eat, how they live, or where they really come from. All we know is that they are here, and they attack anything that moves;

ships, planes, people. Whatever it is, they find a way to destroy it. They run through individual people with the long spear on the front of their bodies. Bigger things they can't stab, like ships, they mass onto until it capsizes. Airplanes, they just fly into."

"They're smart enough to know what to do?"

I shrugged. "I wouldn't call it too smart when they usually die in their attacks, but we just don't know for sure. It's difficult to study them up close. Most scientists that have tried are dead. They've dissected the carcasses of a few dead Rocs, but don't understand what they found. Maybe they're intelligent, maybe not. Either way though, the Rocs have cut off the world's oceans around the equator. We can't ship oil, goods, people, or anything else across the Roc's zone. We don't know how to get around them."

"But you were flying through them, weren't you?"

"We were, but it's dangerous, and not many people do it anymore. We are not an independent company now, but a division of the U.S. government. We get an armed escort. We're more military than civilian now."

"Where were you going?"

"Sydney, Australia. They're hurting even more down there than we are in the northern hemisphere. Famine, drought, power and communications blackouts; Australia's fighting to stay alive. Our flights are among the few contacts the South Pacific has with the rest of the world. That's why we keep doing them."

"Is it enough?"

I shook my head. "Probably not. Within a couple of years, things everywhere will simply fall apart. Some people say it will be the end of civilization. We just can't live with the Rocs here on Earth. Nobody can."

The Chief looked around at the crowd in the shelter. Nearby, one of my passengers moaned quietly, blood seeping from bandages around her arm and legs.

"We do," he said

"Excuse me?"

"We live with them," the Chief reiterated as he stood up. "Stay here. I will be back."

2.50PM

The howl from our damaged engines sounded like a dying animal. We'd left the Rocs behind, but with both engines blown apart, we were gliding toward the ocean below.

"Prepare for ditching," I said. A panicked look crossed Brett's eyes, but he flipped to the appropriate checklist, and started configuring the plane. My heart raced, and I gripped the control wheel with sweaty hands. Damn, damn, damn. Why did this have to happen now? Why didn't I listen to Jennifer?

I reached for the intercom to tell the steward to prep the passengers when something caught my eye. I looked over the glareshield, and my heart skipped a beat. Of course! I'd seen it a hundred times on this route, but hadn't given it any thought until now. Nestled below the scattered cotton ball clouds appeared the verdant green and tan of a small island. Ditching in the open ocean with all these Rocs around meant certain death. If we could get onto that island though…

I made up my mind instantly. "Brett, we're going down there," I said, pointing out the forward window. He looked out and his eyes widened.

"Okay, okay." He nodded rapidly.

I called the back, and told them what to expect.

"Hoku two," I said, calling the remaining fighter. "You still with us?"

"Yes sir."

"We're going down on the island just a few miles ahead. See it?"

"Yes sir."

"You going to join us there?"

"I guess so. I'm low on fuel, and there's nowhere else for me to go. I'll give you cover until you're down, then pop out myself."

"Got it," I said. "Good luck."

We were still at fifteen thousand feet as we crossed over the island. I started a turn to the left to remain over it, and get a good look at where I planned to touch down. It was an atoll, about seven miles long, two miles wide, shaped somewhat like a banana. A narrow lagoon took up the center of the island, with a heavily forested rim around it. When the weather was clear on previous trips, I remembered seeing a small village on the south side of the island. There wouldn't be anyone alive there now.

"I'll come in from the west," I told Brett and Jeff. "If we touch down on the land, the palm trees will rip the shit out of the airplane. I want to touch down on the lagoon, but I'll try to slide up onto the beach so we don't have to swim out of this thing."

They both nodded.

"Are we ready?" I asked.

"I think so," Brett said. "We're configured except for flaps. They'll be slow to extend, so start early. I called oceanic control and told them what happened. They said they'd inform the military, but…"

He didn't have to say more. The Navy wouldn't risk its ships to rescue a handful of survivors. The same went for the Air Force. We were on our own.

7.40PM

I struggled to my feet, leaning on the makeshift crutch they'd given me. The superficial cut on my right foot had been bandaged and when I put a little weight on it, and it seemed okay, so I left the crutch leaning against the corrugated metal wall of the shelter and limped across the room. The sandy floor made the going difficult, but not impossible. I went to our steward, Ken Cochran, who sat tending to one of our passengers.

"How are you doing, Ken?" He looked up, a bandage across his left ear.

"Not bad, I guess." Kenny Sunshine, we sometimes called him; always the optimist. His spiky blonde hair still looked perfect too. That must have been some super-strength hair gel. "Guess I won't be listening to my iPod any time soon," he said with a grin, touching his bandaged ear. "Thanks for the good landing though."

I tried to smile, but it wasn't much. "Sorry it wasn't Sydney."

"Hey, no problem. It's always been a fantasy of mine to be stranded on a tropical island. It really was a good landing too. We're still alive, after all."

I wanted to say 'Most of us are', but couldn't bring myself dampen his spirits. I gave him a pat on the back and straightened up again. Most of the injuries to our passengers were superficial. At least, those inflicted by the crash were.

Next to Ken were two of our passengers, a man and wife, holding each other's hands. I thought about Jennifer, and wondered what she was going through at this moment. She must have been told about our crash by now. Would she have been given any words of encouragement by the airline? Or would they have told her not to hold on to any hope? My heart cried out to her, but she couldn't hear me now. In this day of effortless communication, we were cut off as completely as the ancient Polynesians had been on their long-distance canoe voyages. I felt trapped in the shelter. I needed to get outside and breathe. The confines of this rusty hut had become unbearable.

The blanket over the doorway drifted inwards with the breeze. Outside, the sky had darkened, with a streak of orange resting on the western horizon. I walked toward the door, but was stopped a few feet short by local. Small but muscular, and not much more than a teenager, he wouldn't let me past.

"No go outside," he said.

"I just need some fresh air," I said, trying to keep my voice low.

"No go. Pouakai out there. Wait for Chief."

"Pouakai?"

"The new birds," he explained. "The visitors."

The Rocs.

I couldn't fight my way past this athletic young man, and decided if he was worried about the Rocs, I should be too. What was the Chief doing out there, though? I turned to go back to my spot by the wall just as the Chief came through the doorway, moving as silent as a whisper.

"Captain Boonie," he said quietly. "It is time. Come with me."

3.00PM

I stared ahead at the island and thought, it's too damn small. I was used to seeing two miles of concrete runway on final approach, not a sparkling blue-green lagoon.

"Five thousand feet, flaps full, ditching checklist complete," said Brett.

"Thanks," I replied. "If you guys see anything you don't like, let me know."

"I think that runway ahead looks a little too wet," Jeff said wryly.

Everything was as set as we could make it. It felt strange though; it had only been a few minutes since the impacts with the Rocs, yet it felt like an eternity. Whether it was cliché or not, I did see images of Jennifer, Josh and Kelly in my mind.

"I love you Jennifer," I said out loud for the sake of the cockpit voice recorder, in case the worst happened and the plane was someday recovered. Brett and Jeff both mumbled similar comments into their microphones.

"Two thousand feet," said Brett.

The west end of the island flashed below us, a blur of palm trees, sand, and emerald coral reefs. Then we were over the lagoon. I aimed for the water along the south lagoon shore, next to the abandoned village. We were almost parallel to the southern shore of the lagoon, angled slightly toward the village ahead and to our right. If it all worked correctly, we'd slow down on the water and slide to a stop on the sandy shore. It's not like they teach this kind of maneuver in flight school though. We might be as likely to end up a giant ball of twisted metal and fire in a few seconds.

"Are we going short?" Jeff asked abruptly.

"I don't think so." I wrestled with the plane. The gusty tradewinds made it difficult to keep the wings level. I didn't want to hit the water with one wing down, as we might cartwheel. We had to hit flat, and slow.

The electronic voice of the airplane took over. "Five hundred," it said, relaying our altitude over the water. Small windblown wavelets stood out in my field of view, but the lagoon looked relatively flat. "Two hundred." I started leveling our descent, trying to bleed off as much speed as possible before touching the water. "One hundred." The shoreline near the village loomed directly ahead. We were coming in at a shallow angle to the beach. I didn't want to hit the sand with too much speed, but didn't want to land short and have to swim for it either. How fast would this thing decelerate? I had no idea.

"Fifty, thirty, twenty, ten."

I leveled us over the lagoon, trying to slow some more.

"Damn." Without the landing gear out, the plane bled off speed slower than I'd expected. The beach raced toward us at a frightening clip.

"Get it down, get it down!" Brett yelled.

"Hang on." I relaxed the control wheel just a bit. We were still doing 140 knots.

Bang. I felt a jerk to the right as the engine on that side slapped the water. Instinctively, I stomped on the left rudder pedal, trying to straighten us out. *Bang* again, and we jerked to the left. The nose dropped with a sickening *slam,* and slapped the water. I yanked back on the control wheel to try to keep the nose up. With a brutal jolt, both engines dug into the water. I got jerked around violently in my harness, and it sounded like a bomb went off inside the plane, as everything not bolted down broke loose. I tried to hang on to the control wheel, but it was impossible. I flailed about like a rag doll, and felt an intense deceleration pulling on me as water grabbed at the plane. An explosion of blue gushed over the windscreens, and then with a grinding scrape, we slid onto the beach. We were still moving though, and I caught a glimpse of palm trees on either side. Then with a sickening *crunch* and a flash of pain, we jerked to a stop.

My seat had partially detached from its base, my left shoulder pinned against the glareshield. A stabbing pain tore through that shoulder as I tried to move. Jeff unstrapped from the jumpseat and pulled my chair back. Fire flashed through my shoulder and I saw stars, but tried to concentrate on what I had to do. I grabbed the PA handset with my good hand and shouted "Evacuate, evacuate," but I didn't hear anything over the speakers. Jeff saw the problem, yanked the cockpit door open and screamed into the cabin, "Evacuate!"

"You okay?" Jeff asked as he turned back.

I nodded weakly. "Get the hell out of here." Jeff took off, and Brett clambered over the center console, close behind him.

"You going to be able to get out of that?" Brett asked from the doorway.

"Yep, just give me a second," I grunted. Brett took off, and I twisted the latch on my harness. I stood up unsteadily, grabbing the edge of the cockpit door. My first glance into the cabin didn't make sense, until I realized what I saw: Daylight. The far end of the plane had partially detached, and sunlight streamed in through a foot-wide gap in the ceiling near the last row of seats. Many of the passengers had already made it out the exits. I had to ensure everyone else got out before I left. I grabbed the crash axe from the cockpit, and hobbled down the aisle, climbing over mounds of debris. With only seventy people on a plane designed for two hundred and fifty, it was easy to get out in a hurry. By the time I reached the coach section, everyone had evacuated. An eerie quiet filled the cabin, with just a whisper of wind blowing through the cracked fuselage, and a muted hum from the emergency batteries powering the remaining lights. At the aft end of the cabin I found one passenger, still in his seat, just underneath the gap where sunlight poured in. I went to help him, and then saw why he hadn't moved. A metal beam protruded from his chest. He sat there, eyes glazed, unmoving. The beam came up from the floor behind him, through his seat, and through him. His blood drained down the beam, and pooled against the aft bulkhead. I left him there, and moved to the aft exits.

I reached out to open the door, but when I looked out the small window it was partially underwater. Instead, I went forward to the next set of doors, which were already open. Several passengers and crew members were climbing up the sandy lagoon shore toward the palm trees. I jumped onto the inflatable slide, and bounced down to the sand, right at the water's edge.

7.45PM

Chief Kalahamotu led me out of the shelter, into a rapidly darkening tropical evening. A last band of orange clung to the western horizon, visible through the thin grove of palm trees.

Overhead, massive buildups of cumulus clouds glowed a glorious pink and orange, the salty ocean strong in the air.

"You must be quiet," he whispered. "No talking. Breathe quiet. Walk quiet."

For some reason, his words triggered a memory of Elmer Fudd whispering 'Be vewy vewy qwiet'. I stifled a giggle, then bit my lip, and tried to regain control, something which had slipped away hours ago. We were vulnerable, walking down the crushed coral road. If the Rocs found us here, we'd be dead meat. Somehow though, the Chief engendered trust.

We passed several metal and concrete block buildings. Some appeared to have been abandoned, but most looked lived in. A few houses had open windows with oil lamps flickering inside. I wanted to ask the Chief about them, but kept quiet in deference to his orders. The church stood tall and proud, its garden well tended.

Just past the central square the Chief led me down a path to the steep sandy beach on the ocean side of the atoll. The edge of the reef was visible in the fading light, a couple of hundred yards offshore, waves curling over the coral. It made a calming, soothing noise, and brought back memories of more tranquil times. Between the beach and the breakers a shallow floor of rock and coral led out to the waves, covered with just a few feet of water.

The Chief motioned downward with his hands, and sat in the sand. I did the same, wanting to ask why we were there. I took a deep breath and tried to slow my pounding heart. We were way too exposed, especially sitting down like this; easy pickings for the Rocs. I dug my fingers into the cool, damp sand.

A splash of white light caught my eye. Just above the tops of the palms, a full moon rose. If the situation were different, I'd have called this a truly beautiful, romantic spot.

The Chief pointed to the water, and my heart jumped into my throat. Several Rocs flew just above the surface of the shallow water in front of us. Their wide triangular bodies were about ten feet long, and the wings maybe twenty-five feet wide when fully extended. Glossy black skin reflected the moonlight in a myriad of sparkles. They flapped gently at their wingtips as they descended. The apex of their bodies formed a long, wicked spike that extended another six feet or so out in front of them, flattened top and bottom with a razor sharp edge on both sides. A quick swipe from one of those spikes could cut through almost anything. They looked like armed, flying manta rays.

A tide of fear and anger rose inside me again. Fear at being so close to these things without protection, and anger at them for destroying my life, my career, and possibly my world. My breath quickened. The Chief turned toward me and made the palms-down wave again. Keep quiet. I struggled, but managed to slow my breathing. The closest Rocs touched down in the water mere feet in front of us, mimicking my own landing in the lagoon that afternoon, albeit carrying it off much more successfully. More Rocs followed, filling the shallows with rippling black triangles.

Then I heard them. Quiet, extremely high-pitched, almost beyond the threshold of hearing. A hypersonic cooing, each with a slightly different tone. What amazed me most of all though, was that I was still alive.

3.10PM

I dashed up the beach and leaned against a palm tree, out of breath. I still held the crash axe in my good hand. My left shoulder throbbed, and that arm dangled uselessly at my side. My right foot bled through rips in my shoe. Maybe I was in shock, but I didn't feel any pain from my foot. My shoulder however, pulsed in time with my racing heart.

My passengers and crew had made it up to the trees, and collapsed onto the ground at the top of the beach. I found Brett and Jeff among them, tending to a passenger who bled from her head and arms.

"You okay?" Brett asked as I limped up to him.

"I'll live. You guys?"

Both Brett and Jeff nodded, and then went back to helping the passengers on the ground. Another passenger walked up to me, and without saying a word, hugged me. More pain tore through my shoulder. I glanced at the passenger and felt a shock of recognition.

"Colin!"

"Yep, still here," croaked Colin Benoit, my friend, college roommate, and neighbor from Honolulu. We'd said hello during boarding, but I'd forgotten he was on the flight once the Rocs attacked.

"Thanks," he added.

I grinned at him through the stars of pain from my shoulder. "I'm glad you're okay. Anna would have had my head if I let anything happen to you."

"Same here, Boonie. Thanks for getting us down in one piece."

"Sorry about the detour. Maybe you'll get a chance to study the Rocs here, instead of at Cairns." Colin and his associate from the University of Hawaii, Alan Gee, had been heading down under to study the recent influx of Rocs into Cairns, Australia, farther south then they'd been seen before.

"Where are we?" he asked.

"One of the islands of Tuvalu. I don't know the name, though." We both stared at the lagoon, and the battered carcass of my plane, sitting on the sand like a beached whale of technology, very much out of place.

"How are we going to get out of here?" he asked.

I paused for a moment. I had been so preoccupied with getting us down safely, that I hadn't thought about how to get off. "We're working on that," I lied, and walked over to Jeff and Brett again.

Brett looked up and smiled. "Nice job getting us down, skipper," he said, tilting his head toward the plane.

"Thanks. And thanks for your help. Both of you."

They nodded.

"Now what?" Brett asked.

I shrugged my good shoulder. "I don't know. But the Rocs will be here soon. We have to find some shelter."

Brett's face paled. To him the Rocs were a menace at 35,000 feet, not something to be faced in person, at sea level. He had one of our Emergency Locater Transmitters on a strap over his shoulder. The red light indicated it still worked, transmitting a signal to search and rescue satellites in orbit overhead. At least the outside world would know we were down and possibly safe for now. Whether they would do anything about it was another story.

"We'll find a way off of here, I'm sure," I said.

Brett nodded, but had a sad look on his face.

"Don't worry. You'll see your little girl again."

A small tear formed in the corner of his eye, and he gave me a weak grin before turning away. I had no idea how, but we had to find some way to get us off the island.

Above the whisper of wind in the trees, a ragged whistle grew quickly into a steady roar, and everyone instinctively looked up. Our remaining escort fighter flew overhead and waggled its wings. Some of us waved back. Then his afterburners lit up and he made a hard turn to the right. Rapid puffs of smoke came out of the gun port on the side of the plane. Above the roar of the engines came a sound like a piece of heavy canvas being ripped apart, the pilot firing his guns at something; probably something close.

"Rocs!" I shouted. "Find some shelter, quick!"

Everyone hauled themselves onto their feet, and we made a dash deeper into the grove of palm trees. I didn't know which way the village sat from our location, but it couldn't be too far. We ran in a surge away from the lagoon, some people limping, others in a full-tilt dash.

"Hold it! Hold it!" I shouted. I didn't want everyone scattering in an uncoordinated sprint. "Everyone keep your eyes open for some kind of shelter, anything to protect us from the Rocs!" A few heads had turned toward me and nodded, but most were in panic mode, running through the grove.

Our fighter roared by in a tight turn. I froze as several black triangles flew overhead, diving toward the center of the island.

The roar of our fighter intensified as it banked hard toward us. "Cover now! Everyone!" I shouted. A flock of Rocs speared past the treetops, and a moment later we heard a huge *thump*. The fighter appeared overhead, trailing smoke and fire. It rolled furiously, and arced straight for the lagoon. It exploded as it hit the water a few hundred yards behind our stricken plane, sending shards of burning metal in all directions. At the impact site an oily ball of fire and smoke rolled skyward.

Over the far end of the lagoon a thick black cloud of Rocs dove toward us, just a few minutes away.

7.55PM

The Rocs played in the shallows of the reef, a dozen yards offshore. The splashing droplets of water shimmered in the moonlight like a million diamonds, briefly living out their lives above the ocean. The Rocs floated and bobbed, as if they didn't care we were there. What stopped them from attacking? My heart pounded and cold fear ran through my veins. Yet I trusted the Chief to keep me safe somehow. After all, he had been living with the Rocs for years.

How had he done that? A swarm of other questions circled in my mind too. All I could do though, was watch the Rocs splash in the waves; a lethal terror momentarily held at bay.

The black shapes moved around the reef, occasionally flapping their wings and briefly flying, and then landing back in the water. One of the biggest Rocs swam near the shore. It appeared different from the others, with a row of bulges down its normally smooth back. The creature swam to the edge of the beach just to my left, and rested its long spike on the sand, the remainder of its body barely in the water. It started a rhythmic pulsing motion, which grew in intensity to what I'd call convulsions. My horror grew as one of the bulges on its back popped open with a small spray of goo and out burst a tiny Roc, no more than eight inches long. The baby Roc flopped around on its parent's back for a moment, before it splashed into the sea. It wriggled through the water, and onto the sand in front of me. I felt another rush of fear and started to stand up, when the tiny thing started digging into the sand just a couple of feet from the water. It buried itself, leaving behind a small divot at the edge of the beach.

Another pop sounded from the parent, and then another. Soon, a total of five baby Rocs had come out and flopped their way onto the beach. Frightening and fascinating at the same time, I didn't know what to make of it. The parent Roc slid back into the water and disappeared below the surface. I watched, but it didn't come up again. Had is simply swum away, or had it died reproducing? I hoped for the latter.

A light touch on my shoulder startled me, and I stifled a scream. The Chief had stood and walked up to me without a sound. He motioned for me to stand. I did so on unsteady feet, shaking with adrenaline. We walked up the steep beach, and retraced our path toward the shelter. Along the way, we passed two locals standing in the front yard of a house. They nodded silently to us as we passed.

After the quiet of the beach, even the muted conversation in the shelter sounded like a full-blown riot. When I could finally talk again, I said, "That was unbelievable! They didn't attack! They didn't even notice us! Why are they different here than any place else?"

"I do not think these are different from any others," the Chief replied. "We have just come to know each other. We have learned about them. Maybe they have learned about us."

"That's it? Why haven't we been able to do that anywhere else?"

"When anyone in your world sees a Pouakai, how do they respond?" the Chief asked quietly.

"Nowadays? Scream. Yell. Run away. Call the military."

"Exactly. Noise. Lots of noise and rapid movement. Either it's people screaming, or its ships, planes, missiles and bombs, making more noise than a hundred people could."

"Right," I said, sarcastically. "We just have to shut up, and they'll leave us alone?"

"In essence, yes," the Chief replied, keeping his voice calm. "There is more to it, but that is the heart of living with them."

"So they just showed up one day, and you didn't do anything more than sit on the beach, be quiet, and let them set up house-keeping in your ocean?"

"It was not that easy," the Chief said. "Half my people died learning what we should do, and how we should do it, in the first weeks after the Pouakai came. In the end, we all learned; we and the Pouakai. We had to. There was no choice." The Chief looked around at our group. Most were sleeping after the frightening ordeal they had been through. "It is time to sleep. We will talk more in morning."

He slipped out the door before I could think of more questions for him. So much rolled through my mind that I couldn't keep it straight. In one day I had survived a plane crash, and several close encounters with the Rocs, or Pouakai, or whatever the hell they were called. What would come tomorrow? I couldn't even imagine. I felt utterly exhausted and lay down on the mat in my corner of the shelter. Before I could think of any more questions for the Chief, I fell asleep.

3.15PM

We fled from the beach into a grove of coconut trees. A moment later I saw several small concrete block homes, not more than a hundred yards from us. They were off to our right, away from where my people were running. I had overshot the village on my landing, but not by much.

"Over here!" I shouted, and waved my arms to get everyone's attention. Most of the people saw me, and I tried pointing toward the houses. They got the gist of it, and started running toward me. More yelling followed as people tried to get the others already farther away to turn around.

"This way! This way!" I heard several people shouting.

Fifty yards from the nearest house and at a dead run, I heard a quiet 'whoosh' overhead. A black triangle dove through the trees to my left, and with a meaty thunk, speared into the back of one of my passengers. He let out a terrified scream and blood foamed out of his mouth as he and the Roc tumbled to the ground, a thrashing mass of glossy black skin and spraying blood, the Roc's spike impaled through his chest. More people screamed and a few ran away from the man. Some turned away from the houses.

"No, no!" I shouted at them. "Get to shelter! Into the houses! Go!"

Most people dashed as fast as they could toward the houses, yelling and screaming. Sand covered the ground between the palm trees, with a few green vines and dried coconut husks there too. It wasn't the easiest surface to run on, but we made good time. I looked behind, and saw just a few of our group back there. Most had caught up to me and were making a run for the houses. Brett ran next to me.

"How's your foot?" he asked between gasps of air.

"Can't feel a thing," I panted.

"Good. We're almost…" His eyes widened. "Look out!" he screamed, and pushed me hard with his shoulder. The crash axe spun out of my hand, and I fell, twisting to the ground as a Roc's wingtip slapped the back of my head. Its spike grazed Brett across his neck and shoulder, and blood gushed from a severed artery as he fell to the ground.

"God dammit!" I shouted. "Brett, Brett!"

The Roc ricocheted off the ground and flapped its way back into the air. Brett lay on the ground just feet from me, his eyes wide with terror. His mouth moved, but no sound came out. I stumbled to my feet, grabbed him around the chest with my good arm, and heaved him upright. He held a hand to his neck, but blood poured out of his wound. Together, we stumbled to the doorway of the nearest house, which faced a narrow lane paved with crushed coral. The sturdy little bungalow was made of concrete bricks with a thick metal roof. I heard two more flat thunks, followed by screams. We were losing the battle. My mind reeled as I tried the door; locked. Two Rocs whistled overhead as I put my shoulder to the door, but it didn't budge. We couldn't get in. The windows were open but had heavy steel bars over them.

Just a few straggler Rocs were attacking us, and we were already outnumbered. The big swarm of Rocs I had seen from the lagoon had to be only seconds away, and we had nowhere to hide. Many of our passengers were screaming as they ran up and down the street, looking for any place to hide. Panic rose in my throat, along with a sense of helplessness like I'd never known.

I knew I had really gone 'round the bend when two people I didn't recognize silently sprinted up the road toward us. A pair of young men, dark skinned, dressed in shorts and tattered T-shirts, padded barefoot up to us like soundless wraiths, making shushing motions with their hands. One stopped in the street, motioning people to gather around him. The other ran further down the road, collecting our people and sending them on toward his partner. Within seconds they had rounded up most of our group, and we followed the first young man while the other went looking for stragglers. I held Brett upright, a difficult task with his blood-slickened skin. Together, we limped along with the crowd. In stunned silence we made our way with the newcomer down the road, which ended at a large metal Quonset hut. The young man kept looking at the sky, but didn't say a word as he waved us into the hut. Brett and I stumbled in through the open doorway and fell to the floor. A moment later the other young man showed up with five more of my passengers. The two strangers moved a metal grate across the doorway, and latched it into place.

Brett lay on the sandy ground, blood pouring from his neck. Another young man knelt down beside him, tore off part of his shirt, made a bandage and pressed it against Brett's neck. I stood up, not quite believing or understanding what was going on. My eyes adjusted to the dim interior of the shelter, and I saw several other strangers emerging from the darkness at the far end, carrying blankets, water jugs, and first aid kits.

I looked around and did a quick head count. It took three tries to count everyone, but when I finished I realized that we'd lost only four, including the man who'd been killed inside the airplane. I'd seen one get impaled by a Roc, which meant only two others hadn't made it this far. My friend Colin sat on the floor, as well as his co-worker, Alan Gee, and all the members of my crew.

A loud clang sounded from the roof of the building, followed by the flapping of wings. A Roc. Panic appeared in the eyes of many of my passengers, but our rescuers made the shushing motion again and everyone quieted down. Two more clangs echoed through the shelter, then it sounded like hell's own hailstorm crashed onto the roof. Everyone in the shelter stopped what they were doing and looked up. The roof held, and a minute later a great rushing-wind sound came from above as the Rocs lifted off. For another minute nobody moved or spoke. Then the two men who had rescued us removed the grate from the doorway, and the locals went back to work, tending to our wounded. I stood in the center of the hut, seeing but not believing our good fortune in finding survivors on this supposedly deserted island.

Another local looked at me with quiet concern. Older than me, with a shock of white hair, and a dark, well-muscled physique, he seemed to be supervising the chaos. He stared at me for a moment, and then moved in my direction. Despite my bloody uniform, I was obviously the leader of our group.

With a heavy Polynesian accent, he said "Welcome to Nanumea. I am the Chief."

I couldn't think of anything to say, except a whispered "Thank you." He went back to work, carrying supplies for the people tending to my passengers and crew.

DAY FOUR

Four days after crashing onto the island, depression had set in on many of my group. The batteries in the Emergency Locator Beacon died the day after we landed, and a slow certainty had set in that nobody was coming for us. The Rocs weren't attacking anymore, but that didn't mean we had free reign on the island, either. The people of Nanumea taught us how they lived now, and we had to follow, or risk becoming victims of the invaders.

When we went outside, we travelled in groups of no more than four, walking quietly and slowly. We helped the Nanumeans fish in the morning and evening, and harvest coconuts, taro and other vegetables in the afternoon. The sixty-five of us who'd survived the crash were added to the five hundred locals living on the island. They were gracious about us being there, but mostly kept to themselves. We had a temporary home inside the Quonset hut, but couldn't live that way forever, being too cramped to make it permanent. Eventually we'd have to build our own houses. I saw the inevitability of this; we wouldn't be leaving the island any time soon. Many of my passengers and crew couldn't face that fact yet, but they would have to eventually. There was just no way off the island, and nobody would be coming for us any time soon. Our being here didn't stretch the available resources by too much. We'd survive, but we would all be a lot thinner by the time we got off the island, if that ever happened.

I thought a lot about Jennifer and Josh and Kelly, and made them a silent promise that I'd get back somehow, someday. It wouldn't be soon, but I still promised.

It turns out that Nanumea is about as far from anywhere as we could have found. It's the westernmost island in the tiny island nation of Tuvalu, hundreds of miles from the abandoned capital town of Funafuti, and thousands of miles from any place we knew about where people still lived. I spent the evenings talking quietly with the Chief about life here and abroad, and how everything had changed because of the Rocs. He didn't know of anyone alive on the other islands of Tuvalu, because they didn't have a boat capable of going that far without upsetting the Rocs.

Out of sheer necessity, and with a big dose of luck, they had learned how to be quiet around the Rocs, and how not to disturb them. If you moved slowly and quietly enough, the invaders left you alone. Make a noise, or move too fast, and something was triggered in them that caused a mass hysteria. They would attack in a frenzy, without regard for themselves.

Despite the general gloom, Colin and Alan were thrilled to be here. The two exobiologists were excited because this was the first time they, or anyone else, had ever had a chance to watch the Rocs up close for this long. So instead of trying to study the Rocs amid the panic and confusion of Cairns during an evacuation, they could spend their time out on the beach with the locals, watching the Rocs go through their daily lives.

Around noon on our fourth day on Nanumea, I was avoiding the worst of the tropical heat when Colin plopped down next to me in the sand of the shelter. The skinny, fair-skinned professor had a scorching sunburn, but also a gleam in his eyes that I recognized as pure excitement.

"What's up?" I asked.

"It's just unbelievable, Boonie. The Pouakai are simply amazing! I never thought I'd get a chance to study them like this."

"You're calling them Pouakai? Are you going local on me?"

"It's as good a name as any. I never liked the name 'Rocs' anyway. These things are nothing like real Rocs."

"Rocs never existed. They're a mythological bird. What the hell is a Pouakai anyway?"

"Another mythological creature, also a man-eating bird from Polynesian legend. The Chief said his people started using that name after the first islanders were killed early on. I guess it stuck."

"Roc, Pouakai. Either way, it's an imaginary bird."

Colin shook his head, but had a big grin on his face. "You know what I mean. Unicorns don't exist either, but everyone knows what they look like. Anyway, Alan and I have seen Pouakai behaviors never reported before. We think we understand their energy source too."

"Their what?"

"Where they get their energy. We've never seen them eat. Anywhere. They don't even have mouths as far as we know. Up to now, nobody has discovered how they sustain themselves, but we think we're on to something." He left it hanging, expecting me to prompt him further. I was too exhausted to play along though.

"They're solar powered!"

I did raise an eyebrow at that. "They're what?"

"Their skin. We think it acts like a solar panel. A couple of researchers in Japan had put that forth as a possibility, but none of us took it too seriously. We'd always assumed they ate while underwater. But we've been watching them in the waters around here, and several never leave and never submerge, so they can't be feeding underwater. They just float or flop on the surface all day. We've seen a noticeable decrease in their energy level during the later hours of nighttime too. In the mornings, they align their bodies so they are broadside to the sun as it rises. It really looks like they're using solar power and an organic battery system to power themselves! That might explain some of the really odd organs we've seen on the carcasses we've dissected too."

I took a deep breath, and let it out slowly through pursed lips. I just couldn't get excited about this new information. "This helps us get off the island how?" I asked a little too snidely. Colin didn't seem to notice.

"Everything we learn about the Pouakai helps. Any little bit of data may be the one that opens the door to controlling them."

"I don't want to control them. I want to wipe them off the face of the Earth."

"We might be able to learn a lot from them," Colin said, the smile leaving his face. "After what I've seen here, I'd bet a fortune that they really are extraterrestrial, and that creates a lot more questions. Like, where are they from? How did they get here? Are they intelligent?"

"Questions," I snorted. "What I want are answers."

Colin ignored my slam. "Hell. If they aren't from here, they're the first extraterrestrial organism we've ever encountered. Alan and I are wondering if they're a natural evolution of another species. Or maybe, since they seem to survive on Earth okay, they're an engineered organism."

"A what?"

"An engineered biological entity. Something that isn't natural, but engineered, designed, for its purpose in life."

"Seriously? You think someone *made* these things?"

"Not anyone here," Colin replied, "though maybe something from out there did." He pointed up at the sky.

I shook my head. The last thing I wanted to worry about was the possibility of an alien race having dropped these things off here as some sort of weapon.

"Does it really matter now?" I said. "All I care about is making sure we survive, and find a way off this island."

Colin took a deep breath and then shrugged. "Yeah, you're right. We each have our jobs to do."

I closed my eyes, and leaned my head back against the corrugated wall of the hut. "Sorry. I didn't mean to jump all over you like that."

"No problem buddy. You've had a lot to take care of the past few days."

He stood up and left. I checked the time; ten more minutes until I had to be out at the taro patch to help the locals with weeding and harvesting. My shoulder felt better, and I tried to help out our hosts as much as possible.

A loud peal of thunder rolled across the island. I'd be getting wet outside. At least the Rocs tended to stay put when it rained. Another clap of thunder echoed across the island, as big fat raindrops hit the sandy ground with a hiss, a moment of normalcy in what had been an unreal string of days.

I mused on that thought for a moment. The dark clouds and rain meant less sunshine coming through, and if Colin was right, less energy for them. I told myself to forget it though. That was someone else's job to worry about. My job was, first, to keep us alive. And second, to find a way back home.

DAY FIVE

"Here, hold on to this," Jeff whispered, early the next morning. I grabbed the loose cable he held out to me, and pulled it away from the opening in the floor of the cockpit.

"Jesus Christ," he said quietly, as he withdrew his head from the avionics bay. I poked my head into the opening and looked around. The radio compartment under the cockpit had taken the brunt of the impact as we slid across the water and up onto the beach. It had saved us in the cockpit from certain death, but in the process, the racks holding the radios had ripped apart. It was a jumbled mess of cables, twisted metal, sand, and water.

"I don't suppose you took a class in avionics repair," I sighed.

Jeff shook his head. "The closest I came was trying to build a crystal radio for Boy Scouts. It didn't work. I never got the merit badge."

We both stared at the wreckage.

"I don't think we could have done anything with it anyway," I said. "Unless you know a way to make a coconut battery like they had on Gilligan's Island."

"Yeah," he said, without a hint of a smile. "I guess this was worth a try, but not likely to work."

Jeff had been showing some signs of depression, as were a lot of my passengers and crew. I wanted to restore some hope for my people, if we could get the radio and a battery off the plane. But the radios were smashed beyond our ability to repair, and the main batteries were underwater near the tail.

"Okay," I said. "Let's get the food out of the galley."

Jeff followed me down the aisle. The Rocs had beaten on the fuselage when they were chasing after us that first day. The whole plane now looked like it had been through a boulder attack, with dents over practically every square inch of exposed surface. Jet fuel leaked from the battered engine nacelles, leaving an oily sheen on the lagoon, and a stench of kerosene in the humid air.

"Peanuts, pretzels, and soda pop," Jeff reported, as he opened the galley carts. "All the major food groups."

I smiled. Maybe he hadn't gone completely into a depression yet. "Now if I can only find…Damn," I said.

"What is it?"

"The coffee. The packets are all torn apart. Doesn't look like there's anything salvageable here."

"Shit. Now that is depressing," he replied.

We gathered what we could, put it into a couple of canvas sacks the Chief had given us and, after checking to see if any Rocs were in the area, dropped to the sand. With our meager booty in hand, we hiked back to the village under a scorching sun.

DAY TEN

Five days later, I stood on a rock a few feet from the beach, with a long fishing pole in hand. I cast the lure as far as I could onto the reef, and slowly reeled it back in. The sun had just fallen below the horizon and the first stars were becoming visible. After spending more than a week on the island, it felt like we were settling into a routine. A few people were still recovering from injuries sustained in the crash but everyone else had healed up nicely, thanks to the Nanumeans. That didn't mean we were all helping out with daily life though. Half my crew and passengers were in a deep depression I couldn't do anything about. They moped about the shelter and did little work. The rest of us pitched in as best as we could, remaining quiet while outside, the whoosh of a passing Roc hardly even noticed now.

With so much time spent taking care of my passengers and crew, fishing was one of the few times I could be alone to think. I tried not to dwell on the flight and crash, but it was like an itch that wouldn't go away. In an endless loop, I wondered why I hadn't listened to Jennifer and only worked the safe trips. Had I been trying to thumb my nose at the Rocs? Had I actually flown these trips to prove to myself that they didn't have the upper hand yet? Normally I'd have said no, but in these quiet reflections, I had to admit to myself that it was a possibility.

At least while fishing I could get a little enjoyment out of our situation. I did a lot of surf fishing at home in Hawaii to relax. A lone Roc passed overhead in the dying light, heading out to the far end of the island. It all seemed so strange, yet peaceful. Here I stood, fishing like nothing unusual had happened, while a Roc sailed by. Was there actually a way to co-exist with these things? Could we learn to live alongside the Rocs? Big cities would certainly have to change, or not exist where the Rocs settled. Smaller outposts like this might survive, given the right information.

These thoughts were rolling around in my head when a strange shape appeared in the water. At first it looked like another pregnant Roc, but it had only one lump, and I couldn't see the wings or spike. It dipped below the surface, and then appeared a few feet closer, heading straight toward me. The darkening skies reflected sapphire and orange on the ripples of water, and I couldn't see what lay below the surface. The lump reappeared twenty feet away, and then rose out of the ocean. My heart skipped a beat. Colin's suggestions about the Rocs being created by something else raced through my mind, and for an instant I felt a rush of panic. Then I recognized the lump.

It was a man. A man in a high-tech scuba outfit, carrying a rifle. More men rose out of the ocean around him and stood waist-deep in the waters of the reef. Seeing half a dozen armed men appear in front of me was not what I'd expected that day.

"Are you from the crashed aircraft?" he asked, in a voice that rolled like thunder.

"Shhhhh!" I whispered as loudly as I dared. I waved him closer, and lay my fishing pole on the rock. He waded through the water as I glanced around. No Rocs yet, so I took a deep breath. He came up next to me, his rifle held across his chest.

"Yes, I am. Have your men follow me," I whispered. "Make sure they don't talk, don't make any noise at all. And if you want to stay alive, for God's sake, don't fire those weapons."

He turned to his men and made some quick signs with his hand, and then nodded to me. Shaking, I climbed the shore toward the village. When I turned back, they looked like half a dozen shadows following me. In the fading light, I couldn't make out any details. One could have been standing in the shadow of a palm tree, and I'd never have known it. If they were who I thought they were, we might yet get off this island.

I walked them to the shelter, and as we entered, a silent riot erupted. Everyone dashed over to us, most in shock to see someone new. Even the worst victims of depression had a look of hope on their faces. I shushed them all and turned to the leader. Salt water still dripped from his wetsuit, as well as from the small, high tech modules attached to the webbing on his chest and waist. He had pulled his facemask back on his head, and carried his rifle with practiced ease.

"Navy Seals?" I asked. The leader nodded, and a small smile crossed his face.

"You are the survivors of the crash?" he asked, looking around at us.

"We are. Sixty-five out of the seventy that were onboard."

He looked at me, positively appraising my efforts. "Nice job."

"Thanks. How did you get here? I didn't think the Navy sent any ships down this way."

His smile grew a little wider. "We don't, but submarines do come this way, a lot."

My jaw dropped. I'd been an idiot. A submarine—I hadn't even thought about that.

"Can you get us out of here?" one of my passengers asked breathlessly.

"Certainly," he replied. "That is why we're here, assuming you want to be—" He turned as the Chief entered the shelter, followed by a couple of dozen locals. The Seals stiffened, but did not otherwise react.

"Chief," I said, hoping to avoid any sort of distrust from either side. "These men are from the US Navy, and are here to rescue us." I turned to the leader of the Seals, and motioned to the Chief. "This is the leader of the island, Chief Kalahamotu. Chief, this is—"

"Lieutenant Hanson," the leader said. "US Navy." Hanson held out his hand, and the Chief took it.

"Welcome to Nanumea," the Chief said.

"Thanks," Hanson replied, flustered. "We didn't expect to find anyone else here with the survivors."

"You are the second set of unexpected guests we've had this month. Welcome."

Hanson looked around at the locals. "How many of you are there?"

"Five hundred twelve."

Hanson looked thoughtful for a few seconds. "We weren't planning on rescuing that many people. The sub won't be able to hold all of you."

"Oh no," said the Chief. "We do not wish to be rescued. This is our home. We are fine here."

The lieutenant raised an eyebrow. "But, the Rocs—"

"Lieutenant," I said. "I'll explain later. I agree with the Chief, though. If they don't want to be rescued, we don't have to take them along."

"They won't survive down here with the Rocs around. There's nobody alive anywhere down here. No survivors anywhere in the central Pacific."

"They have survived here," I said, pointing at the Chief, "and for all we know, there may be others around the world. It's a long story, but we have the trip home to talk about it. For now, just believe me. They have been living with the Rocs for years, and will be fine. But we have information that is vitally important to get back home, and I'm sure that we're all more than ready to get going."

DAY ELEVEN

We shuttled out to the sub the next evening in a rubber boat with a silent electric motor. The sound of the wind and the slap of the waves on the reef were louder than the boat's passage. I remained on the shore until the last group was picked up. Before climbing in, I shook hands with the Chief.

"Thanks," I whispered. He nodded, but kept quiet. "Good luck," I added, and climbed into the boat.

We slipped over the reef, and bounced through the waves of the open ocean. Spray flew through the air, and soaked us. Without the moon it was pitch dark, and I didn't see the sub until we were almost on top of it. A huge black bulk rising out of the water, it stretched a hundred feet in either direction. The sail towered overhead, fins protruding like wings. Many hands were there to lift us out of the boat and onto the deck. Within seconds I was ushered through a hatch and down into the bowels of the sub. Dim red lighting greeted us once we got inside. A strong mixture of smells permeated the air; diesel fumes, electronics, and sweat. I heard men talking above us on the deck, then they climbed down too, and the heavy hatch shut with a metallic clang.

The Captain of the sub came up to me and shook my hand. "You are the Captain of the aircraft that crashed?"

I nodded. "Mark Boone, sir."

"Baker," he said. "Riley Baker. Captain of the *USS Ohio*. Welcome aboard."

Short and lean, Captain Baker wore wire rimmed half-glasses perched on his nose. He moved quickly and purposefully.

"We're pretty damn happy to be here," I said. "Thanks."

"You're welcome. Having an extra sixty-five people down here will be a tight squeeze. We took three of your people to the infirmary, but the rest of your group is in the enlisted mess. That's the biggest area we have. We'll be back in Hawaii in six days. I hope you can put up with the cramped quarters for a while."

"It's all fine with us, Captain. We're just happy you found us."

"It wasn't us. The search and rescue people picked up the signal from your beacon. The coordinates moved around a bit on the island before the signal faded, so they assumed someone was still alive and carrying the beacon with them. We were on patrol east of Hawaii, and they dispatched us to take a look."

"However it happened, we're glad. Thanks."

The Captain took us toward the mess. The inside of the sub was small and densely packed with pipes and wiring, but spotlessly clean.

"I can't believe there have been people living on Nanumea all this time," the Captain said, as we walked down the corridor.

"They got lucky," I replied. "They did all the right things, although they didn't know it at the time. They stayed quiet and didn't disturb the Rocs."

"That's really all it took?"

"Apparently, yes. We learned what to do from the locals, and even in the short time we had on the island, I got a chance to watch the Rocs up close, without them attacking me. We have two biologists, Benoit and Gee, with us too. They've been studying the things around the clock and it sounds like they have come on some important finds."

"Anything we could use to wipe them out?" the Captain asked, as we ducked under a set of black pipes.

"I don't know. You'd have to ask them. They did say they thought the Rocs get their energy from sunlight."

"I see. If we could put up some sort of sunshade in orbit, that might do it."

"I don't know. It would have to be huge. Bigger than anything we've done before by several orders of magnitude. If we did that, how would it affect the rest of the Earth? Plants and animals that depend on sunlight. The Rocs are killing us, but some of the cures may be worse than the problem."

"It's us versus them, Captain Boone. We have to do something. Nobody can live with those damn things around."

With a look back at what had happened over that past couple of weeks, I wasn't so sure that wiping them out was the only right move. "Some people have learned to live with them," I suggested, echoing the Chief. "There are other alternatives we should consider first."

"Really? Have you seen the condition of the world today?"

"Of course I have," I said, as we walked into the mess. My crew and passengers were crowded into the small room, sitting on the tables, benches, and the floor. "My career is dependent on getting rid of them. So is the world's economy. My whole life would be better if they were gone. I'm just asking if there are alternatives we haven't thought of yet."

"That's for people at a higher pay grade than us to figure out," the Captain said, with a thin smile.

I was happy to be on the sub, and on my way to Hawaii, but after being on the island and in a position to learn about the Rocs, it felt like control of the situation was slipping away again. The last thing I wanted to do, though, was get into an argument with the man who had rescued us.

The Captain glanced at our group crowded into the mess, and then back at me. "Enjoy your stay here on the *Ohio,* Captain Boone. If there's anything you need, let me know."

"Thank you, Captain. I'll do that."

He left, and a feeling of calm settled on me. I sat at one of the tables and nibbled on a tuna sandwich. Next to me were Colin and Alan, who furiously scribbled their observations into a pair of notebooks borrowed from the sub's crew. They wrote feverishly as they tried to organize their thoughts. That information could lead to our salvation from the Rocs, or the destruction of the Earth, or both. There were too many variables, and I was too exhausted to think about it all. I'd been through a lot in the past eleven days, and all I wanted was to go home, to live my life in peace and quiet.

Perhaps, I thought, the Rocs felt the same way.

I closed my eyes, and listened to the strange sounds of this technological marvel that was taking me home.

PART 2
OAHU

1

Trade winds swirled around the lanai as Jennifer set a platter of steaks on the table. The palm trees in our back yard slapped and clicked in the breeze.

"Real steaks?" Colin asked.

Jennifer smiled and nodded. "They were the last ones at Foodland, but they still looked okay."

We passed the meat, along with bowls of rice, green beans, and teriyaki sauce, around the table. I picked up my knife and fork just as Anna spoke up.

"To the man who saved my husband's life," she said, raising her glass of wine. The wind played with her long blonde hair.

"Hear hear," Colin added, lifting his glass high.

"Aw, shucks guys," I said with mock modesty. "'Twasn't nuthin'."

"No, of course not," said Colin. "Just another day at the office; ditching your plane on an island, dodging Pouakai, saving the lives of so many people." He tipped his glass toward me, and then grinned. "Nothing at all."

I smiled back, and raised my wine glass to meet the rest.

"Cheers," chorused my wife and friends. I took a sip, and then reached for the bottle of expensive French wine Colin and Anna had brought with them. Bringing a makana—a gift—to dinner was a Hawaiian custom, but this bottle must have cost a small fortune.

"You guys didn't really have to do this," I said, tilting the bottle toward them.

"Yes we did," Anna replied. "For keeping Colin alive."

"Besides," Colin said, "I had to bring something. That makes the score, what, about two hundred to zero?" He flashed a sly grin.

"Yeah, I know, I forget to bring a makana now and then."

"Now and then?" Jennifer scoffed. "Unless I'm with you, you forget every time."

She had a smile on her face, but steely anger lingered behind those beautiful brown eyes. My return home three weeks earlier had been a mixture of tears, hugs, and rage for putting her and the kids through so much panic. It had softened over time, but uncertainty about my job and the future of Hawaii kept her on edge.

Anna leaned toward Jennifer. "Was this really the last of the meat in the store?"

Jennifer nodded. "The store manager said he hoped to have another shipment in from San Francisco next week, but the refrigerated deliveries were coming in slower these days. He didn't know when the next one after that would arrive."

"What's next?" Anna asked sullenly. "Food rationing? Gas stamp books?"

"Not likely," said Colin.

"Why not?"

"People are leaving faster than we're losing shipments. Fewer supplies are coming across the Pacific, but there are fewer people here to buy them too."

I looked down the hill from our backyard, along the Niu valley and out to the waters of the Pacific. The sun had just set and a golden glow enveloped the misty air. The waters of the ocean shimmered like hammered gold. Another glow emerged over the ridges to the west—the lights of Honolulu coming on in the twilight.

"When will it end?" Anna asked quietly.

"I don't know if it does," Jennifer replied.

"It has to! We can't live like this forever."

I leaned back in my chair and stared at the wine glass still in my hand as the discussion continued, the same argument heard around the world for the last three years. *We can't live this way, and yet there's nothing we can do about it.*

"Then what do we do?" Jennifer said. "What options do we have?"

Anna sank back in her chair, clearly exhausted and frustrated. "It's not fair," she whispered.

"No, it's not," I said. "It's a no-win situation. We don't have a clue how to get rid of them, so until we do, we'll have to change the way, and places, we live." I looked at Colin, who shrugged.

"We have a conference in Tokyo next week," he said. "The paper Alan and I wrote for *Nature* was fast-tracked, and will be published while we are at the conference. We're hoping it will generate some new ideas."

"Any other scientists with new ideas like yours?" Jennifer asked.

Colin shook his head. "There's none that I know of. We're still hampered by our inability to take our time dissecting a dead Pouakai."

"Why?"

"They degrade too fast. Something in them is triggered when they die, and the body decomposes within an hour. It's weird, since it doesn't make any sense biologically, but when they die, there's an immediate reaction that begins to dissolve the tissues. Within an hour the carcass becomes too difficult to handle, and within two hours, it's just a pile of gloop."

"You can't learn anything from the gloop?" Jennifer asked.

"Not much. We've learned the basic elemental makeup, but it's pretty much like any other life here; carbon, nitrogen, oxygen, hydrogen, a little sulfur, and some trace elements. Whatever complex molecules they have are broken down before we can test them. We can't get a handle on what they're made of, or what makes them tick."

"Maybe that's the point," I said. Everyone at the table looked at me.

"What do you mean," Anna asked.

"Colin said it himself, back on Nanumea. Maybe they're an engineered organism. Maybe somebody designed it so we couldn't figure out what makes them tick, so we couldn't invent a defense against them."

Colin shook his head. "I know I said that, but it was one of the more extreme theories. We haven't found anything that would favor that theory over another."

"I read about that last week," Anna said.

"Really? Where?"

"Cosmo."

Colin almost choked on his wine.

"Don't laugh," Anna said. "It was a good article. They talked about all the theories of where the Rocs—sorry sweetie—Pouakai, came from. Several of them were versions of that theory: that someone or something created them for whatever job they do, and that maybe they came from space."

"Did the article include ten ways to come on to a lonely Pouakai?" Colin asked with a grin.

Anna glared at Colin, threw her napkin at him, and stuck her tongue out. Then she smiled and laughed.

"Where in the world did you find her?" I mockingly asked.

"Oh, you know the old story," Colin said. "Geeky exobiologist goes for a haircut, falls in love with the girl cutting his hair, they marry, end of story."

"It's more like he came in for a haircut every month for two years before he even got up the nerve to ask me out," Anna replied. "At least Cosmo was giving out some real information. Better than all that crap being sent out by the doomsday churches."

We all went quiet, the playfulness of the moment gone again.

"There was a big gathering at Ala Moana Park this morning," Jennifer said. "Did you see the posters advertising it? Some sort of prayer vigil to rid the Earth of the devil. I assume they meant the Pouakai."

"Couldn't hurt," Anna said.

"Couldn't help," I corrected. "I don't think prayer is going to do it this time."

I looked at Colin, but he sat deep in thought. A growing frustration filled my mind, and wondered if we would ever have a conversation that went for more than two minutes without touching on the Pouakai.

I cut into my steak and chewed without tasting it, lost in thought.

2

I stood at the sink and dried the dishes after Jennifer washed them. She hadn't said anything since Colin and Anna left, and I knew better than to try to force the issue. The only sounds were the clink of dishes on the counter and the wind in the palm trees.

The phone rang, and I almost dropped the dish in my hand. Jennifer looked at the phone.

"Kelly," she said, and pushed the talk button. "Hi sweetie. How was class today?"

I looked at the time; just past midnight in Colorado. She had been the strict clock-watcher at home, but I remembered how college had changed me too.

"Yes, your dad's here. No more trips until next week. No, he's not going to Australia again. I think it's San Francisco."

Their conversation continued for a while as I put the dishes away. Along the way I gathered that the classes Kelly had quit after my accident wouldn't count against her GPA, and she could re-take them next semester. Finally Jennifer handed me the phone.

"Hi, angel," I said. "How's life in the frozen wasteland?"

"Fine, dad. How's life at home? Mom talking to you yet? Or is she still in pissed-off mode?"

"It's chilly, but the spring thaw is on the way."

"Good. You two had better work it out, or I'm coming back for summer break to knock some sense into both of you."

"I'm sure you could do it, too," I said. Then I tried to change the subject. "I gather you can make up the classes you dropped?"

"Yeah, my guidance counselor has been a life saver. When he heard you had disappeared, he talked to someone in the registrar's office, and it was all taken care of."

"Great."

"Yeah. Then after you were rescued and I came back here, they sent someone from the school paper to interview me. They had a pretty nice write-up about your crash, along with my interview. You're a hero to my friends now."

"I've been getting a lot of that lately," I said, looking at last week's Time magazine, sitting on the counter. *'Rocs gaining ground'* read the cover article, along with a photo taken by one of my passengers of our plane on the beach at Nanumea.

"So you're not going to do any more Australia trips, right?" she said, more in the form of a statement than a question.

"No angel, not any more. The airline suspended all flights through the Roc's zone for now, and may not restart them again, depending on a review from the Air Force on the safety of continuing their escort flights."

"Good. I lost you once, and can't imagine losing you again."

"That's sweet of you," I said quietly. "No, the farthest afield I'm going is the mainland, or maybe Japan, but that's about it. No more Rocs for me."

I watched Jennifer's back as she sat at the table and mindlessly stirred a cup of coffee. It almost seemed like I could see the tension in her shoulders relax a tiny bit. Maybe.

A long moment of silence came across the phone, and I began to wonder if the line had gone dead. Then Kelly spoke.

"Dad, what's going to happen, really?" she asked quietly.

"I don't know, angel, I just don't know."

I looked out the kitchen window at the lights on the hillside leading down to the ocean. It appeared so normal. Inside, I felt nothing but hopelessness, but I didn't want to pass that on to Kelly.

"We had dinner with Colin and Anna tonight," I continued. "He was talking about some of the ideas they came up with while we were on the island. He is going to a conference in Japan next week to go over all their data, plus that of other scientists. Hopefully they'll come up with something."

"Yeah, I hope so," she said, in a tone that showed she didn't believe it either.

"Angel, we didn't become humans without learning how to adapt to changes in our environment. Somehow, someway, we'll find a way to keep going, no matter how bad it gets." I said the words, just like I'd said them to her so many times before. Yet now they felt hollow. For the first time, I couldn't convince myself that what I said was true, and it frightened me.

"Thanks Dad. I needed to hear that."

Her reply only made me feel worse.

"Sleep tight, Kelly. Don't pull an all-nighter for finals again like you did last year."

"No way. I learned my lesson."

We said our goodnights, and then hung up.

Jennifer had left the kitchen lights off. I only saw her outline, sitting at the table, a cup of coffee gripped tight in her hands. I wanted to say something, but was afraid of opening the wound again. Her long straight black hair, inherited from her Japanese mother, reflected the light coming in from the living room. A Hapa, as we said in Hawaii; she'd inherited her father's Swedish reserve, and her mother's steel will. I'd fallen in love with her the day I met her at the University in Honolulu. I'd been working on a Masters in Engineering while flying for the Hawaii Air National Guard. She was finishing up her PhD in Economics and wanted to single-handedly put Wall Street on the right track. Fate intervened though, in the form of my roommate Colin Benoit, who, for reasons unknown, thought we would make a good couple and set us up on a blind date. By some strange magic Colin, who couldn't find himself a date to save his life, matched us up and we clicked immediately. Twenty-something years later I still haven't actually said thank you, but I think he gets the idea.

Since my return from Nanumea however, that fiery anger Jennifer usually kept on a tight rein had fallen on me several times. It would eventually fade away, but I had no idea when. Any attempt to defuse it would just make it worse. I walked toward the living room, but as I passed her, Jennifer raised her hand in front of me, and I rocked to a stop. She didn't look at me, but kept a tight grip on the coffee cup.

"Did you mean it?" she asked quietly.

"Mean what?" I replied.

"What you told Kelly. That you wouldn't take any more flights through the Rocs."

"Yes, I did. Just like I said to you yesterday, and last week too." I grimaced, afraid I'd gone too far and the arguments would ignite again. She didn't raise her voice though, or even glare at me. Instead she took a deep breath, and in the dim light I saw her shoulders relax. She let go of the cup, and stood up.

"Okay," she whispered. "Okay."

She stepped forward and put her arms around my waist. I wrapped her up in my arms, as she put her cheek against my shoulder.

"Don't leave me again," she whispered. "Ever."

"No sweetie, I won't. That's a promise."

We stood like that for several minutes, rocking slowly to our own internal beat. Eventually, I looked down and kissed the top of her head. I slowly ran a couple of fingers from behind her ear, down the back of her neck, and along her spine. She responded by dropping her hands to my rear and pulling me harder into her. As she looked up at me, I kissed her softly, and she kissed back more forcefully. I could see where this was going, and let her take the lead as we slowly dropped to the floor.

3

"This can't be good," Jim Reynolds said.

We were both looking at a hastily written notice posted on the crewroom wall. Jim and I had just returned from San Francisco to find the message posted all over the place. 'Mandatory pilot meeting, today, 2pm.' It was signed by our V.P. of Flight Operations.

"It's another furlough," Jim added.

"Don't go borrowing trouble," I said. "Maybe we're getting more work from the government."

"Fat chance. They're cutting back again." Jim sighed and tossed his hat onto the worn leather sofa in the corner of the lounge. He had been a junior Captain before the Rocs started to play havoc with our careers. As the airline shrank and pilots were laid-off, he moved further down the seniority list. Now near the bottom of the co-pilot list, he would be the next to get laid off if we shrank any more.

I checked my watch; just over an hour until the meeting.

"Let's get some lunch," I said. "My treat."

Still a young-looking forty, his broad-shouldered form used to be a regular sight around the airport with a young flight attendant or two trailing along at his elbow. The cutbacks had taken their toll, however. I hadn't seen his smile in months. He'd taken the demotion to co-pilot hard, as had a lot of the pilots here. I was grateful for my seniority, and that I could hold on to my position for now. I understood how the more junior guys felt, but they needed to try to be more thankful for what they still had, like I was trying to.

We wandered up to the concourse, where most of the restaurants had been shuttered due to the decreased tourist trade. The choices were pizza or Chinese. I got a slice of pepperoni, Jim picked up a plate of orange chicken & rice. We chose a plastic table in the nearly deserted seating area. The Honolulu airport used to be filled with excited families, happy newlyweds, and fast-talking businessmen. Now only a few grim-faced passengers sat silently, contemplating the dangers they were about to face by taking to the sky. More than half the lunch customers were airport workers.

Jim stared into the distance, and ate his lunch slowly. I knew what he felt, and didn't want to intrude. I'd been lucky to get him to accompany me. His guess of an impending furlough was probably correct, but I didn't want to let my mind wander too far in that direction. That course led to fear and hopelessness. We ate in silence until both of our lunches were gone. I leaned back and looked at my empty plate, and then had a sudden flash of a memory from college; an empty pizza box, several dozen beer bottles, good friends laughing at a raunchy movie we'd rented. I wondered when, or if, I would ever feel that free and relaxed again.

"What are you going to do?" Jim asked, looking out across the nearly empty ramp.

"Do for what?"

"When it's all gone. When the airline shuts down and everybody has to leave the islands."

I shook my head. "I don't think it'll come to that."

"Of course it will. There's no stopping these things. They'll keep moving, growing, expanding. They'll hit here and make us move out. They'll move up the Caribbean and get Florida, then Texas. The ones in the Pacific will go to Mexico, and California. They'll find a way to live farther from the water." His voice grew edgier and louder. A couple of heads turned our way. "They'll hit us where it hurts; refineries, manufacturing, energy. We can't stop them. We can't! There's no way we are going to survive. We're just fooling ourselves and looking the other way while they take over the world and wipe us out."

"Jim, take it easy."

"Easy? Shit, we're sitting here like it's just another day on the job, while the world is falling down around us. Get it? The fucking world is coming apart and we're sitting here eating this slop like there's nothing wrong. Like we're not going to hear about more job cuts and furloughs. Like we're not going to be driven off these islands. Like those goddamn things aren't going to erase us from the face of the earth!"

Across the aisle, a young mother held her infant close to her chest, tears streaming down her face. I glared at Jim with my best Stern Captain face, and caught his eye. He looked at me as I subtly shook my head, and threw a glance at the young woman. Jim took a deep breath, and caught my meaning as he leaned back in the hard plastic chair.

"Sorry," he whispered.

"Let's get moving." I knew what he was going through. We all did. It was still taboo to rant about the Pouakai, even though most people did it internally or with close friends.

We walked back to the crewroom, where a majority of our pilots had shown up. These meetings used to be handled by memos, but there was no normal any more. We used to have over five hundred pilots. Now down to two hundred and five, those of us who weren't out on trips, sick, or on vacation, easily fit into the large lounge under the main concourse.

Jack Ching, our V.P. of Flight Operations stood behind a table at the far end of the room. Bob Lucas, the Chief Pilot, towered next to him. Knots of people stood around the room, deep in discussion. By looking at who stood in each group, I could pretty much tell what was being said, since the conversations didn't change from day to day. In one corner was the 'arm ourselves' coalition, who'd been advocating mounting missiles and guns on all our planes. Despite the dire situation, the FAA did not look favorably on a fleet of armed passenger aircraft. Next to the coffee maker stood the 'surf patrol', local guys who'd do anything to get the world back to normal so they could hit the beach again without worry. On and on, groups of pilots who had their own ideas of how to handle the situation huddled with like-minded friends, certain their suggestions would work. The thing about pilots is that we're never lacking in attitude or ideas. Our main focus at work is problem-solving; from one second to another, the changing conditions of flight means that we are constantly evaluating our position, attitude, progress, and course. Hundreds, maybe thousands of decisions are made each hour. I don't know of an industry with a higher percentage of Type-A personalities. It also means that most pilots can't leave their attitude in the cockpit. Put a couple of hundred people into the same room, who each feel they know best how to handle a situation, and there is bound to be friction.

Jack Ching tapped a thick manila folder on the table, but nobody paid attention.

"Hey jokers," Bob, the Chief Pilot shouted. "Shut up and sit down. Jack's got a few words to say so no mouthing off until he's done." Nobody had ever accused Bob of being subtle, either in the office or at the controls. Maybe it was in everyone's best interest that he didn't fly much these days. The murmur of voices faded, and most people took a seat.

"Thanks," Jack said. "I'm sure you are wondering what this is all about…"

"Not really," Jim said under his breath.

"We just heard from the Department of Defense. They've decided not to allow any more escort flights through the Roc's territory."

"Shit," came a loud voice. I looked to my right, and saw the petite Annette Wilson glaring at Jack. "Goddammit, what the hell are people down there supposed to do? Fucking swim here?" Annette had family in New Zealand, and had been one of my regular co-pilots down to Sydney and Auckland over the past few years. She also had a vocabulary that could peel the rust off of a sunken battleship.

"Annie, shut up and let Jack finish," Bob said.

She stayed quiet, but I could see she was really steaming.

"Without the DoD escort," Jack continued, "we won't be making any more flights south of here."

"Then put the guns on our planes like we've been saying," said Kelii Rogers. "We can do the flights on our own. We don't need the freaking military."

"You too Rogers," said Bob, pointing a finger at Kelii. "I mean it people. Shut up or you're going to get booted out of here. Jack has more to say, so let him say it."

An uneasy silence settled on the group. This wasn't going to be pretty.

"Thanks Bob," Jack said, his fingers nervously strumming on the folder in his hands. "The point is that we can't do these flights south, so they're gone as of now. Also, we've seen a marked reduction in load factor coming from the mainland, especially from some of the smaller markets. People simply aren't coming here for vacation and a lot of the locals have left for good. We received word today from Washington that they are reducing our subsidies, and eliminating them completely for markets that don't meet a certain average load factor. As of now it looks like we'll have to stop service to Salt Lake City, Boise, and Toronto."

"Cut to the chase," Jim Reynolds said as he stood up. "How many of us are getting cut."

Jack cleared his throat.

"This is preliminary of course, based on projections for staffing the remaining flights, plus expected attrition and retirements, along with our current negotiations to pick up some of the routes from our competitors like…"

"How many?" Jim repeated again, in an even tone.

Jack cleared his throat again and looked at the file in his hand.

"Eighty five furloughs, effective in two months."

Silence filled the room for several seconds, followed by a loud "Fuck!" from Annette as she stormed out of the room. She would be on the furlough list.

"That leaves one hundred twenty active on the list," continued Jack. "There will have to be some retraining because a higher percentage of those being furloughed are on our inter-island aircraft, and the staffing will have to shift. The bid period is open for one week from today. Training for those shifted to different aircraft will begin immediately after. I'm sorry guys, but there's nothing we can do about it. We're at the mercy of the government now, and if they say we don't fly, we don't. We'll have a copy of the new bid out tomorrow, and if you have any questions, call my office."

Jack and Bob hurried out through the crowd, and amazingly enough, nobody tried to deck them as they walked by. I think we were too numb.

Jim looked at me, a resigned stare in his eyes.

"Are you going to get bounced back to co-pilot?" he asked.

I did some quick mental math.

"No, I don't think so. I'm number forty-two, so I should still hold on to Captain."

Jim nodded, and then looked around with just a tiny hint of a smile on his face.

"Maverick, you have the number of that truck driving school we saw on TV? Truck Masters, I think it was? I think I'm gonna need that."

"No problem Goose," I said, following his lead on the Top Gun quote. "I got your six."

4

Colin waved at me from across the dock, a big grin on his face. A cryptic phone message said to meet him at the university's dock in Honolulu harbor. I hadn't heard from him since he'd returned from the conference in Tokyo a month earlier. Sometimes he gets wrapped up in his work, but this had been a longer stretch of quiet than usual.

"What's up?" I asked as I walked closer.

We shook hands, but he didn't say anything. He just kept that goofy grin on as he motioned for me to follow. We turned the corner and walked next to the university's research ship, the *R/V Kilo Moana.* Its broad twin hulls rubbed against the fenders with a slow creak. The trade winds had eased, and the heat from the summer sun pressed down hard on us. The sharp tang of creosote and salt water filled the air.

"Come on, Colin, where are we going?"

"Right here," he said as he turned around. We stood between an orange shipping container and the ship.

"What's here?" I asked.

"This." He pointed to the container.

"Something inside it?"

"No, the container itself," Colin said, practically giddy.

"This isn't a game of chess," I said. "Tell me what's going on."

A standard seagoing shipping unit, the container stretched forty-eight feet long, and a square eight feet high and wide. Painted bright orange, it had 'Property of the University of Hawaii, Manoa' stenciled on the side. The name of the previous owners, a now-defunct ocean cargo company, had been hastily painted over, leaving orange splotches of a different shade on the sides and end.

"Okay," said Colin. "What's our number one problem right now?"

"Your bad breath?" I said, suppressing a grin.

"Yeah, fine, number two problem," he replied, not falling for my bait.

"The Pouakai?"

"Yes, but more than that, the problem is that we haven't been able to study them. We haven't had enough time to examine a live subject close up to determine behavior, biology, habits, chemistry, or anything else. What we need is a live, captive Pouakai."

I hesitated for a moment and looked at the container. Then the bottom dropped out of my stomach. "You don't have a live Pouakai in that container, do you?"

"Not yet, but hopefully we will soon."

"How the hell do you expect to do that?"

"Come here," he said. "Let me show you."

We walked around to the open end. Instead of a bare metal interior, it had thick black padding on all sides, floor, ceiling, and ends. Even the inside of the doors had the padding installed. Colin grinned from ear to ear.

"It's nice, but what do you do? Send out invitations?" I said.

"At the conference last month, our paper was very well received. By the end of the week everyone had agreed that the Pouakai derive at least some, or maybe even all their energy from the sun. The next step was to consider how to make a closer study of them. That's where Alan came in, because he was originally an engineering major before he got into biology. He designed this thing for us, with the help of some naval architects. We started with three problems. One, how to attract a Pouakai; two, how to capture it; and three, how to keep it alive long enough to study it. Step one is simple enough. We just have to make a lot of noise while the Pouakai are nearby. Steps two and three were harder, but that's where this container comes it."

He hopped up into the container, each step springy on the padded material. I followed him in.

"So here's the plan," he continued. "We take this container to an island at the edge of the Pouakai's territory. It will sit on a raft just a few feet from the shore. Once the ship has dropped it off they'll hightail it back north, out of the Pouakai's range. Alan and I will be onboard a Navy sub just offshore, monitoring the container. Built into the end of the container are some flat speakers hooked up to a small computer. It can play a variety of sounds, from machines to music. The whole device is run by remote control. Once the Pouakai are nearby, we'll arm the doors, which have hydraulic rams to slam them shut. Then we turn on the sounds to attract a Pouakai inside. There are cameras that work both in visible light as well as infrared and ultraviolet behind that clear panel up on the ceiling." He pointed to a smooth square above us. "Once we know the Pouakai is inside we trigger the doors. They'll slam shut, trapping the thing inside."

"Won't the other Pouakai attack the container?"

Colin shrugged. "Probably. We armored the inside before we attached the padding, however. The padding is Kevlar lined too, so the thing's beak can't tear it apart. It should keep the Pouakai from flailing itself to death inside here. It's also watertight so it can't sink if it falls off the raft. It will be in shallow enough water so that if it does capsize, we can recover it once the rest of the Pouakai have left.

"Hopefully, the darkness inside will cause it to slow down, to keep it from beating itself up. We have lights up there behind the Lexan too; different wavelengths that we can use to see what kind of light the Pouakai need to live. There are armored manipulator arms under that hatch there," he said, pointing to another flat spot in the ceiling. "If the Pouakai calms down enough, we can use them to hold it in place and do an exam."

"What if it dies?"

Colin shrugged. "We'll do an autopsy immediately, which should give us enough time to study it better than we have before. Then we open the doors, toss the thing into the water, and arm the container to capture another one. Eventually we hope to have it set up semi-permanently as a research station somewhere down south."

As I looked around the container, a thought hit me, and I grinned.

"What?" Colin asked.

"Build a better mousetrap…" I said, as I started laughing. Colin joined in too. For the first time in weeks, I felt a break in the tension.

5

I cast the line into the surf and set the reel. Using the tip of the rod, I jigged and pulled, making the small lure look like an injured fish to any hungry, bigger fish nearby. I'd already pulled in two nice papio, but wanted more to throw in the freezer.

Jennifer sat in the sand behind me, her long, tan legs crossed as she read the newspaper. The morning had started out nice and cool, but now the sun began to beat down on us. I didn't want to be out here sweating all afternoon.

The next few casts didn't bring in anything, so I sat in the sand next to Jennifer. She put the paper on her lap and watched the surf roll in.

"Peter and Kailani are moving to LA," she said, without looking at me.

"What? When?"

"Next week."

"But his job at the city was secure. Hell, the emergency services division is the only part that's still growing. What happened?"

"It isn't Peter's job. Kailani just couldn't take the stress of living here anymore. I saw her working in the yard yesterday. She was crying, so I went over to talk to her. She's scared, Mark. So are a lot of people. She knows what's coming, and wants to be gone before the Rocs get here."

"They're not coming right away," I said. "It could be years. Maybe never."

"Or it could be tomorrow," she said. "You may have spent time with them, but you don't know what they are really doing."

"But Colin doesn't think..."

"It's all just guessing," she said more forcefully. "They don't *know* for sure what those things will do next. Kailani is scared to death. She doesn't want to be here when they arrive, whether it's tomorrow or in ten years."

"She grew up here. This is her home."

"That doesn't mean we want to be targets. We're scared, Mark. You may think you can live with them, but we don't."

She crumpled the newspaper onto the ground and stood up, shaking. I had no idea what to say to her. She walked to the edge of the water and looked out to sea, her arms crossed tightly over her chest.

I came up behind her and put my hands on her shoulders.

"You said we?"

She nodded.

"You're scared too?"

"What the hell do you think?" she said, still looking out to the ocean. "They're going to come. Anyone who thinks differently is just fooling themselves."

"We don't know for sure."

"We know enough."

We stood like that for a while, looking at the ocean, contemplating what lay beyond that horizon, literally and figuratively.

"What do you want to do?" I finally asked. She didn't reply so I circled around in front of her, and looked into her eyes.

"What do you want to do?" I repeated.

She didn't even appear to see me. Her eyes were focused right through me, into infinity. I held on to her tightly, and we rocked gently with the rhythm of the waves. Then she said something so softly I couldn't understand.

"What was that?" I asked.

"I want to leave," she said.

"Okay," I replied quietly, as I picked up my fishing rod. "Let's go."

"No," she said. "I want to leave. I want to leave Hawaii."

I stepped back unsteadily, and closed my eyes. The ocean roared in my ears, and I felt dizzy.

This had been coming for a long time. Too many of our friends had already left; cousins, neighbors, and co-workers. Now our friends across the street had decided to head to the mainland too. With my airline shrinking, the odds for its long-term survival were not good.

But this was our home.

"We don't know what's coming," I insisted. "Colin says it could be years, if ever, before they make it this far north. We shouldn't rush a decision like this without knowing what's ahead."

"Listen to yourself," Jennifer shouted at me, taking a step back. "You always do what you want, without listening to anyone else. You think you're bulletproof, but you're not. Being a Captain doesn't mean everything in the world bows to your command!"

"I don't do that."

She lowered her voice, and looked at the sand. "Yes, you do. You don't see it, and most of the time it doesn't matter, but you've been doing this since I met you. You try to control what goes on around you, and blast ahead without thinking of the consequences. Maybe it helps you in your job, but not with me."

I looked at her, and saw a fear in her eyes I'd never seen before. This was her home too, born and raised here, and it scared her to think of moving away. Yet the fear of what could happen was worse. Those two sides had been pulling on her for much longer than I'd known. Wrapped up in my job, I'd ignored the signs, her changes in mood, and subtle hints. I'd dismissed her discussion of moving in past months as idle talk, brought on by so many of our friends heading away. She'd tried to tell me what she felt, but I'd discounted her words because they'd conflicted with what I wanted, which was to fly. Always and forever I'd been chasing that dream. How much had I missed in that single-minded pursuit? How had Jennifer accepted me putting my career first? How had I not seen what an ass I'd been?

"You really want to leave here? Move to the mainland?" I asked, voice quavering. She nodded.

"Lisa offered us her place for as long as we want it," she said. "It's plenty big, and we'd only be an hour away from Kelly. Plus Josh would be just a day's drive away in Missoula."

I looked over her head, and up into the hard blue sky.

"You'd like Denver," she continued. "It's not all that bad, just a little cold. You like my cousins. It will be easier this way."

I heard the hope in her voice, and it tore at my heart. Had I really been that blind to her wishes? I thought I'd been brave on many occasions in the past, but I finally realized it had been the bravado of someone in control of a situation that might turn unstable. This was very different. For the first time I knew what it meant to be really scared, to face an unknown that you had no control over, or to have choices without a predictable outcome.

I hugged her, my heart pounding like crazy.

"Okay," I whispered. "We'll go."

I looked over my shoulder and across the waves. The Pouakai were out there, somewhere. They'd won again. I felt the old bitterness rising against them, stronger than it had since they smashed into my plane last spring. Now they were forcing this drastic change in my life, and I hated them, more than anything else in my life. Wherever we ended up, I'd find a way to get rid of them for good.

6

Colin and I sat in the two remaining recliner chairs in our living room, each of us with a cold beer in hand. The mound of boxes that had started the morning piled against the far wall had grown smaller during the day as we moved them into the portable storage container. Although smaller than the one Colin had used for his Pouakai trap, it still dominated our driveway. Almost done with the big stuff, what remained were mostly personal belongings; photo albums, computers, and clothing we were taking with us to Colorado. Jennifer would take her time packing that away in the next few days.

I shifted in my seat. "Ow," I said to no one in particular.

"Ow," Colin added as he tried to reach for the bowl of edamame at his feet, but failed. "Seriously," he said, glaring at me. "How much stuff can one family accumulate?"

I shook my head. "Not that much, compared to our parents. The longer you stay together, the more you have. It's a law of physics. I think Einstein discovered it after helping his grandparents move, and came up with the idea of black holes."

"Funny," he said with a straight face.

Jennifer came over and squeezed into the big recliner with me. She deftly pulled the beer from my hand, and took a long swig. Then she looked at me.

"You stink," she said with a grin.

"You're not exactly a plumeria blossom yourself, sweetie." I didn't have to tell her how good she looked in her shorts and T-shirt. She knew it, and enjoyed letting me ogle her. Even dusty and sweaty she looked a decade younger than her forty-seven years. Ever since I'd agreed to leave Hawaii, the spark of fun had returned to her eyes.

She took another long pull from the bottle, and then handed it back to me. Her head tilted onto my shoulder, with her smooth legs on top of mine. We sat there for several minutes enjoying the down time.

"Before I melt into this chair permanently," Colin said, "is there anything else for me to move?"

"I don't think so," Jennifer replied. "I took a swing through all the rooms before I sat down, and didn't see anything big or obvious."

She gave a little sigh as I ran my fingers through her straight black hair. "If there's anything left it'll be small," she continued. "Mark can stow it himself before they pick up the container tomorrow."

"Slave driver," I said.

"And don't you forget it."

We sat there for several minutes, enjoying the breeze coming through the open windows, letting the soreness ebb from our muscles. I looked down at the carpet, and traced the indentations from the bookcases. How many years had they sat in that same spot? I'd forgotten how much darker the carpet had been when we'd installed it years ago, but that small patch under the shelves had remained a golden-beige while the rest of the room slowly faded in the sunlight and constant traffic. The books laid out a timeline too, as I'd packed them away a few days earlier: Some kids books left over from when Josh and Kelly were young, novels I'd loved, manuals for airplanes I hadn't flown in years, and flyers from old vacations. Now they all sat in a couple of dozen boxes inside the shipping container on our driveway, waiting to be taken to a warehouse and stored for…What? Our return? The demise of the Pouakai? Or would they remain there until some natural disaster leveled the warehouse, centuries after mankind had been erased from history?

"So when do you leave?" Colin's voice brought me out of my fog.

"Some time next week," Jennifer replied.

"After my last trip." I added. "One more San Francisco round trip starting tomorrow. I'll be back Sunday afternoon, and then I'm done."

"And then you're off to the frozen tundra of Colorado," Colin said with a sad smile.

I shrugged. "Hopefully it's only temporary."

"Hopefully," Colin replied.

"Hopefully," Jennifer echoed.

After another minute of silence I asked Colin, "When do you and Anna leave Hawaii?"

A grin spread across his face. "When they make us."

"You're really going to stay?" Jennifer asked. "What about Anna? Doesn't she want to get out of here too?"

Colin shrugged. "She does, but she wants to stay with me more. She said that if anyone was going to find a way to get rid of these things it was me, and she wanted to stay and let me do that."

"Aren't you going out on the ship soon?"

Colin nodded. "About ten more days and we should have everything loaded up. The trap is ready, and we're getting our supplies lined up. Once the Navy is ready to accompany us with their sub, we're off."

"Anna will be here by herself?" Jennifer asked quietly.

"Her mom is here now. She moved over from the big island last month. They'll hang out together until I get back."

Jennifer shook her head. "Brave girl."

Colin nodded. He reached down and snagged the bowl of edamame. He had again remembered to bring makana, a gift, when he came over. The bowl of fresh-cooked soybeans with a little garlic and sesame oil made a perfect snack on a day like this. One of these days I'd remember to bring something when I went to their house. Maybe.

"Aren't you scared," Jennifer finally asked.

Colin nodded again. "Sure. I've seen what the Pouakai can do. But someone has to stop them. I guess I'm in the right position for it now." He put a couple of empty soybean pods back into the bowl and took out another one. "It's not like I volunteered for this. I'd much rather be going over data from the planet finder satellites. Sometimes though, you just have things thrust on you, and you deal with what you've got." He dropped several more soybeans in his mouth, and smiled.

I never knew Colin was that brave. Either that or he really didn't understand the dangers. I chose to believe the first one.

"If you guys don't have anything more to move, I should be going," he said, struggling out of the recliner.

"No, that should do it," I said.

We shook hands, and then hugged. Jennifer reached in and hugged both of us.

"You be careful," she said.

"Don't worry. I'm more of a coward than either of you. I'll be hiding inside that nice steel tube of a submarine most of the time. It'll be cramped, but safe."

"Tell Anna to call us anytime. Please," Jennifer said.

"You too," I added. "I want to hear how the great Pouakai hunt is going."

"Sure thing. Don't worry, I'll be fine. We'll get it figured out soon, then things will be back to normal."

"We're counting on it."

Colin took off down the hill, in his rusty old Toyota. We stood in the doorway for a long time after that, listening to the sounds of the world; the tradewinds blowing down the valley, the distant surf at the beach, birds in the trees.

"He's a brave man," Jennifer finally said.

"Yeah, he is," I added. We needed more like him, but I had a feeling that trying to eliminate the Pouakai was like shooting arrows into the dark; you might hit your target, but just as likely you'd end up nailing a friend instead. I hugged Jennifer, who stood up on her tiptoes to kiss me.

I felt horrible about leaving Hawaii, but we had to do it. My first duty was to my family. The rest of the world came second. If that made me a coward and Colin a hero, so be it. Soon enough we'd be on the mainland, away from any immediate danger. Then, maybe, I could find some way to help.

At least we'd be safe in Colorado, I thought.

7

Sunlight reflected off of the low scattered clouds and ocean swells of the Pacific, a sight I'd never gotten tired of. The view out the cockpit window took on a more melancholy tone though, as it might be many years, if ever, before I saw it again.

My last flight: I never thought it would come this soon. I had been planning to fly until mandatory retirement at sixty-five, nearly fifteen years in the future. For now though, this was it.

We'd taken off from San Francisco into the typical summer morning fog, and popped up through it to a brilliant blue sky. The towers of the Golden Gate Bridge stood out of the fog like two orange spikes, signposts for what lay beneath. Now, four hours into the flight, I had just an hour left in my career as a pilot, and try as I might, I couldn't shake the feeling of failure.

Jeff Lee was my co-pilot, the first time we'd flown together since crashing on Nanumea in the spring. He offered to let me fly both legs, but with his furlough coming in another week, I said no. He flew into SFO while I took the leg home. We'd chatted all the way over the previous afternoon, but this last leg was mostly in silence. We both had a lot to think about.

We passed the last waypoint before calling Honolulu center on the radio, and Jeff sent our position report.

"Last time for that too," he said with a smile. Trying to talk to controllers in San Francisco over the High Frequency radio was the equivalent of shouting to your neighbor across the street during a windstorm. The technology hadn't changed much since the 1930s, and sometimes the static made meaningful communications impossible.

"Any plans after you get moved?" he asked.

"No, not really. Just hunker down and see what happens, I guess. You?"

"Alaska. I've got a cabin outside of Fairbanks that I usually go to in the summer for fishing and hunting. I'll just hang out there until things calm down."

"Not much of a party scene for you out there," I said with a grin.

"Just me and the ptarmigan, bears, and moose," he laughed. "I need some down time anyway." He placed the flight plan and report sheets into the envelope for our dispatch office records.

The ACARS chime dinged, signaling that we had a text message from our dispatch office. I was getting my approach charts for Honolulu out and arranged, so Jeff printed the message and started reading it out loud.

"Attention all aircraft inbound Hawaii," he began, and then went silent. I turned to him and all I saw was a blank stare on his face.

"What is it?"

He handed me the message:

> ATTN ALL ACFT INBOUND HAWAII. ROCS POSITIVELY IDENTIFIED WEST OF KONA MOVING NORTH. ONE NAVY DESTROYER SUNK. IF YOU HAVE NOT REACHED ETP, RETURN TO MAINLAND. IF YOU ARE PAST ETP, CONTINUE INBOUND. BE PREPARED FOR DIVERSION. DISPATCH. HOLLY.

"Holy shit," I said.

"Here we go again," Jeff added, his face a ghostly pale color. I probably looked the same.

One thought overwhelmed my mind; Jennifer. If the Pouakai were around, I hoped she would remember to be quiet, and stay hidden. If she'd been listening to my stories from Nanumea, she would.

8

"All aircraft just shut up!"

I'd never heard an air traffic controller use language like that, but I'd never been in a situation like this, either. We were descending toward Honolulu, all eyes searching for Pouakai. Seventeen aircraft had been enroute to Hawaii and too far to turn around. The military had wanted to make us all turn back, but saner heads prevailed, since most of us would have run out of fuel short of the mainland.

"No more replies unless it's an emergency," the approach controller continued, obviously stressed by the situation. "United eighty-five, turn right heading three-five-zero, cleared for approach runway eight left, American two fifteen, descend and maintain three thousand." His rapid-fire directions were an attempt to clear the skies as soon as possible. We'd just watched another airline's plane make a sharp turn and steep descent into the airport.

"Jeez, he's going fast," Jeff said, while looking at that plane.

"Everyone's in panic mode."

"They'd better keep it together. No use in banging up an airplane by hurrying."

After a couple of interminable minutes, the controller turned us toward the airport. "Palm Tree twenty-two turn right heading three-five-zero, cleared for visual approach, runway eight left."

I turned the plane right, and as we rolled level Jeff said, "Oh shit."

Adrenaline kicked in, and my heart raced. "Pouakai?"

"No, look." He pointed toward the airport. A thick column of black smoke rose from the far end of the runway.

"Son of a bitch. Did the Pouakai get him?"

"No, I don't think so. It's the guy we saw making a steep approach. He was going too fast and ran off the end of the runway."

Just then I heard the United ahead of us call approach control. "There's an overrun at the airport. It looks like the runway is closed."

"No shit," Jeff said under his breath.

"All aircraft maintain altitude, approach clearances cancelled."

I leveled off and overflew the runway. Another airline's 767 sat nose down in the grass at the end of the runway. The escape slides were out with a horde of people standing on the taxiway nearby. The right wingtip had broken off and flames engulfed the wing and grass. "At least it looks like most of them got out," I said.

Decision time.

"Approach, Palm Tree twenty-two," I said. "We're declaring a fuel emergency. We need an immediate approach."

"Unable, Palm Tree. The tower called and said the field is closed to civilian traffic because of the overrun. They've got a ton of rescue equipment down at the far end of the runway. The only open airport is Lihue."

"Lihue is twenty minutes away," I replied, trying to hold my voice steady. "Unless you want the rest of us to go and ditch these planes, I'd suggest letting us land."

The radio stayed silent for what seemed like an eternity. Finally I keyed the mike.

"Approach, you still there?"

"Standby."

After another few moments of silence, I was about to turn for Honolulu, controllers be dammed, when the radio came alive.

"All aircraft, Honolulu will take you now. Be sure to land as short as possible and avoid the rescue efforts at the east end of the runway."

"Thank God," Jeff muttered.

Another string of rapid-fire instructions followed to get us in some semblance of order and heading in line back toward the airport.

Jeff reprogrammed the computer with our new route.

"How does the fuel look?" I asked.

"Marginal, but okay. Don't do any more go-arounds though."

"Got it." After holding for an hour while the air traffic controllers figured out what to do with us when we first arrived in the islands, our fuel reserves had dwindled to the bare minimum.

We lined up five miles behind the United 777 and followed the directions from the controller. Jeff called the company operations center to tell them we were coming in, but nobody answered. Hopefully someone knew we were coming and would have a crew ready to meet us. If the Pouakai were in the area though, they may all be in a shelter somewhere, unable to help us. We flew west along the Honolulu shoreline low and slow, burning up even more precious fuel. The controllers wouldn't let us out of line from behind the United, however.

"Keep your eyes open," I said. Jeff nodded. He didn't have to be told what to look out for. We'd both seen Pouakai from the air.

"Caution all aircraft, fighters launching from the Air Guard base in three minutes."

"Seriously?" Jeff asked as we made the turn to cross the west shoreline of Oahu. "That's right when we get there."

"Approach, Palm Tree twenty-two. We don't have the fuel for a go-around, no matter what the fighters are doing."

"Palm Tree, we're letting you in here against all normal regulations. Just be glad we let you in at all."

Jeff and I looked at each other. "And fuck you very much," Jeff said, pretending to key the microphone. "Asshole."

We configured for landing, trying to remain close to the United jet ahead of us. In the distance, beyond the rising smoke from the burning plane, were the verdant ridges at the east end of Honolulu.

Jennifer was just over that last ridge, hopefully hiding someplace safe inside our house. We hadn't been able to get details on how long the alert had been out, or how many Pouakai had actually been sighted in Honolulu. Our operations frequency remained frustratingly quiet.

The approach controller turned us over to the tower, who cleared us to land. The United landed hard, two puffs of tire smoke curling in its wake as it hit the concrete. We bounced in the normal tradewind turbulence; the blue of the ocean to our right and green trees below felt unnaturally bright, as if mocking our grim situation.

"Any Pouakai in sight?" I asked.

"Nothing yet."

Five hundred feet above the ground we crossed the entrance channel to Pearl Harbor, emptied now of almost all Navy vessels.

"Dammit," said Jeff. "Here come the Guard fighters."

I looked to the right of the runway. Six F-22s were taxiing at high speed toward our runway, and it looked like we'd meet at the same place and time. As if on cue, the tower called.

"Palm Tree twenty-two, go around for fighter departure. Turn right heading one four zero, maintain three thousand feet."

I keyed the mike. "Unable. We've declared a low fuel emergency."

"Palm Tree twenty-two, the Guard has emergency priority. A large swarm of Rocs is at the east shore, and they have to go now!"

"Unless you want two hundred and fifty dead people on your hands, we're landing now. The fighters will have to wait just a few seconds, that's all."

"Palm Tree, go around!"

We crossed the threshold of the runway.

"Hold on, Jeff."

The lead fighter crossed the hold-short line on the taxiway ahead of me, and bobbed to a stop as the pilot stomped on his brakes. I eased my plane to the left side of the runway as I flared for the landing, flashing past the fighters, just a couple of dozen feet from my right wingtip. Years of practice took over and I made the landing, possibly my last ever, as smooth as glass. Then I jumped on the brakes and slowed quickly, turning off at my normal spot.

"Tell the fighters, thank you," I said to the tower.

"The FAA will be contacting you," came the icy reply.

I turned to Jeff. "What are they going to do? Pull my license?"

He grinned as he switched to the ground frequency. They directed us to a nearby gate. There wasn't anyone to marshal us in, but I'd done it so many times I didn't need them. I stopped when I pulled even with the jetway and shut down the engines.

"Now what?" Jeff asked.

"Call ops, see if they can get someone up here to move the jetway for us."

Nobody answered in ops. Just before I went to blow the escape slide for everyone to exit down however, a young agent showed up in the jetway and moved it toward the plane.

When she opened the door I could tell she had been crying. A look of fear filled her eyes.

"Thanks for moving the jetway," I said.

"The Rocs are coming," she replied, "I saw you pull in and didn't want to leave you out here, but you have to get everyone to safety." She dashed down the jetway.

"Wait! Where should we all go?"

"Everyone is in the main concourse, hiding. I have to go, please. I don't want them to get me…"

She turned and ran back into the terminal.

"Get everyone off the plane and into the terminal," I said quietly to the lead flight attendant.

The passengers streamed off the plane, most with fear in their eyes or tears on their faces. I wanted to comfort them, to tell them it would be all right, but one overriding thought raced through my head.

Jennifer.

9

The terminal had been sealed tight by airport security. I managed to make it to the crewroom with my ID, but couldn't get outside to the parking lot. There was no way to get home. Jeff and I stood with a couple of other pilots that had made it in, and watched the TV news.

"Remember the most important measures, in case you see a Roc in the vicinity," said an overly-caffeinated local newsreader. "Stay quiet. If you're in your car, pull to the shoulder and shut everything off. Stay inside and don't move. If you're outside on foot, slowly and quietly make your way to shelter. Don't run, and don't scream."

Jeff groaned. "Here's where they pull out the old footage of us." As if on cue one of the many interviews Jeff and I did after returning to Oahu appeared on the screen.

"Yep. Always refer to the experts." I rolled my eyes at Jeff, and he grimly shook his head.

"Remember," said the TV anchor, "people have survived around the Rocs before. Here is an interview with Captain Mark Boone and Co-Pilot Jeff Lee who kept most of their passengers alive after crashing onto a Roc-infested island in the South Pacific a few months ago."

Jeff and I both walked away from the TV. We'd seen that interview too many times already. The other pilots in the room knew enough not to kid us about it like they had in the past.

I phoned home again. About half my tries had been met with a fast busy signal, and those that had gone through ended up at the answering machine. Jennifer's cell phone went straight to voicemail. She was either hiding, or at a friend's house. At least, I hoped so.

I got the answering machine again. "Dammit."

Fear for Jennifer kept me pacing as if I were a caged animal. Airport security had an armed guard posted at every exit, and they were deadly serious about not letting anyone outside. I turned to the TV again.

"HPD has closed off all streets and freeways," said the TV newsreader. "Remain where you are until the all-clear has sounded."

"Yeah right," said Jeff. "You think the police are sitting outside with those things around?"

I thought about that for a minute. "You may be right."

"Huh?"

"If I could get outside, I don't think anyone would stop me from getting home."

"Don't be an idiot, Boonie. There could be roadblocks, or accidents, or you could get stuck in traffic with the other loons and be a sitting target for the Pouakai."

"Look at the traffic cams," I said, pointing to the status monitors at the back of the crew room. "Nobody's out there. They're all holed up somewhere. But there's no Pouakai showing up here either. If I could just get to my car I could get home and make sure Jennifer is safe, instead of sitting here, being useless."

"All it takes is one Pouakai for you to have a really bad day. Remember what happened to Brett."

I shrugged, but couldn't shake the feeling that I had to get home.

"It doesn't matter anyway," Jeff continued. "You can't get out of the terminal."

"There's got to be a way, somehow," I said quietly.

I left the crew room and wandered around, my mind spinning. I went to the Chief Pilot's office, but it being Sunday, the door was locked. The main lounge had several leather sofas and chairs, computers for pulling up flight plans, and the TV. Jeff and the others huddled around the set, watching the unfolding drama. So far though, nothing had happened in Honolulu. The only action was the sinking of the Navy ship off the coast of the Big Island, well south of us. A huge swarm of Pouakai was out there, somewhere around the east end of our island. According to the TV however, nobody had reported seeing more than a couple of Pouakai in Honolulu yet.

I walked through the locker room and into the bathroom, needing to relieve myself. As I stood at the urinal, I glanced over at the wall next to me. The passenger parking lot sat on the other side of that wall, and beyond that, the employee lot with my car, ready to take me to Jennifer. If I could only get past that concrete barrier, I could get to her.

I looked up, and took in a breath. An old louver window was set into the wall. Welded shut and painted over years ago, I'd never really noticed it before. Without even washing my hands, I zipped up and climbed onto the bench below the window. The louvers were held shut with a steel bar welded into the frame, but the frame itself was screwed into the wall with what looked like standard Phillips-head screws.

Feeling like I had a secret nobody else knew, I walked back to the crew room, looking for the tool kit we used for fixing broken suitcases and headsets. I hadn't pulled it out in years, and wondered if there would be a screwdriver big enough. The rusty red case had a thick coating of dust on it, but inside sat a decent sized screwdriver. I palmed it, and nonchalantly wandered back to the bathroom, my heart pounding.

I climbed back up on the bench to work on the six screws standing between me and Jennifer. The first one had several coats of paint over it, but the moist tropical environment had softened the layers, and they peeled off easily. The screw was tight, but I got it out, and started on the second.

"This looks like a bad prison movie," Jeff said from behind me. I jumped and almost dropped the screwdriver.

"Shit. Don't scare me like that."

"You were way too obvious in trying to be casual. I could tell something was up. Are you really going to drive home with the Pouakai out there?"

"I have to make sure Jennifer is okay. She's not answering the phone and I can't take just sitting here."

"Well, hell, hang on," he said. "I'll keep an eye out for anyone else on this side. If I cough, get down and pee or something."

"Thanks." I got back to digging out the ancient window frame. A few minutes later the screws were out and I jiggled the window. It didn't budge, but the welded bar made a nice handhold. I grabbed it and yanked harder. With a grinding scrape the window moved back an inch.

"So much for the TSA's security," Jeff said from the bathroom doorway. "Be careful Boonie. I know you've been around these things before, but this isn't Nanumea. They could act a lot different here."

"Thanks," I said. "I'll be careful, and I'll give you a call once I get home, let you know I made it safely. Just help me here, and put this thing back in place after I'm out."

Jeff and I pulled the window out of the frame. It felt a lot heavier than I'd expected, but we caught it, and set it on the bench. I poked my head out into the hot and humid air. Nobody was around, so I scrambled through the opening and dropped to the ground in the planter bed that lined the wall. I heard Jeff grunting, and then the scraping sound of the window as it slid into place. I was on my own.

10

I ripped down the empty freeway toward Honolulu doing ninety, about as fast as my little econobox could go. The wind roared outside the open passenger window like a hurricane. I passed two on-ramps with police cruisers sitting on them, but their lights were off, and nobody followed me. The Honolulu traffic had eased over the past year as people moved away, but I had never seen the freeway so completely deserted like this.

The radio blasted another high-pitched warning signal, and a scratchy voice came on.

"This is a statement from the joint emergency preparedness office. A large swarm of Rocs has been positively identified over east Oahu, extending from Makapuu Point to Hawaii Kai. The Rocs are heading west, toward downtown Honolulu. Everyone take shelter now, remain quiet and keep listening for further updates."

"Son of a bitch," I mumbled. If the Pouakai kept closing in like that, I'd have to stop and hide before I got home.

I hadn't been looking in my rear-view mirror, concentrating instead on the freeway ahead. So I got a jolt of adrenaline as a police cruiser blasted past me, doing well over a hundred. For a moment I thought he would try to pull me over, but he kept on moving, raising a cloud of dust every time he bounced through a dip in the road. His lights and sirens were off; a good idea since they'd attract the Pouakai that much faster. Maybe he was trying to get home like me.

The freeway curved sharply onto an overpass as it went by the University. Just beyond the crest of the overpass a plume of dust billowed skyward. I slammed on the brakes just in time to avoid a pile of three cars smashed into each other, including the police car that had just passed me. Flames burst from the wreckage as I veered around the twisted metal scattered across the only open lane. If the police car hadn't passed me, it might have been me that plowed into the two vehicles already smashed up on the freeway.

I didn't look into any of the cars as I went by, and a feeling of shame washed over me. I should have stopped to see if anyone had survived. One part of my mind screamed to go help them, but the other forced me to continue because I didn't know where Jennifer was. I drove on.

I soared over another rise less than a minute later, and I saw the Pouakai, the same gray cloud that I'd seen from my plane over Nanumea.

"Son of a bitch," I shouted, and hit the steering wheel with my palm. I slammed on the brakes and slewed over to the exit I was just passing. My car screamed down the ramp and across the intersection, all against red lights. I pulled onto the road that ran under the elevated freeway, and skidded to a stop next to the Kahala mall. I stopped under the cover of the freeway, protected from whatever flew directly above me, but I could still see out to either side of the road. The mall sat to the right, and a residential neighborhood to the left.

"Damn, damn, damn," I whispered to myself. The overworked engine pinged and hissed quietly as I waited. I dialed my home number, but got the fast-busy signal. I tried again and it started ringing.

"Come on Jen," I whispered to myself, "answer the phone."

"Hi, you've reached Mark and Jennifer. Please leave…" I hung up, and hit the steering wheel several times.

"God dammit. Answer the fucking phone!"

A quiet whoosh outside the passenger window startled me. A black triangle streaked by, not a hundred feet away. My heart pounded as I leaned over and rolled up the window. I hunkered down in my seat, wanting to disappear from view. A large towel lay folded on the rear seat from an aborted day at the beach several weeks ago. I pulled it over myself, hoping that if a Pouakai didn't see a person inside, they might not attack the car. I wrapped the end of the towel around my head, leaving an opening for my eyes, and scrunched as low as I could into the driver's seat. It quickly warmed up inside my cocoon, but I didn't dare open a window.

Several minutes went by with no movement outside. Then a Pouakai appeared in the distance over the mall, and then another. Within seconds a huge swarm of them wheeled about in the sky. Several flew under the freeway and over my car. I slid further down in the seat, my knees against the bolster.

Wham. I stifled a scream as a Pouakai bounced off the top of my car. It flew down the road, bouncing its way along the abandoned cars under the freeway. *Wham* again, as another Pouakai slammed the roof of my car, caving in the thin sheet metal. A rough scraping noise came from overhead. The thing was still there. Its wings drooped over both sides of the car windows, blocking out some of the light. High-pitched whistles came through the roof in a couple of different tones. There were two of the monsters on top of my car. They shook and rattled the vehicle, and I hoped they didn't work themselves into a rage on their own. *Fly away, fly away*, I thought. Just get the hell off of my car.

Crash. One of the Pouakai smashed its long spike onto my windshield, shattering the safety glass. It held in place, but little bits of glass rained down on the towel. I held the car keys in my hand, desperately wanting to get out of this spot. If I did anything though, I'd be killed in seconds by this flock of frenzied Pouakai.

A louder screech pierced the air, and several more Pouakai flew in to land on my car. The suspension creaked under the load, and the car rocked at they fought. Two creatures rolled off the roof and onto the hood, pushing the shattered windshield in that much more. I peeked out with one eye at the ebon monsters wrestling right in front of me. *Go away. Go away. Go away.* A third Pouakai dove in from the side, and buried its spike through the hood and into the engine compartment. A cloud of steam billowed out from underneath, and the Pouakai all whistled as the one pulled its spike out and shook like a dog. The wing that had been covering the passenger window lifted, revealing a ghastly flock of Pouakai, as thick as bees around a hive, circling the mall parking lot. Several seemed to be heading toward my car. *I'm going to die here, and Jennifer will never know what happened. She'll never know I did this for her. Why didn't I listen to Jeff…?*

A loud screech echoed under the freeway, sounding like the creatures were beginning another attack. Then I recognized the noise as tires squealing. The mass of Pouakai on top of my car flew off in a rush of wind, and I dared to peek out from under the towel. Someone else had done the same thing I did, hiding themselves inside their car in the mall parking lot. Instead of staying hidden though, they must have thought they could outrun the creatures. They peeled out of the mall lot and onto the freeway, several thousand Pouakai in furious pursuit.

The air cleared of most of the creatures, and soon the only sound was the hiss of steam from under the hood of my wounded car. A few Pouakai stragglers flew westward over the mall until the skies emptied. I waited another ten minutes, but the sky remained clear.

Gingerly, I pulled the towel off of me, soaking wet from sweat. Little bits of glass rolled onto the floor around my feet. I sat up, and bumped my head into the roof that had been shoved down by the fighting Pouakai. My door wouldn't open, but the window still rolled down, so I climbed out that way. My heart pounded as I looked for any sign of the creatures.

The air stunk of engine coolant and steam, and a large puddle of green water flowed from under my car. Oil mixed in too, giving it a rainbow sheen. My car was most definitely dead.

A four-foot piece of rusty steel pipe lay in the gutter next to my car. I picked it up as a weapon, but deep down I knew it wouldn't do more than delay my demise by a few seconds if the Pouakai returned.

It was just over four miles from the mall to my house, a route I'd driven hundreds of times in the past. I'd never walked it though, and in the sweltering midday heat, it would take over an hour. Too drained to jog the distance, I set a steady brisk pace toward home, the rusty pipe swinging close by my side. My head swiveling back and forth, I emerged from under the freeway and followed the sidewalk eastward. Nothing moved, and an eerie quiet blanketed the city. Only the blustery tradewind made a sound as it passed through the palm trees.

The cloud of Pouakai had disappeared already, not even visible on the eastern horizon. The empty streets looked odd. I caught a glimpse of two people peeking out of an apartment window, but they dove inside when they saw me. I stepped over the broken bottles and trash alongside the road, jumping every time I heard a noise. Even the wind made me think of the whoosh of a Pouakai's wings.

Passing the Waialae golf club, I realized that the greens weren't mowed, while leaves and branches covered the fairways. So many people had left Honolulu that the club had closed. We were falling ever deeper into a state of abandonment, tipping into a bottomless pit of hopelessness. The Pouakai were turning us into an empty shell of what we had been.

Crack. I nearly jumped out of my skin. I whirled around, pipe in hand, ready to smash a Pouakai. Instead, a tiny old Japanese man crossed the street behind me, his dog on a leash. He'd stepped on a downed palm frond. He looked at me and bowed slightly under his wide straw hat. I nodded back, breathing hard, before turning and continuing toward my neighborhood. Didn't he know about the Pouakai, or did he simply not care?

The highway paralleled the ocean along the south shore of Oahu, and a perfect set of mid-sized waves rolled over the reef. At least the hardcore surfers hadn't risked themselves to enjoy the waves as the water was completely empty. Or, more likely, the Pouakai had already taken out any surfers that had been in the water.

I passed several more neighborhoods and I sped up my pace. Nobody was outside, but the all-clear sirens hadn't sounded yet either. There had to be thousands of people holed up inside their houses here, but from what I was seeing, the entire island could be lifeless.

Sweat rolled off my forehead as I turned up the hill into my neighborhood in the Niu Valley. I started a moderate jog up the road toward home. Seven blocks to go as I ran; six; five. I broke into a dash and dropped the rusty pipe with a loud clang.

The road turned and I saw my house a couple of blocks up the hill, looking peaceful. Jen's car sat in the driveway, undamaged. Good. It looked like the swarm had missed this area.

I dashed up the last steep incline and into my driveway.

"Jen!" I called through the door. "Jen, I'm here!"

I fumbled for my keys, but then I saw the front door was ajar. I pushed it open.

"Jen? I'm home! Where are you?"

Silence. The answering machine in the hallway blinked with seven new messages; probably all the ones I'd left for her.

I walked into the kitchen and something crunched underfoot. I picked up my foot and saw shards of broken glass.

"Jenn!"

An electrical cord stretched from the kitchen wall into the living room. The floor lamp lay on its side and more broken glass littered the floor. A big brown stain covered the carpet as I turned into the room. Jennifer lay at one end of the stain, her arms and legs twisted into a grotesque position.

"*JEN!*"

I dashed in and dropped to the floor next to her, turning her head toward me. Her eyes were open but lifeless, her hands and face cold. A huge gash opened across her stomach, blood crusted around the edges. More blood was smeared across her legs, arms, and face.

"No, no," I cried, cradling her head, and bursting into tears. "No, no, no."

I rocked back and forth for a long time, my mind hit by shocks every time I opened my eyes. The shattered remains of the big picture window at the far end of the living room were piled on the floor, and both recliners lay on their backs, the fabric torn to shreds.

"What happened?" I whispered. "What happened?" It couldn't be true. She couldn't be gone.

The truth lay in my arms, a cold and bitter reminder.

Her iPod still strapped around her bicep, the thin wires for the ear buds twisted around her arm and neck. She wore a T-shirt and jogging shorts. Had she been exercising? The vacuum lay in a corner, its cord stretching into the kitchen. Jen often wore her exercise clothes and listened to music while doing housework. She must have been trying to finish the clean-up before we left for the mainland.

I held her head tight to my chest. "No, no," I sobbed over and over. My fault, I thought. My fault. I should have been home. I should have listened to her long ago, when she wanted to leave.

What had happened? I stood up, and pain shot through my left knee. I'd knelt down in the broken glass and cut myself. I ignored the gash and looked around. The front window was smashed, the glass mostly inside the living room. Something had come in that way. The furniture tossed and torn, it showed there had been a huge struggle. Jen wasn't a weak woman.

The vacuum lay behind one of the fallen recliners. I looked at it again, and took in a sharp breath. Something else lay behind the recliner too, besides the vacuum. It looked like a sheet of black goo spread over the suction end of the machine. I took two steps toward it then stopped. It was the remains of a Pouakai.

"God dammit!" I backed up and shouted. "You son of a bitch! You fucking alien bastard! Why here? Why the hell did you have to come here?"

I staggered back, and the picture suddenly came into view. Jenn had been cleaning in preparation for us leaving Hawaii. She'd had her iPod buds in her ears, and she rarely watched TV, so she wouldn't have known about the Pouakai swarm unless someone told her. She'd been vacuuming, and the noise had attracted the Pouakai. The struggle had killed both of them.

"Oh my god," I whispered as I looked at her. "Jen, I'm sorry. I'm so sorry."

I sank to the floor again, and held her hand in mine, wishing I could change what had happened. But there was no change, and as the light slowly faded into evening, I sat on the floor, crying as never before.

11

Night had already fallen when I heard a car drive up to the house, and a door slam.

"Boonie?"

I sat on the floor, Jen's head in my lap. The voice didn't register.

"Boonie? Jennifer? You guys here?"

I looked up. Something clicked; the door being pushed open.

"In here," I croaked.

"That you, Boonie?" the voice asked.

"In here," I repeated. Footsteps, and then someone at the doorway to the kitchen.

"Oh my god, what the hell…" It was Jeff Lee. He ran into the living room and stopped just past the entrance.

"Jesus Christ," he said quietly. "What happened?"

"Too late, too late," I whispered. "We were too late, Jeff. When we landed, we were already too late."

"Boonie, I'm so sorry," he said, kneeling down next to me. "You didn't call to tell me you were okay and I got worried. When they let us leave the airport…"

"Too late," I whispered again, rocking gently with Jennifer's cold head in my lap. Jeff backed out to the kitchen, and I heard the quiet beeps of a cell phone. The rest of the evening was a blur to me. I remember a lot of waiting, and I remember the police showing up well after midnight. There were a lot of people coming and going, and a harried police counselor tried to talk me out of following the ambulance carrying Jennifer away. She won out, and after a sergeant spent half an hour questioning me and Jeff, she left me with a card and phone number to call. I could find out what had happened with Jennifer later in the morning. I don't remember calling anyone, though it may have been Jeff's doing, but soon there were several friends in the house helping clean up the mess, including the puddle of Pouakai goo.

The sun had just come up over the hills when Colin and Anna showed up. They were both crying, and we all sat together, not saying anything, just buried in our grief.

Then came the hardest part, calling Kelly and Josh, telling them their mother was dead. Kelly wouldn't stop crying, and it took Anna's soothing voice to get her to calm down enough to talk to me again. Josh sounded like his usual stoic self, even though I could tell he was crying too. I spent over an hour on the phone with each of them, as friends came and went from our house. Someone put a sheet of plywood over the broken window, and others picked up the mess in the living room. Even the puddle of blood had disappeared; the carpet just damp, and smelling of disinfectant. Who had done all this for me? I couldn't remember. Lots of familiar faces, but faces that I couldn't name just then.

Colin and Anna stayed, and while Anna busied herself in the kitchen, Colin sat with me in the living room, neither of us talking.

We turned on the TV, and watched the nonstop news as the local stations cataloged the damage. At least two hundred and fifty dead, many more still unaccounted for. There was minimal damage at the airport, since we'd all had time to shut the planes down and leave them inert. Heavy damage was reported at a wastewater treatment plant, which had still been running when the attack started, and at a power plant that hadn't been able to shut down in time. Oddly enough, a lot of the damage had been concentrated at the military's satellite tracking antennas at Kaena Point. There were a number of vehicle wrecks on the island's highways and side roads, the source of most of the fatalities. About twenty homes had been invaded, like mine, and the death toll there was at least forty.

Anna brought in three bowls of chicken stir-fry and rice. I ate slowly, without tasting it. Colin and Anna talked quietly in the kitchen while I finished eating, but I couldn't hear what they were discussing.

I felt numb, and infinitely tired. The clock said three pm, and all I wanted to do was climb into bed. I mumbled something to Colin that must have made sense, and worked my way to the back of the house. I closed the door to my room and crawled onto the bed without taking anything off.

When I woke it was dark again outside. My shoes and socks were off, but I still wore my blood-crusted uniform. The clock said four thirty, and I realized it was early morning. I'd been asleep for more than twelve hours. I padded out to the living room in my bare feet and heard snoring. I found Colin curled up in one of the shredded recliners, an old blanket from the guest room tangled around his legs.

I stood in the doorway, and looked the room over. It was too neat and orderly, with a disinfectant smell in the air, and plywood over the window.

Jen was gone.

My mouth tasted like an old garbage can. I couldn't shake the draggy feeling in my bones, as I stood over the damp spot in the carpet and looked down. She was gone, and it hurt like hell, as if someone had poured hot oil onto my soul. I remembered the drive home, the escape from the Pouakai, the discovery, and everything that came after; the people showing up, helping, cleaning, holding, crying. I remembered it now, even if it didn't register at the time.

"How are you doing?" Colin said from behind me.

He was still in the chair, looking at me with the disheveled hair and skewed glasses I remembered from college.

"Numb, I guess."

He nodded and stood up, folding the blanket.

"What are you doing here?" I asked.

"Anna and I have been trading shifts. We didn't think you should be alone right now."

"You didn't have to do that."

"Yes, we did." He gave me a firm stare.

Yes, I guess they did.

12

Jennifer's funeral, five days later, was another rough day. The government had clamped a travel ban inbound to Hawaii, so Josh and Kelly couldn't get in for the service. I begged and pleaded right to the top, even calling the Governor's office. In the end he said no, so it was just me and a small group of our friends on a sunny, crystal clear morning that said goodbye to my love.

We gathered at my house afterwards, not for a formal wake, but just as a group of friends, holding each other together. Eventually most of them drifted off, needing to get home before the sunset curfew. Colin and Anna stayed behind as they had every night since the attack. I'd tried to tell them they didn't have to stay, but I didn't try too hard. So we sat on the back deck, listening to the breeze, not saying much. Finally, Colin leaned forward, elbows on his knees, hands clasped.

"We caught one, you know," he said.

"One what?"

"A Pouakai."

It took me a moment to sift through what he said, before it hit me.

"Wait a minute. Are you talking about your trap? The shipping container?"

Colin nodded.

"I didn't want to tell you right after the attack, because of what happened to Jennifer. But when we knew the swarm was coming, Alan and I ran down to the docks, armed the trap, and hid out in the ship. It worked perfectly, and we now have a living subject."

Anger raged up inside me, and caught me completely unaware.

"Fucking murderers," I said too loudly. Anna and Colin both looked away, and as quickly as it rose, the anger faded. I didn't like being this out of control, but had no idea how to handle it. Embarrassed, I quietly said, "Sorry."

"Mark," Anna replied, "if you didn't have an angry reaction to these things, I'd be a lot more worried about you."

I nodded grimly.

"Boonie," Colin said, "I know it's only been a short time, but have you thought about what's next?"

"For me?"

He nodded.

I took a deep breath, and stared at the floor. "My job is over. I've already quit, and the paperwork is in and signed. Anyway, I don't think the airline would let me back into the cockpit for a while after what's happened this week."

Colin looked at Anna, and after a moment, she gave him a slight nod of the head.

"What?" I asked.

"Boonie, there's something we've been talking about for a few days, that I want to ask you."

"Something from you and Anna?"

"No," he said, "but she knows about it, and I wanted her approval before we talked."

I felt a little numb and confused. None of this made sense.

"Just tell me."

Anna gave another nod, and Colin smiled.

"First off, things have been moving pretty fast here the last few days."

Anna added, "Yeah, I don't think he's been home more than five minutes all week."

"I told you guys you didn't have to stay with me."

"No, no," Colin said, hands waving in front of him. "It's not that. Being here has been the most restful part of our days. What I'm talking about is the Pouakai, the one we caught."

"You've learned something?"

"Yes, but it's more than that. The government saw how easily we caught the Pouakai with our trap, and has agreed to fund us as much as we need. The trip down south with the ship, trap, and sub is on for next week."

"Congrats," I said quietly. "I'll miss you."

"You don't have to miss me. I want you to join us."

After a long pause, "You want me to what?"

"I know it's too soon, but our schedule is set and we're leaving next week. I'd rather you had some time to regroup and get it together, but we don't have that option. I think you should come with us, Boonie, down to the South Pacific."

"What the hell for?"

"For a lot of reasons. You and Alan and I each have more experience dealing with the Pouakai than the rest of the crew combined. I trust you and your judgment. You've been in the military, and you've ridden on this sub so you know what to expect. I think you'd be an asset to the trip. Finally, both Anna and I think it would be good for you to get out of here. There's nothing you can do here in Hawaii, but you can do a lot of good if you come with me."

I stared into space for a long minute.

"Why would the Navy let me come along?" I finally asked.

"Because I'm in charge of the mission, and what I say goes. Technically, the University is in charge, but that means me. The Navy is just giving us a ride wherever we need to go."

I got up and walked to the edge of the yard, looking over the fence and down to the ocean. The sunset more muted than usual, it colored the sky mostly gray instead of orange and red. Too many questions rolled around in my mind, and I honestly didn't know what to do. The grass in my yard grew too long, and spots covered the papaya leaves. It was hard to connect the little things of everyday life with what was going on in the world. When I looked back to the house though, what I felt most of all was how empty it was without Jennifer. Colin and Anna were right–something had to change.

"What are your plans?" I asked as I walked back to the lanai.

"There's a lot we hope to do," Colin said, "and it's a bit open-ended. We're going down to Palmyra Atoll to place the trap. That's about eleven hundred miles south of here. Then the university's ship will head back here and we'll move to the sub. Depending on what we find, we'll either have the sub stay there with the trap to catch more Pouakai, or we'll move further south, and investigate more islands in the heart of the Pouakai's territory. After that, who knows? It will depend on what we find. The general idea is to check other locations around the South Pacific to see what has happened over the past few years, and document any interactions between humans and the Pouakai. Maybe there are other communities that have found the secret that the Nanumeans did to living with them. There hasn't been a systematic survey done of that region in recent times. Since that is where the first sightings were, whatever source the Pouakai came from should be there somewhere."

I sat down in a chair and closed my eyes.

"That's a lot to think about," I said.

"I know you can't make a decision right now, Boonie, but we are leaving a week from tomorrow, and to get you clearance to ride on the sub. I'll need to know in the next few days."

"No," I said, "it's not that I need time to decide, it's just a lot to think about."

Colin looked at me quizzically.

"I'll go with you," I said with a forced smile. "There isn't anything here for me now. I should do this."

"I'm proud of you Boonie," Anna said, jumping up to give me a big hug. "You took care of Colin last time. I want you to do the same this time too."

"I will, I promise," I said. I hoped I could live up to what I'd just promised.

13

Navy headquarters at Pearl Harbor bristled with a new deployment of heavy anti-aircraft batteries. They surrounded the facility in several arcs, although what good they'd do against an angry swarm of Pouakai, I didn't know.

We had to stop at the gate for a moment, but Colin must have already added my name to the approved list. The guard let us through, and after parking the car, we entered the building. We took an elevator several floors underground, and then went through another security check. Finally we were led into a conference room with large monitors on all four walls. At least a dozen military officials were seated at the polished wood table, along with Alan Gee. All of the military officials were high-ranking; more brass at the table than in a marching band.

Colin showed me where to sit, and plopped into the chair next to me.

"Professor," said an Air Force General across the table, nodding at Colin.

"Morning, General," Colin nodded back while pulling out his computer from its case.

An Admiral stood up, and everyone quieted.

"Gentlemen, we should begin," he said. Older than me, but lean and muscular, he hadn't been spending all of his time behind a desk.

"Doctor Benoit, introductions?" the Admiral said.

Colin stood up. "Gentlemen, this is Captain Mark Boone. You may remember him from the stories about our crash on Nanumea this spring. I've decided that since he isn't working for the airline any more, and has a lot of experience with the Pouakai from our time on the island, he would be an asset to this mission."

Colin sat down, and most of the men around the table nodded, and then turned their attention back to the Admiral.

"Welcome, Captain Boone. I am Admiral Bianchi, Commander, Pacific Fleet. We've all read your dossier, and as far as I know, there are no qualms about your joining this mission."

I looked around again, and recognized Riley Baker, Captain of the *USS Ohio*. He was scowling and pointedly not looking at me.

"Captain Baker, status of the *Ohio*?"

Baker glanced at the Admiral.

"We'll be ready by Wednesday, sir. We're just waiting for the *Georgia* to pull into port so we can get the spare generator equipment they're carrying. The electronics team has finished installing the communications link and display equipment to sync with the trap."

"Thanks, Captain. Doctor Benoit?"

"The *Kilo Moana* is ready to go," Colin said. "The trap is loaded onboard and the raft is attached. Just let us know when to go and we'll be underway."

"Okay. Commander Abraham, what about the extra SEAL detachment?"

"They're fully equipped, ready to go."

I looked at Colin, and tilted my head. He leaned toward me.

"They're sending an extra team of SEALs along with us," he whispered. "They didn't want to be left out of a fight."

"Really?" I whispered back. "What good will they do against a swarm of Pouakai?"

Colin shrugged. "I've learned never to question the military's motives, especially the SEALs. If everything goes according to plan, we won't have to fight the Pouakai. That's the last thing I want to do."

The Admiral continued questioning the men around the table. Colin hadn't told me what the meeting was all about, but obviously it was a final status briefing regarding our mission. I had thought we were just going in to meet the brass and get my final clearance to go on the mission. As the questions moved to people with a more peripheral duty to the trip, I looked at the status monitors on the wall. Some were symbolic representations of fleet locations around the world, and others showed real-time views of the Pacific from a satellite.

The meeting soon ended. I had to respect the Admiral even more for that; he didn't let it drag on like so many others I had attended while in the military. Colin stood up, and so did I. Captain Baker of the *Ohio* had moved to a corner, looking through a thick folder of paperwork as I walked up to him.

"Captain Baker," I said. "It's good to see you again."

He looked at me over his glasses. "Yeah," he said gruffly, and then went back to his reading.

"I'm sorry. Is there a problem?"

He closed the folder. Despite his short stature, he had cultivated the image of leadership well. "You don't get it, do you?" he said evenly.

"Get what?"

"That you're not needed here. That this entire mission is a waste of our time and resources. That we have a lot more important things to do than chase theories of where these things came from and what they are."

"Wait a minute. You don't want to be on this mission? Then why the hell are you here?"

He looked over my shoulder, then back at me.

"It's the mission I've been assigned, and I'll do it to the best of my ability."

"You don't think we should be going?"

He sighed.

"There's a world of hurt going on out there, Major," he said, using my old rank from the Air Guard. "China is making noises we don't like, because they're running out of oil. They're getting aggressive with Japan and Korea. Our own relationship with Canada is near the breaking point over energy. Several million Australians are slowly starving to death, and a billion Indians are about to pour over the borders into China and Pakistan because they're starving too. And here I am, about to go on a butterfly hunt with you and your buddies. So no, Major, I don't think we should be going."

"You think that starting a shooting war would really be the best thing for us right now?" I asked, a little too loudly.

Captain Baker glanced around, but nobody was looking toward us. He pointedly lowered his voice.

"My job is to defend the United States from all enemies, foreign and domestic. If my superiors say that my best duty is to drag your asses around the South Pacific, then so be it. I may personally have different ideas, but I'll do as I'm ordered."

"Wouldn't the best thing for everyone be to get rid of the Pouakai?"

Baker grimaced. "Sure. It's been such an easy job so far, hasn't it?"

The back of my neck got hot, and I struggled to keep my voice down.

"Let me tell you what I want," I said. "These things killed my wife. They ripped her belly apart like she was a side of beef on a hook, spilled her guts on the floor, and left her to bleed to death in our living room. We don't have any way to stop them right now, and if we don't find what makes them tick, where they came from, and how to stop them, it won't matter that China is mad at Japan, or that Canada can't sell us the oil we want, or that India is starving. None of that will matter because none of us will be here. Every one of us is going to end up like my wife, ripped to shreds and left to die. But when the last of us is gone the Pouakai won't be crying over our remains. Our number one priority *must* be to find a way to get rid of these things, because if we don't, your little gun club here won't be able to fire a spitwad at…"

The Captain looked over my shoulder again, and then at me with a tiny shake of his head. I got his drift and held my tirade in check, even though I was still shaking. Colin came up behind me, smiling.

"Hey guys. Together again, just like old times," he said.

Captain Baker smiled with practiced ease.

"Just another cruise in the sunshine," he said, and then he strode over to the Admiral, all pent-up power and determination.

"Don't let Roger Ramjet get to you," Colin said quietly, once Baker had walked out of earshot. "I heard a bit of your discussion. I've had pretty much the same one with him myself."

I kept looking at Captain Baker. "You think he'll be a problem for us?"

"No. The Admiral pulled me aside last week, specifically to warn me about him. He said he's a bulldog, but the one thing he wouldn't do is go against orders. The Admiral said he'll bluster and grumble, but he will do what we need him to do. Apparently he's got a closet full of medals from his stint as a sub commander, so he knows what he's doing. We're supposed to steer clear of him as much as possible, but we don't have to worry about him surprising us."

I took in a deep breath. The room smelled of electronics and leather chairs. I remembered the smell of the *Ohio* from earlier in the year; machines, oil, ozone, and disinfectant. I'd miss the outdoors, stuffed into that metal tube under the ocean. That made me think of being on the beach with Jennifer, and a familiar wave of sorrow and anger flooded over me again. I tried to channel that anger toward the mission, but I simply felt tired, and mad at the world. Finally, I let the breath out and turned to Colin.

"Come on," I said. "What else do we need to do here?"

The rest of the day was a nightmare of paperwork. To allow me a spot on the sub, I'd been reactivated into the Air Guard without my knowledge. Being active military made it possible, but it still wasn't easy. Five hours later, my hand cramped and mind numb, Colin drove me home. He left me with a list of what to bring, and what to leave behind, for the ship and the sub. I was an active Major in the Air Guard again, which I'd never thought would happen. I was planning on riding a ship into Pouakai territory, and hitching passage on a submarine after that. My life had spiraled out of control, but I had no idea where I could have stopped it from following this path.

I called Kelly, and talked to her for two hours, and then spent another hour on the phone with Josh. They were both far more open with me than I'd expected. Neither wanted me to go, but they knew I had to do it for myself, as well as for the rest of the world. They'd lost one parent already, and didn't want to lose the other. Somehow though, it felt like I was already gone. I promised them the Navy would allow me to contact them while I was out. Actually, I had no idea if it was possible or not, but I had to ease them down somehow. If nothing else, Colin had his satellite phone. We could use that when we weren't inside the sub.

Darkness filled the house when I finished the calls. I hadn't eaten all day, but I wasn't hungry. Tired, sore, and drained, but not hungry. The black of the moonless evening enveloped me, and I left the lanai lights off as I sat there, looking toward the ocean. I felt Jennifer's presence there, reminding me of all I'd lost. Despite the aching loss I still felt, I tried to focus on the Pouakai. They'd taken my career, my life, and my love. For all of Colin's talk and the attention they got in the media, we still didn't know much about them. That was why I wanted to go. To clear up the fear and uncertainty, we had to learn the truth of the Pouakai and what drove them. It might even help us survive them.

You are out there somewhere, and I'm coming to get you.

PART 3
POLYNESIA

1

Half a day into the voyage south, I realized why I'd never owned a boat. The Pacific Ocean is calm in name only. Big swells, pushed up by a thousand miles of tradewinds, heaved the *Kilo Moana* up and down. Even though the ship's submerged twin hulls supposedly made it a stable platform for research, the ocean took no notice. I downed a pill supplied the by ship's medic, and stood at the bow, eyes on the horizon, willing my stomach to calm down. How could I roll and loop a fighter jet around the sky without a hint of queasiness, but fall victim to a bad case of seasickness on a slow moving ship? I'll never know.

Colin and Alan had set up shop in one of the research labs, and invited me to look at everything they'd gathered on the Pouakai so far. However, I wasn't going anyplace where I couldn't see the horizon until I felt better. Out on the deck, the fresh air and salt spray kept me from losing my breakfast until the pill took effect.

Off to our left, I spotted the periscope and radar mast of the *Ohio* cutting through the waves. Just a mile away, they were already difficult to see. I had a hard time imagining the giant black cylinder of the sub moving below the waves. Deep blue water surrounded us, the swells topped with an occasional whitecap. The lighter blue sky held a few small cumulus clouds and an occasional sea bird. The steady breeze from our twelve-knot passage south and the occasional splash and hiss from a passing wave sounded a rhythm that helped soothe my rebellious stomach.

Lunch-time rolled around, and I started feeling more human. I went downstairs to find Colin, Alan, and their assistants. The mostly empty ship had an abandoned feel to it. A skeleton crew, earning triple-time hazardous duty pay, was taking us to Palmyra Atoll. They would drop us off, along with the trap, and then get the hell out of the Pouakai's territory. The only others aboard were one of the three SEAL squads assigned to the mission. The other two squads were onboard the *Ohio*. Eight well-equipped laboratories covered the main deck of the *Kilo Moana*, but only one was in use. I found Colin, Alan and the others in the Hydrographic lab, a series of nautical charts, laptops, and thick binders scattered across the table. Colin looked up with an evil grin as I wobbled through the hatch.

"He's alive!"

"Remind me to kick your ass once I feel better," I replied.

"If you're going to puke, the sink is over there."

"I think I'd rather puke on you."

"Not a chance. I've got my sea legs, and you don't. I can outrun you."

"Don't worry Boonie," Alan chimed in. "Everyone gets it on their first open-ocean trip. You'll feel better by tomorrow."

"I hope so. Or the doc had better have a big supply of these pills."

"You'll be fine," Colin said. "Come over here, and let me show you what we've got."

He turned one of the laptops toward me, displaying an aerial photograph of a shoreline, showing a beach and fringing reef. The colors were off though, as if it had been taken through a filter. A few green dots shone brightly in the waters of the reef.

"What is it?"

"It's a satellite photo of a beach on Nanumea, taken yesterday afternoon," Colin said as he stared at the photo, a frown on his face.

"And…?" I prodded.

"The problem we've had in the past is that none of the reconnaissance satellites could see the Pouakai. The creatures are plenty big enough, and they should have shown up, but we'd never seen them, even in places where we had evidence they were present.

Once we got our first Pouakai in the trap however, we ran a full spectral analysis on it. That skin of theirs absorbs almost all wavelengths of light, which makes it a very efficient solar panel. It has made it nearly impossible to get a good image of them, or identify where they are by satellite. What we found though is that there is a narrow band of light reflected by their skin in the near infrared spectrum. The National Reconnaissance Office retuned one of their KH-11 satellites, and this is the result."

He pointed to the image on the laptop.

"The green dots are the Pouakai," he said. "We got the first set of images two days ago, and this is one of them."

"That's great," I said. "Now we can see where the Pouakai are, and avoid those areas."

Colin shook his head.

"We think it's not accurate yet. We seem to be missing a lot of them with this method."

"How?"

"Alan and I took careful surveys of the Pouakai population on Nanumea when we were there. The totals were consistent from day to day, and the locals confirmed that the numbers didn't change much. These images however, don't show the same density of creatures that we saw on the island."

"So the satellites can't see all the Pouakai?"

"Apparently not."

"But it does see some?"

"Yes."

"That should be of some help. If we see a few, we know there are probably more around, and if we don't see any, it should be clear."

"We hope so. We're counting on the satellite to give us an idea of whether we can proceed all the way to Palmyra. If the Pouakai are too thick to approach, we'll have to try somewhere else."

The ship rolled over a big swell, and we held on to the table until we were level again.

Steve, one of the two graduate assistants with us, grabbed a stack of binders as they threatened to slide off the table. With a bushy red beard and baggy T-shirt, he fit my image of a typical college student. He put the stack back on the table and grinned.

"Gotta love the ride!" he said.

"Not really," I countered.

The other assistant was Mina, a quiet, mousy little Korean woman. She sat next to Alan, typing away on her laptop. I hadn't heard her utter a single word since we'd boarded. I don't know what prompted these two kids to come along on the voyage, but it must have been some powerful need, considering the dangers involved. Maybe it was just that youthful feeling of invincibility.

"Come on everyone," Colin said. "It's lunch time."

"What's on the menu?" Steve asked.

"Fish stew."

Something lurched in my stomach. "I think I'll pass. I'll be outside."

2

By dinner-time the pills had taken full effect, and I felt human again. I nibbled on some grilled chicken and rice, before joining the rest of the team in the conference room, one deck up. Colin sat at the table, talking to someone on the satellite phone, the other three either on their laptops or writing in notebooks. I sank onto a couch along the outside wall. The constant rumble of the engines faded to background noise as I closed my eyes. A spectacular sunset streamed orange through the windows, a glow I could see even through my closed eyelids. The seas had calmed as we moved farther south, chugging steadily toward the equator. As I lay back in the comfortable couch, I thought about Jennifer, and a veil of sorrow draped over me again. I was out of my element here; I wasn't a Captain in charge, I wasn't a pilot any more, I wasn't a scientist. Hell, I didn't even know what I was supposed to do here. Why had I agreed to do this?

"Boonie? You still with us?"

Colin had finished his call, and roused me out of my stupor. The pills had taken away the seasickness, but left a side effect of drowsiness.

"Yep. Present," I said, pulling myself upright.

"Feeling better?"

"I'll live."

"You'll be fine," Alan said, looking up from his laptop. "Like I said, everyone gets it."

I sat next to Colin at the table. "Okay, I'm here. I don't know why, but I'm here."

"Because I asked you to come along," he said with a grin.

"Yeah, I'll be a big help writing your papers."

"Boonie, you're here because we need you. You have as much experience with the Pouakai as Alan and I do. You're used to dealing with unusual situations, and know how to lead if necessary. Anna and I felt it would be a lot better for you if came with us instead of moping around Honolulu."

"Jennifer died!" I said sharply. "I think I have a right to be upset."

Colin put his hands up.

"Sorry, sorry. I know it's been horrible on you. We just thought it would be healthier if you were involved in something, anything, rather than sitting at home."

I hated losing control so easily. "Sorry. I shouldn't snap like that."

"No problem, buddy. So here's what's going on." He pointed to a screen on the wall with an electronic navigation chart. A blinking red dot showed south of Hawaii, less than a quarter of the way to Palmyra. "We're here," he said, pointing at the dot. "We'll cruise through the night then stop for the day."

"Stop?"

"The sub has their radar going full time looking for Pouakai. They haven't seen any yet, but we're close enough to their territory that being underway during the daytime would be foolish. Out here in the fringe areas of their habitat, there haven't been any reports of Pouakai attacking ships this size while underway at night. The same goes for standing still during the day, so we're going to use that to our advantage. We cruise at night, and float in the daytime."

"How long to get to Palmyra then?"

"About seven or eight days. Normally it would take about four days if we cruised straight through."

I thought for a moment.

"Why can't the tankers and freighters use this method?"

Colin shrugged. "They did try it, but the size of the craft must be a factor. Ships our size aren't attacked if they not underway. Anything bigger is swarmed though, even if it's just floating. It only works out here in the fringe anyway. Down in the heart of the Pouakai territory, just south of the equator, everything gets attacked."

"Do we know why?"

Alan laughed.

"If we did, we'd be a lot further on our way to understanding these things," Colin's chubby co-worker said. "If you have a theory, we'd love to hear it."

I shook my head. "No theories from me. I'm the action hero, remember?"

All four of them laughed.

"Come on," Colin said. "Let's go outside. These guys have everything under control, and I need some fresh air."

We walked downstairs, and out onto the aft deck. The trap sat lashed to the deck underneath the hydraulic crane. I leaned against the railing at the back of the deck, and watched the water slip around the two bulbous, submerged hulls. A small flock of sea birds followed us, and I wondered what they were doing so far from land. The ship ran smoothly across the ocean, and somehow everything seemed calm. Colin crossed his arms on top of the railing, and peered over the side at the passing ocean.

"I don't know why you think I should be here." I said.

Colin sighed. "I know you, Boonie, I know your moods. Hell, after rooming with you for two years in college, I could tell exactly what you'd done the night before by what you ate for breakfast."

I raised an eyebrow at him.

"Cold cereal after a normal night studying," he continued. "Spam and eggs after a late evening baseball practice, and pancakes with Portuguese sausage if you'd gotten lucky with your girlfriend."

"Come on, I wasn't that predictable, was I?"

Colin shrugged, and looked at the ocean. "You need this trip, Boonie. I think without it, you might end up broken."

He paused a moment, then looked at me. "I need you here, Boonie. You're my good luck charm. You're the one that finally talked me into asking Anna out. You got me safely down onto Nanumea, where we learned far more than we ever would have in Cairns. You got me safely back home to Anna. For all of that, I'll be forever thankful."

That was about as close to an emotional outpouring as I'd ever heard from Colin. We both stared at the ocean and the hypnotically smooth wake trailing behind the ship. One of the birds following in our wake screeched at us, passed overhead, and backed off again.

"Okay," I said. "Tell me everything."

"About what?"

"The Pouakai. Tell me what you've found with the one you captured. Tell me what you guys are thinking. Tell me what other scientists are thinking. Tell me what we're going to do if we capture a bunch of these things on Palmyra, and how we can use that info to eliminate them."

A grin slid across Colin's face.

"They don't have cells," he said.

"Huh?"

"Their tissue isn't made up of cells like ours is. Its structure is actually fairly simple, relative to ours. There are different compounds in there, and there are structures analogous to muscle, nerve fiber, and a flexible supporting framework that resembles ceramic fibers, but no individual cells. We haven't found anything in there that might work as genetic material."

"So how do they have babies, like the ones I saw on Nanumea?"

A bigger smile appeared on Colin's face.

"We did all sorts of scans on the one we caught in Honolulu before it died. And, by the way, it took nearly sixty hours of pitch black before it kicked the bucket."

I gave a low whistle.

"Almost any amount of light, even equivalent to moonlight, was enough to keep it alive, if not moving."

"So much for Captain Baker's idea of a sunshade," I said.

Colin nodded. "Regarding the baby Pouakai however, we found something even stranger. The scans we did included everything we could think of; CT, MRI, PET, nucleotide tracers, and sonogram. As soon as it died we were able to capture it with a scanning electron microscope too. We imaged this thing down to the fraction of a micron. What we found was that it was born pregnant."

"Really? Like a hermaphrodite?"

"No, hermaphrodites will get themselves pregnant. These things are already born that way, with their offspring already inside them. Let me ask you this; when we were on Nanumea, how many Pouakai babies did you see being born at once?"

"Depends. Anywhere from two to five. Is that important?"

"It might be, because the scans we did showed that our captured Pouakai had three offspring in the sacs on its back. The scans were detailed enough that we could get a clear image of the unborn Pouakai, and what we found was that each of them had two tiny sacs on their back, and at the highest resolution, we saw that each of those sacs had very tiny Pouakai with one sac each."

"One less baby with each generation?"

Colin nodded.

"Maybe they grow additional offspring as they get bigger?" I said.

"Maybe, but the problem with that idea is that the three unborn Pouakai on the back of our captive seemed to have all of their body structures in place, only smaller in comparison to an adult's. The same applied to the two grandchildren Pouakai on the backs of each of the unborn children. When we looked over our data from Nanumea and from these tests, we couldn't find anything suggesting that the Pouakai develop additional organs, structures, or features after they're born. They do grow in size, but all the parts are there on the day they're born."

"That doesn't make sense," I said. "If they have one less offspring each generation, they'd die out. That sounds like a pretty ineffective strategy for survival."

Colin nodded. "You're right. It would be stupid, if the idea was to perpetuate the species." His eyes were bright as he talked about their discoveries.

"Another problem is that, according to what the Nanumeans said, a typical Pouakai takes about three months to go from newborn to having it babies. Then it dies. We weren't on Nanumea long enough to see this through, but I don't doubt what they were saying."

"How could they tell the lifespan of an individual?" I asked. "They couldn't follow a single Pouakai for three straight months."

"Not normally, but occasionally one would come by with some identifiable mark, like a scar or an oddly shaped spike. They were observant enough to be able to track them that way."

I looked up at the emerging stars, and did some mental math.

"Wait a minute," I said. "If each generation lasts only three months, then even if you start with a Pouakai giving birth to five babies, and they all give birth to four, and so on, there's only six generations before they die out."

Colin nodded in agreement.

"At three months per generation that's just a year and a half," I continued.

More nodding.

"So how do we still have Pouakai three years after they were first seen?" I asked.

"That is the trillion dollar question," he responded. "Nobody, anywhere, has reported seeing a Pouakai give birth to more than five babies, and that has only been here in the central Pacific basin. The reports from elsewhere are scattered, and some are suspect, but from the trustworthy data, the most they've seen in the Indian Ocean is four, the Mediterranean is three, and the Atlantic is two. So the farther you get from where we first found them, the fewer babies they have."

"Something had to give birth to those Pouakai that had five babies."

"Give birth, or make them, somehow."

"Make them?"

"It's a theory. Or there could be a giant hive queen, like in *Aliens*, squeezing these things out at a prodigious rate."

I looked at him, and raised an eyebrow. He tried keeping a serious face, then burst out laughing.

"Sorry bud. I had to do that," he said through the laughter.

"What if it really happens that way?" I asked, still shivering at the thought of that memorable movie image.

"Then we call in the Marines, or the SEALs, in our case, and do away with her."

I took a couple of deep breaths, and tried to rid my mind of thoughts of the *Alien* queen. I also wondered again why Scott, my friend in fourth grade, decided it would be a good movie to watch with me one evening when his parents were out. The nightmares took a long time to subside after that experience. Apparently it had been a mistake to tell Colin about that night years later too.

"So we really don't know what we're looking for, specifically," he said. "They must be coming from somewhere. What we're trying to do is understand them, their life cycle, and anything else to help find a weak spot. By coming down here, into their territory, maybe we can find that source: queen, nest, or whatever it is that they come from."

"Anything else you guys have come up with?" I asked, trying to move the subject away from alien queens.

"Well, there have been some changes to the Pouakai over time, too."

"Like what?"

"When they were first seen, in Vanuatu, three and a half years ago, they weren't as strong, or vicious. They did attack loud objects, but didn't seem able to keep their strength up for as long. A few months later however, they got bigger, and stronger too. That's when we really started having problems with them."

"Why didn't you scientists go check them out before they became dangerous?" I asked.

"Because we didn't believe the stories at first. Do you know how many elaborate hoaxes and false reports the scientific community sees every day? Even with all the technology we take for granted today, Vanuatu is a poor and technology-limited country. By the time video of the Pouakai came out, it was too late. They were already beginning to sink ships and down airplanes."

"Oh."

The ocean below had darkened from deep blue to nearly black, with only the white of our wake visible beyond the stern. We remained quiet for several minutes, as brilliant stars twinkled in the sky. The ship ran with all lights off, glowing displays shielded and curtains over the windows of occupied rooms. Somewhere nearby, the *Ohio* kept pace with us, watching the skies for Pouakai. For all I could see though, we were alone in a black hole, in the middle of the ocean.

"I just don't get it," I finally said. "I mean, I remember my basic biology. I thought there had to be a reason for certain kinds of evolution. Like the moth that changed colors when smoke from the industrial revolution turned the bark of trees from white to black."

Colin nodded.

"So what is the reason for the Pouakai's existence?" I continued. "What is its purpose in life? I thought the most basic reason for existence was to perpetuate the species. If the Pouakai die out after a few generations, what is its purpose? If it doesn't have DNA or cells, how did it come to exist in the first place?"

"I'm proud of you, Boonie," Colin said quietly. "You're beginning to think like a scientist. That's why we're down here; to answer those questions."

Those were answers I very much wanted to have.

3

A week later we dropped anchor a few hundred yards offshore from Palmyra. Smaller than Nanumea, the sandy atoll had a central lagoon dotted with tiny islets and a rim of coconut palms. The whole thing, including fringing reefs, was about six miles long, and two miles wide. Just like Nanumea, nothing stood taller than the palm trees.

The engines stopped twenty minutes before sunrise, followed by the anchor chain rattling down to the sandy bottom. A pink glow filled the sky, reflecting off the small puffy clouds overhead. The wind had died down, and the waves were mercifully small.

After a radio conference with Captain Baker on the *Ohio*, the Captain of the *Kilo Moana* decided to go ahead and move the trap into the lagoon right away.

I watched from the railing as the crew used the big crane to lower the container, with its attached raft, into the water between the hulls.

"Easy, easy," the Captain shouted from the deck above. "Just let it edge into the water."

Colin, Alan, their assistants Steve and Mina, and I watched the sailors work. Off to the west a short black line lay on the horizon; the *Ohio*. They were staying in deeper water in case the Pouakai forced them to make a quick dive. Two rubber inflatables from the sub, like the ones that had brought us from Nanumea, were waiting nearby, ready to maneuver the trap into the lagoon.

"Anything on the radar?" Colin asked into a handheld radio.

"Nothing at all," replied a voice from the *Ohio*. "All clear to at least fifty miles."

Colin looked up at the Captain, giving him a thumbs-up.

The trap bobbed in the small waves a minute later. Once the Navy workers had nudged their inflatables up to the bulky raft, the crane pulled its cable away.

"Let's get going," Colin said.

We dropped our duffle bags over the side, into another small inflatable, and climbed a rope ladder down the side of the *Kilo Moana.* We wouldn't be coming back. From here on, we were at the mercy of Captain Baker, the *Ohio*, and the Pouakai.

The university was understandably reluctant to leave their expensive and unarmed research ship in the Pouakai's territory any longer than necessary. It would head back to Hawaii, with another sub escorting it, as soon as they had unloaded the trap.

The Navy crew had already pulled the trap from between the twin hulls of the ship and were moving it slowly toward the narrow channel cut through the west end of the reef. The sun rose quickly, the temperature climbing. I was glad I'd slathered on sunscreen before the day began. With Alan running the boat, we followed the trap as the Navy men herded the unwieldy box into the channel. Their small inflatable boats weren't designed as tugs, but they did the job.

The lagoon was a silky smooth blue, and the wakes from our passage were the biggest disturbance in the water.

"What the hell is that?" I asked, pointing toward the northern island.

"What do you mean?" Colin said.

"That structure."

"Oh, that's the dock where we're going to set up the trap."

"A dock? You didn't say anyone lives here."

"They don't, at least not any more. Palmyra Atoll is a territory of the U.S., but nobody lives here permanently. A lot of the set-up was completed by the Nature Conservancy, and they bought most of the island a couple of decades ago. Since then, they've run a research station here. There's a good-sized airstrip just on the other side of those buildings too. Before the Pouakai showed up, this was a world-class research facility. Once they started attacking though, all the researchers pulled out. Nobody's been here for at least two years."

Alan slowed the boat, and we watched the Navy crew push the trap up to the dock, where they lashed it into place. They waved when they finished before speeding off toward the sub. Within seconds, silence descended on the lagoon.

"Let's get to work," Colin said.

We pulled up to the dock, just behind the trap, and stepped ashore. My legs told me the dock still rolled like a ship.

"Submarine, this is survey leader," Colin said into his radio.

"Go ahead," came a scratchy reply.

"The trap is secure, and the inflatables are heading your way. Any sign of Pouakai?"

"Nothing on the screen. All clear to fifty miles."

"Sounds good. We'll set up the trap, then make a survey of the island. Let us know if anything shows up."

"Roger."

I looked at Colin. "Why didn't you call it the *Ohio*?"

"Captain's rules. We can't use names on an unsecured radio."

"And I thought the Air Force was paranoid."

Arming the trap involved climbing a ladder and using a hand crank to open the doors against their powerful springs. Colin and I sweated through that task as the tropical sun beat down on us. Alan, Steve and Mina went inside the trap to turn on the electronics. The solar panels on the top of the trap had kept the batteries charged as we steamed south from Hawaii, so it took only ten minutes to get the equipment working. After Colin and I climbed down, we pulled our daypacks from the duffle bags, and made sure our water bottles were filled.

"You guys go west," Colin said to Alan and the assistants. "We'll get the cameras installed, then go check out the airstrip. If there's any word from the *Ohio* about Pouakai, head straight back here. If they say the Pouakai are within ten miles, find shelter wherever you are. You know the drill. Stay still, and stay quiet."

"Got it," Alan said. They took off toward the west end of the atoll.

"Come on," Colin said. "Let's get the cameras up and running."

He pulled two waterproof cases from the equipment duffel and opened them to remove the camera gear. We carried it to a weather-beaten building inland from the dock. It was a heavy-equipment shop, with wheels, grease, cables, and barrels all over the interior, as well as an ancient pickup truck and a rusty bulldozer. The front of the building, facing towards the dock, had several large posts holding up the roof, but no wall. It was open-air toward the lagoon. Colin brought out a set of clamps, to attach the camera gear, transmitters, and antennas to the posts.

"What's all this for?" I asked.

"It's so we can see what's going on around the trap, not just from the cameras on the trap itself. These will transmit to the *Ohio*, along with the data from the trap."

"Sounds reasonable," I grunted, as I torqued the bolts on a camera bracket to a rusty steel post.

The modular equipment snapped together quickly, so we had the four cameras mounted in a few minutes.

"Time for a walk," Colin said.

We took off down a rough sandy road, surrounded by thick vegetation. With no breeze, the humid air hung over us like a steaming wet towel.

"What are we looking for?" I asked.

"Any signs of Pouakai, or anything else unusual."

Pouakai signs? He might as well have asked me to translate his thesis into Arabic.

The path led past a small cluster of buildings, with vegetation growing right up to the walls. Two years of neglect in a tropical environment had taken its toll. Beyond the buildings sat a small signpost, pointing toward the airstrip. Another sign, a few hundred yards down the path, read 'Welcome to Palmyra. Population: 4'.

"The people who worked here had to have a sense of humor," Colin said.

A few minutes later we came to a rough scar cut through the jungle; the airstrip. It didn't look like any of the smoothly paved runways I'd flown from in the past, as it was made of packed sand and crushed coral. To my right, the runway ended at the lagoon's edge, and to the left, the uneven surface rolled off into the distance. At the edge of the runway, a dozen feet away, a dark splotch glistened in the sunlight. It was in the shape of a Pouakai, wings spread.

"Colin, look," I said, pointing.

He walked over to it, and nodded.

"This is what remains after a Pouakai dies," he said. "They die, dissolve, then as the moisture evaporates, all that's left is this outline of dried gunk."

We both stared at it for a moment before I turned to look east, down the length of the runway. Twenty feet away were two more dark blotches.

"There's more."

Colin jogged over and knelt down, gently touching the remains. It turned to powder as it sifted through his fingers.

"How long have these been here?" I asked.

"Don't know," he said with a shrug. "We've never run tests on the decay rate. But considering how powdery it is, it couldn't have been more than a few days."

"Why?"

"If a storm came through, the wind would have blown all this away, or the rain would have washed it into the lagoon." He picked up some of the remains and let them fall to the ground. The dust drifted several feet in the light breeze.

I looked up again, and peered along the runway. "Jesus, there's hundreds out here."

Colin stood up next to me, one hand shading his eyes. Then he picked up the radio.

"Team B, this is survey leader."

A crackle of static, then, "Go ahead."

"We've found the remains of well over a hundred dead Pouakai on the runway."

"I was just about to call you. We found the same thing here in a couple of clearings, and at the top of the beaches too. They're all over the place."

Colin held the radio next to his mouth, but didn't say anything, a glazed look in his eyes.

"Did you copy?" Alan asked over the radio.

"Sorry, yes, I did. Head back to the dock. We need to talk."

I followed Colin up the road again, wondering just what the hell was going on.

"Submarine to survey leader," crackled the radio.

"Go ahead."

"Single target on radar, moving toward the island. Radar signature positively identified as Pouakai."

"Shit," Colin said, and then keyed the radio. "How long to arrival?"

"Estimate ten minutes."

"Fifty miles in ten minutes?"

"Target is only five miles from the island. It's a single target, not a large group of Pouakai. That's as close as we can identify a single target."

"Maintain radio silence," Colin said. "We'll find shelter and call you once the Pouakai is away from us."

"The Captain has ordered a dive. We'll call when we surface again."

"I understand," replied Colin.

"We heard that," came Alan's voice over the radio. "There's an old concrete bunker next to us. We'll hide out there until it's clear."

"Sounds good," Colin said. "Keep your radio as low as possible. Don't make any noise."

"Will do."

My heart thumped as Colin turned toward me.

"Run," he said.

We dashed up the road, past the overgrown buildings, and within a couple of minutes made it back to the trap. Colin ran to the dock where our duffle bags lay, and grabbed another waterproof case. He carried it to the equipment shop where we'd set up the cameras. We slid under the pickup truck, and dropped into a grease pit. Standing up, we peered over the edge, still under the chassis of the truck. There wasn't a wall on the side of the building facing the dock, so we had a clear view of the lagoon. The bottom of the pit was ankle deep in muck and water, but I didn't care. I felt protected there, as I tried to catch my breath.

Colin opened the case and pulled out an electronic control box that looked like a glorified RC airplane transmitter.

"Is that for the trap?" I asked between heavy breaths.

He nodded. "The main controller is onboard the *Ohio*, but this is a backup. We can use it to catch this straggler if it shows up here."

"So now what?" I asked.

"We wait."

"Great. Love being a sitting target."

"We're okay. We've been around these things before. Stay quiet, and remember what we did on Nanumea. We'll be fine." He had that look of excitement in his eyes again, so I took a deep breath, and watched the sky for movement. I jerked as I saw some motion out of the corner of my eye, but it turned out to be a sea bird circling the lagoon. We waited for several minutes in silence.

"Maybe it won't come," I whispered.

"Don't know," Colin whispered back. "They never seem to fly in a predictable pattern."

The lagoon shimmered as the late morning trade winds picked up. Palm trees swayed gently, and our Pouakai trap squeaked as its raft slowly rubbed against the dock. Colin and I both scanned the lagoon, looking for movement.

Then, in the distance over the lagoon, a black triangle swooped and dipped above the water.

"That's odd," Colin whispered.

"What?"

"I've never seen one fly like that."

Colin handed me his binoculars. The Pouakai dipped toward the water, thrashed upward, and fell downward again.

"What should we do?"

"This," he said, and flipped a switch on the controller. A deep thrumming sound echoed from the trap, like an amplified bass guitar. I kept an eye on the Pouakai.

"It's turning," I said. The creature veered from its westerly course and toward us on the north shore of the lagoon. I had to remind myself that I'd been through this before on Nanumea. As long as I remained quiet, it shouldn't hurt me. Then again, I'd never been around a machine trying to attract one either.

I handed the binoculars back to Colin, and watched the black speck grow larger, flopping awkwardly toward us.

"Come on, come on," Colin whispered. He put one hand on the controller, ready to slam the doors shut.

The Pouakai dipped closer, disappearing from view behind the trap for a moment. Then it reappeared, much nearer. It flew toward the trap, but instead of going into the open door, it bounced off the roof of the container, and rolled in a heap onto the sandy ground next to the dock.

"Son of a bitch," Colin said.

The creature flopped wildly on the ground, but couldn't get itself airborne again. The thrashing black animal moved closer to our hiding spot under the pickup truck.

"Oh no."

"Shit!"

The Pouakai kept bouncing towards us. In a few seconds it had rolled under the front awning of the shop, a dozen feet away from us. We backed up to the far side of the pit, but it was still too close.

Slam. The Pouakai smashed its six-foot long spike into the side of the pickup truck. Colin and I scrambled out of the pit, trying not to make any noise, but our grunts were as loud as cannon shots. The pickup shook several times as the creature banged against it. A splash sounded, as the trap controller fell into the pit, and sank into the muck at the bottom. A huge boom came from the trap as the doors slammed shut.

"Look out!" Colin whispered frantically. The Pouakai's wings were wrapping over the bed of the truck, and it looked like the creature was trying to pull itself upward. We ran to the back of the shop, and out an open doorway. We weren't supposed to be running near a Pouakai, but this felt different from what we'd encountered on Nanumea. Something was wrong with this one.

Colin motioned for me to follow him, and we tiptoed around the side of the shop. We heard the creature thrashing on the ground, so I risked a peek around the corner of the wall. The Pouakai had flopped back out onto the sand in front of the shop, convulsing like mad. Little sprays of sand flew up every time it tried to move, but it just couldn't get itself upright. Without feet to stand on, they have to use their wings to push themselves up enough to begin flying. This one couldn't do it though.

Colin brushed past me as he raced toward the Pouakai, a thick metal rod in his hand.

"No!" I whispered as loud as I could, but he was already in motion. With one swift move he brought the pointed end of the rod over his head and down through the center of the Pouakai's belly. It let out a piercing whistle, and flapped like mad. The thing's spike swung savagely back and forth, but Colin had run up from behind, so it didn't get him. The Pouakai was impaled into the ground with the rod. Colin fell backwards and scrambled, crab-like, away from the monster.

The steel rod wavered as the thing thrashed.

"Pin it down," Colin shouted out loud.

I ran into the shop, and found several five-gallon buckets of paint, still sealed shut. I heaved two of them out to where the Pouakai lay flopping in the sand. Colin grabbed one.

"Try and get them on top of the wings," he panted.

He approached from one side, and I came in from the other. Colin tried to set his down first, but the Pouakai batted it away, out of his hands. He got the bucket back, and looked at me.

"Two on one wing first," I said. He nodded and circled around to where I stood. Together, we cautiously approached the Pouakai.

"One, two, three!" I whispered, and then we hefted the buckets upward, letting them fall on one of the wings. One landed upright, and the other tipped over, but they both stayed where they landed, pinning the wing down.

"Two more buckets," Colin said.

I grabbed them, and we repeated the process on the other wing. Just to make sure it wouldn't move, we put two additional buckets on each wing. Once we had a couple hundred pounds on each side of the creature, as well as the steel spike through its middle, we backed up a dozen feet, and sat down on the sand.

"Son of a bitch," Colin said, still out of breath.

"Yeah, you son of a bitch," I snapped at him. "What the hell were you thinking, attacking a Pouakai?"

He heaved a big sigh, and lay back on the sand, propped up on his elbows.

"Something is wrong with that one. It isn't acting normally, and I couldn't trust it to behave like the ones on Nanumea. It didn't go into the trap, which I didn't expect. We didn't have good shelter, and it wasn't contained. Our only options were to kill it, or restrain it."

"So your idea of restraint was to go Rambo on me and stab it?"

A big grin spread across his face. "It was the logical thing to do."

I let out another breath, and looked at the creature. Its thrashing had subsided, and it only twitched a little.

After we caught our breath, Colin pulled out the radio.

"Survey leader to submarine."

No answer.

"They're probably still submerged," I said.

"Team B, you on?"

"We're here," the radio crackled. "How are you two?"

"Alive, with a prize. I need you here right away, but with the sub underwater, we won't know if other Pouakai are around. Be very careful."

"Will do," Alan answered.

Colin stood up, and jogged to the pile of duffle bags still lying next to the dock. He pulled out yet another waterproof case, and brought it back to where I sat. It held a mass of stainless surgical instruments, from tiny scalpels to a vicious-looking bone saw.

He knelt down next to the Pouakai, making sure to stay clear of the still-twitching spike. With the scalpel, he sliced open the back of the creature. It didn't make any noises, but seemed to tense up for a moment. A tremor ran through its body and out to the wings, then it lay still. Colin pulled the scalpel back a moment and looked at the incision.

"Damn," he said.

"What?"

"I didn't want it to die that fast. Others have taken a lot more damage before they kicked the bucket."

"It's dead already?"

"Yes. There's a series of narrow tubes right here in the back," he said as he pointed them out. "See these? They act like a primitive heart, pulsating to circulate fluid around their body. If they're not pumping, it's dead."

"Why did you want it still alive?"

"So Alan could watch as I took it apart. If they don't get here soon, it will start dissolving before he can see it." He looked around for a moment. "Grab one of those cameras off the post and start filming what I'm doing."

I ran to the video cameras we'd set up less than an hour earlier, and detached one from its post.

"Got it," I said, running back to Colin.

"Okay. Push that red button, and aim it at what I'm doing."

"Yes, sir."

He leaned forward and started cutting, delicately, moving bits of its innards aside, probing deeper into its body. I hovered over him, aiming the camera at what he was doing. Thin yellowish fluid dripped out of the opening, and seeped into the sandy ground.

"Yes, yes," Colin whispered.

"What?"

"It's a zero."

"What's a zero?"

There was a crashing in the jungle behind us, and a moment later Alan, Steve, and Mina stepped into view. Alan saw us, and a big grin spread across his chubby face. Steve's eyes got wide, and Mina let out a short gasp. Colin looked up.

"Al, get the hell over here."

Alan puffed his way over, and knelt next to Colin.

"It's a zero," Colin repeated.

"Great."

"What's a zero?" I asked again.

"It's a Pouakai that doesn't have any babies growing on its back," Steve said from behind me. "The last of its line."

"Why is that special?"

"Watch," Steve said.

Colin kept cutting farther forward, toward the head end of the Pouakai. They didn't have heads as such; the body just tapered from its wide point in the middle down to where the spike began. As he cut closer to the spike, Colin got excited.

"See Al, see? Look at the size of that thing!"

Steve and Mina leaned in to look.

"Son of a bitch," Steve said.

"Boonie, you still recording this?" Colin asked.

"Yep."

I didn't know what it was, but for Colin's sake, I kept pointing the camera at the open gash on top of the Pouakai. He set the scalpel down, and reached one hand into the open wound. Soon he was buried up to his elbow. Stringy yellow fibers filled the opening, a little like the inside of an unripened pumpkin, all floating in the pale yellow liquid. I had an uneasy feeling about what he was doing; it just seemed so unnatural.

"Got it," Colin said. He pulled his arm out, and stood up, holding a horror in his hands: A misshapen ball of yellow goo that somehow held together.

"It's at least five pounds," he said.

Alan nodded. "Probably three times the size of the one from home."

"What is it?" I asked.

"It's a Pouakai brain, we think," Colin replied, holding it up like a trophy fish. Alan stood next to Colin, and I aimed the camera at the two of them. They posed like big game hunters, a surreal moment in an unreal day. Mina pulled out a big SLR camera, and took pictures too.

"The Pouakai is beginning to dissolve," Steve said.

We all turned back to the creature. The wings were damp, and wobbled like jelly at Colin's touch.

"Shit. It shouldn't happen this fast," Alan said.

Colin went back to dissecting the body of the Pouakai with the scalpel. A minute later, he had the rest of its innards exposed. Then he sat down on the sand, shaking his head.

"Nothing else unusual," he said.

"You've got a really weird sense of what's usual, buddy," I quipped. Colin looked up at me and grinned.

4

We watched the Pouakai disintegrate. Within five minutes the body had turned to a mass of jelly, and after another five minutes, it was an unidentifiable puddle of black goo. Only the rough shape of the Pouakai remained.

When there wasn't anything left to watch, we all went back to the shop, and sat down in the shade of its awning. Colin tried calling the sub, but they didn't answer.

Alan passed lunch around–granola bars, apples, and milk cartons. I looked at the five of us sitting in the sand, eating like we were on a school field trip, and started thinking about the Pouakai. I'd just seen one taken apart, killed by a rod through its body, as well as a knife to its back. I'd thought I would feel more satisfaction at seeing one split open, suffering like Jennifer had, but all I felt was empty, incomplete. There was too much still unknown about them, and too many of them left out there for me to feel any happiness at the death of just one.

I looked at the drying puddle of the Pouakai. "So what's up with the brain?"

"It's big," Alan said, after swallowing the last of his milk.

"So?"

"So," Colin replied, "it confirms a theory we had about them."

I raised an eyebrow until he continued.

"There have been about half a dozen Pouakai dissected by scientists so far. That isn't a lot of data of course, because they decay so fast after death. Most were dead ones that happened to be found by scientists after an attack, just in time to take a cursory look. They didn't get all that much information, but one thing that stood out was the fetus/brain correlation."

"Which is?" I prompted.

"The more baby Pouakai it has on its back, the smaller its brain. Nobody has dissected a one or zero before. That is, a Pouakai that didn't have any babies growing on its back. Of the Pouakai that have been dissected, there were two fives, and a handful of twos and threes. It began to look like the size of the brain grew in each generation going forward. It correlated with other reports said that when baby Pouakai were born, the size of the head region was bigger if they were born in fewer numbers."

"You lost me," I said.

"When a Pouakai gives birth to five babies, they have small heads. If it gave birth to three babies, the newborn have bigger heads; even larger for a litter of two, and so on. We theorized, based on our observations on Nanumea, as well as the Pouakai we dissected and the few others that received cursory examinations, that the bigger heads mean bigger brains. Nobody had seen a one give birth to a zero, but here we are today, with a zero."

"Its brain fits the theory perfectly," Alan added. "At five pounds, it's about two pounds heavier than the brains of the twos that had been dissected. Most likely, a one would have a brain a little over four pounds."

"They get heavier at each generation?" I asked.

"We think so, yes."

"Why?"

All four of them looked at each other, then back at me.

"More room for brain matter? More brain tissue?" Colin said. "Hell if I know. The biological material from the dead Pouakai is not stable enough to study."

I took a deep breath. "You mean we nearly got ourselves killed, to substantiate a theory?"

"I wouldn't put it that way," Colin began. "This is all about gathering information, so we can…"

"Son of a bitch," I interrupted. "You really don't have a clue what you're doing, do you?"

"Boonie…"

"No, you brought me down here on a wild goose chase. You don't have anything solid, only have an untested theory about brains. How is this theory going to get rid of them?"

I glared at the four of them. Mina looked down, tears welling up in her eyes. Alan and Steve were shaking their heads, but Colin held my gaze.

"Boonie, this is how science works. We gather data. We look for correlations and trends. We come up with questions, and try to find ways to answer them. It's not all brilliant discoveries and eureka moments. It's a hard slog through hundreds of wrong turns and incorrect hypotheses. We get piles of information, reams of notes, and computers full of data. Somewhere deep inside that pile of data we may find what we're looking for. Getting the right information out of mountains of data points is hard work."

I let out a long breath. "Sorry. I didn't realize it wasn't clear cut; I thought you were on to something with the brain size thing."

"I understand, Boonie. You're new at this. It takes time to go through the data and make sense of it. That's all."

I nodded, and turned to stare across the lagoon, into the midday heat. I realized what an enormous task lay ahead for my friends. All this data they had been gathering…it had to be stored, retrieved, analyzed, tabulated, organized, and correlated. Each day brought more data to be stored and collated.

It would take a big computer to store all that info, and it would have to get bigger with each new theory or discovery. All the little computers out here in the field would have to feed their information into a bigger computer, so the information would be available in one place.

Bigger. Just like the Pouakai's brain.

I sat back, staring across the sapphire blue lagoon. It couldn't be that simple, could it?

"Colin, have you guys figured out what an individual Pouakai does with those bigger brains?"

"No. As far we've seen, all their behaviors remain the same, no matter which generation they are."

I hesitated. I didn't want to look like a fool, even if I didn't know these people all that well.

"What is it Boonie?" Colin asked.

I shook my head, and looked back at the lagoon.

"Never hold an idea back," Colin continued. "What may seem silly to you, could be the heart of a great theory."

"Okay. This is probably stupid, but…first off, are you guys sure that the glob you pulled out is a brain?"

"We're pretty sure. We tracked electrical activity inside the one we captured in Honolulu, and that organ was the center of it all. It appeared similar to the activity we see in animal brains."

"So if it is a brain, it could store data, right?"

"Sure."

"And bigger brains can store more data."

"Yes, in theory."

"Well, you said that each of the unborn Pouakai appeared fully formed, even down to the smallest ones you could see."

"That's right."

"So what if all the memories of the parent Pouakai were passed down to the children. They'd need bigger brains, not only to store their parent's memories, but their own too. Then they pass those memories on to their children."

Colin's face took on a glazed look. Alan looked up at the corrugated metal roof of the shop. Steve grinned at me, and Mina had covered her mouth with her hands.

"Un-frickin believable," Alan finally said.

My heart sank. They were laughing at me. Why the hell had I decided to come along, when I had nothing to contribute? I was more than useless here, I…

"Boonie," Colin said quietly, "that's brilliant!"

"Huh?"

"Dammit, I should have thought of it sooner. That's the best explanation I've heard yet."

"I agree," Alan said. "It makes complete sense that they transfer information to each other."

"It's not just data transfer," Steve responded. "They're scouts. They go out, gather information, and pass it on to their offspring."

"That is their purpose," Colin said, glassy-eyed again "They're biological machines. Biological data-gathering and storage machines! Dammit. I knew they were too simple to have spontaneously evolved this way. I just couldn't figure out what their purpose was." He grinned, and slapped me on the shoulder.

"That would explain the distribution difference too," Alan added.

"The what?" I asked.

"It's what I mentioned back on the *Kilo Moana*," Colin said. "The question of why we only found Pouakai that give birth to five babies in the Pacific basin, four both here and farther out toward the Indian Ocean, two in the Mediterranean, and so on, until there are only ones and zeros in the Caribbean."

"I don't get it."

"If they're constructed entities, biological machines acting as scouts, it would be a way of gathering information. Whoever, or whatever created these things, would send out these scouts, and see what information they bring back. If they don't come back, they'd create new ones that would have additional generations living past the original ones. Program them to search in one direction, until you've created enough generations to circle the globe. The ones that made it all the way around would have a memory of everything its parents and ancestors did. Where they swam, what they encountered, and what the world was like."

"They're Magellan," Steve said, "circling the globe, and reporting back what they find."

Everyone smiled, except me.

"That's great," I said, "but who, or what, is receiving that information at the end of the trip?"

Their smiles fell, and silence filled the air.

The radio squawked, and everyone jumped. "Submarine to survey leader, submarine to survey leader."

Colin picked up the radio. "Survey leader here."

"What is your status?"

"We are all okay. One Pouakai is dead, and we have information we need to pass along."

"Roger. We'll send the boat for you. There's a priority message for you too."

"What is it?"

"Unable to relay by radio. It's for your eyes only."

There was a pause as Colin stared at the radio, as if he could get the message just by wishing for it.

"The inflatables will be there in thirty minutes," the voice from the submarine continued. "Prepare your boat, and follow them back as soon as they arrive. Radar is clear, but the Captain doesn't want the inflatables away from here any longer than necessary."

"We'll be ready. Survey leader out." He looked at all of us. "When it rains, it pours," he said with a shrug. "Come on; let's get the trap set up again before our ride gets here."

5

Colin raced down the hatch when we reached the *Ohio*. I followed him down, through the control room, and forward to a small communications room. Colin went through the hatch, and I reached in to go through too.

"Sorry, sir," an armed Marine said, stopping me from entering. "Authorized personnel only."

"He's with me," Colin said from inside.

"Sorry, sir," the Marine reiterated. "Captain's orders. Only you are allowed in the comm center."

I shrugged my shoulders. "Don't worry, I'll head back to the mess."

The Captain had reserved one table in the crew mess for us 'non-quals', as we were called. Non-qualified riders, we ranked somewhere below a wharf rat, but above pond scum in the tightly ordered world of submariners.

We'd been through the two-day basic sub training required by the Navy, but there was so much about this ruthless weapon we didn't know yet. I fingered the radiation detector we'd been given as we boarded. Of all the things I had to worry about, it was just one more layer of concern. I didn't want to end up glowing green.

Thirty minutes later Colin walked into the mess, and joined us at our table, a thick manila folder in hand. He had a curious look on his face.

"What's up?" Alan asked.

"This." He opened the folder, removed a photograph, and set it on the table. "The National Reconnaissance Office sent these to me." They were satellite photographs of Palmyra, flecked with the same green dots as before, representing the Pouakai.

"This one was taken three days ago. The count is over three thousand Pouakai on Palmyra. Because of cloud cover and the satellite's orbit, we didn't get another photo until about twenty four hours ago, and that's this one." He put a second photo on the table. "It's the one we got before deciding to bring the *Kilo Moana* in and unload the trap."

Alan nodded. "They had left. That's why we decided to continue."

"They didn't leave," Colin said. "I think they died there, and dissolved. That's why we didn't see them in the satellite photos."

Everybody stared at the photographs.

"Remember last week, when we noticed that there weren't enough Pouakai in the photos? The trend has accelerated. These are the newest ones, taken today." He dropped the photos, one by one, on the table. "Samoa, Fiji, Solomons, Tuvalu, Kiribati, Indonesia, Seychelles."

We picked up the photos and looked at them. It didn't matter which one we had, we all had to be thinking the same thing.

"Can we be sure the satellite isn't losing the ability to identify them?" Steve asked.

Colin shook his head, discounting Steve's thought. "Here's the kicker," he said, dropping one more photo on the table. "This was taken earlier this afternoon, just before our encounter with the Pouakai."

The photo showed Palmyra, with one single green dot just south of the island.

"Our Pouakai was identified, so the satellite is still picking them up," Colin said quietly.

It took a moment for that to settle into our thoughts.

Mina looked up at Colin. "They are dying?" she asked in an ever-so-soft voice.

"I don't want to jump to conclusions, especially ones we really want to be true, but the evidence seems to point to the Pouakai disappearing."

We all sat back in our chairs in unison, and the magical feeling of relief began to spread across the room. It seemed too good to be true.

"H. G. Wells was right," Steve said. "It's the War of the Worlds. Something from here is killing them off."

"I don't know. We haven't seen anything to suggest that over another theory," Colin said.

I picked up one of the photos, but as I looked at it, another thought was bothering me.

"If the Pouakai are biological machines," I said, "perhaps they're dying because their job is complete, and they aren't needed any more."

"If that's true," Colin asked, "what comes next?"

Nobody else spoke for a long time.

6

We sat offshore of Palmyra for several more days, waiting for a Pouakai to show up at the trap. Colin, Alan, and Steve took eight-hour shifts, monitoring the cameras we'd set up by the trap, waiting for a victim. All they saw was an occasional sea bird, and one lonely turtle that kept bumping against the trap. The *Ohio's* radar scanned the skies, but it drew a blank too.

Submarines don't do well when sitting still. The round hull wallows in any waves, making for a sickening ride. I took my medicine so I didn't get ill. The crewmen didn't get sick either, but they were not having a good time.

I didn't have anything specific to do onboard, and turned to exploring the sub. More than half the boat was off-limits to me however, from the missile launch tubes in the mid-section to the reactor and engineering spaces at the aft end. The crew acted friendly at first, but distant. After a couple of days in though, they barely had a word to say to any of us. Having been in the military myself, I knew a widespread attitude change like this could only come from the top. Soon enough, I discovered the reason.

Every few hours, an emergency drill sounded onboard the sub. Whether it was a simulated fire in the torpedo room, a steam leak from the nuclear reactor, or even a collision with a surface ship, the emergency bells and sirens went on and off, signaling yet another drill. A booming voice came over the speaker system announcing the type of emergency. The crewmen tumbled out of their bunks, grabbed their emergency equipment, and dashed to their stations. Some time later, from a few minutes to half an hour, the voice would come over the speakers again, and tell the crew to return to their watch stations. I had no idea if this was a normal training cycle, or if the Captain was just being sadistic. Either way though, it usually interrupted a meal, or sleep, or both. The crewmen worked harder every day, and it coincided with them becoming distant to us. It seemed everyone felt the pressure to perform while parked next to Palmyra. Captain Baker's mood was blacker than ever. He had a perpetual scowl when we passed in the corridors.

At the end of the third day, Colin and I were eating dinner at our table. The crew had just finished another drill, this one being a reactor scram. Several crewmembers, enlisted and officers alike, were walking through the mess, back to their normal positions. The Captain blasted into the mess, unannounced. Everyone, except us, snapped to attention.

"Lieutenant Ainsworth," Baker shouted as he entered. "That scram took sixteen seconds longer to stabilize than yesterday. That is unacceptable."

A young, bespectacled officer stared straight ahead, the Captain in his face.

"Yes sir," the crewman shouted.

"You are relieved. Lieutenant Werner is now the EEOD."

"Yes sir."

Baker strode out, favoring us with a withering glare.

There was five seconds of silence once the Captain left, before the crewmen started to move. I looked at Colin, who rolled his eyes. Then I saw a familiar face.

"Lieutenant Hanson," I greeted the Navy SEAL walking by. He held a mug of coffee, and moved slowly through the mess. He looked down, and smiled.

"Good evening, sir," he replied.

I offered a seat, and after a momentary hesitation, he sat down.

"I gotta run," Colin said, wolfing down the last of his mashed potatoes. "It's time for my shift at the monitor."

"Happy hunting."

"Have a good evening, sir," Hanson added.

Colin left, and Hanson carefully studied his chipped coffee mug. I looked around the room and saw a lot of unhappy faces. I had no idea what was going on, and Hanson wasn't saying anything. The uncomfortable silence dragged on.

"I've never said thank you for rescuing us from Nanumea. So, thank you."

"No problem, sir. Just doing my job."

"Is your team always assigned to the *Ohio*?"

"Yes sir, for now, sir. My squads are assigned to the *Ohio*, and we are used wherever necessary."

The muscular Lieutenant didn't look at me as he talked, but fidgeted with his coffee mug. Something wasn't right, and I wanted to know more about what was going on with the crew. I wasn't sure how to approach the subject, however. From my own days in the Air Guard, I knew that everyone complained about their superior officers, so I tried that tack.

"So what's got into the Captain?"

"Bad performance on the reactor scram," he replied, still staring at the mug.

"So he demotes one of the reactor operators, and rides roughshod over the crew?"

Hanson shrugged. "They have performance standards to keep up."

"It just seems the Captain is being harder on the crew, compared to when you rescued us."

After nearly a minute of silence, he looked at me. "Sir, how much do you know about submarine ops?"

"Only what they taught us in the two days at Pearl Harbor."

He sighed, and shook his head. "When a submarine puts out to sea, the Captain gets a packet of orders. It's a list of tasks to be accomplished while out on patrol. Always, number one on the list is 'remain undetected'. That's the primary goal of any sub cruise. When we were assigned to support your operation however, we couldn't do that. We had to cruise near the surface on the way down here, so the radar would work. We have to stay stationary on the surface here too, so you guys can communicate with your trap. All that goes against what the crew has been trained to do, which is to hunt the enemy, and not get caught."

"Why would anyone want to catch us here? We're trying to do something to save the world."

"You know the saying about poking an angry animal? There are other countries that are hurting because of what the Rocs have done. They're like an angry animal, and we're poking at them just because we have what they want. The U.S has got oil, coal, gas, and other things they want, so they get angry. We need it for ourselves, and it's not enough, but they want it."

"What does that have to do with us?"

"This sub is a symbol. We're a target, sitting here. The *Ohio* is supposed to be unseen, submerged, protecting what's important to America, but we've been visible, and surfaced, for most of the trip so far."

He looked around casually. Most of the others had left the mess. A few sullen crewmen sat at the far end, drinking coffee.

"Do you know what this sub is designed to do?" he asked quietly.

"Lob nukes at our enemies?"

Hanson shook his head. "No, not any more. It used to though. The *Ohio* was originally a Trident ballistic missile sub. However this one, and three others, have been modified. They're set up now for more modern warfare. They carry cruise missiles instead of the ballistic ones. Some of the cruise missiles are nuclear, but the *Ohio* can deliver conventional weapons too. There's also equipment for delivering our SEAL teams ashore without being detected. Plus lots of equipment for, um, other types of operations."

"You guys fight terrorists?"

"Among other targets, yes. The whole point of this sub though, is to remain quiet, and undetected, while getting us close enough to the target to do our job. What the Captain is required to do by helping you goes against everything he's learned and trained for as a submariner."

"Son of a bitch," I said quietly.

"There have been rumors," Hanson continued, "that subs from Russia, China, and North Korea are all nearby, watching us, gathering data on us."

"They're trying to figure out what we're doing here?"

"No, they are watching the *Ohio*. They're probably wondering if they should take the chance to fire on us."

My stomach flopped. "But we're trying to help the whole world, including them!"

Hanson looked around, and shook his head minutely. Don't talk so loud he seemed to be suggesting.

"It's not about the Rocs. It's about getting the upper hand against us. The Rocs have changed the way the world works. Nothing is the same any more. Everyone is scrambling to survive, which puts everyone on a short trigger. Everything we're doing is to protect our country. It's the same for them. They are all about getting what we have, and what they think they need."

Three senior officers walked through the mess on their way to the reactor control room. Hanson downed the rest of his coffee and, without a word, left me sitting alone. How could a mission of discovery about humanity's common enemy become just another bit of international intrigue?

7

There were simply no Pouakai showing up at Palmyra. The world's news sites buzzed continuously about the missing Pouakai. Big die-offs were happening everywhere, and people were speculating why. The church groups took credit for their prayer meetings, and said it was God's will that the devil had left. Others thought it had to be biological, while a few insisted it was a hoax from the beginning, fabricated to allow prices to be jacked up. If that was true, that was one hell of a hoax Colin speared on Palmyra.

Colin, Alan, Mina and I sat at our table the next morning, poring over the news reports. Steve was on duty at the trap controls. Colin also had a running email discussion going on with several other scientists. Everyone had a different opinion, but nobody had credible data to back up their thoughts.

"Great," Alan said, "look at this, Colin. It's only been a couple of days, and the oil companies are already pressing governments to let them run their tankers across the equator."

"That won't happen right away. It's too soon. There could be a huge flock of Pouakai we don't know about."

"Tell that to the oil shippers. They want to get back into business before they go broke."

"It's too fast. We just don't know enough."

"People are excited," Mina said. "There is hope, which they have not had for a long time."

Colin shook his head. "It has only been a few days since we noticed the die-off. The Pouakai have been here for three years. It's happening too fast to make big decisions yet."

We went back to our online reading. I found an article complaining about the lack of knowledge regarding the Pouakai. It read like it had been written by one of Colin's scientist buddies. The main point was that we had no information on what preceded the Pouakai's disappearance. Nobody knew whether there had been a gradual decline leading up to now, or if it had happened all of a sudden. The data from the newly tuned satellites didn't go back far enough.

As I read that statement, I realized there were people who might know the answers to that question.

"Colin, read this." I turned my laptop toward him.

After finishing it, he said, "That's what I've been saying all day."

"So let's do something about it."

"We are. We're trying to pull all the information we have together, to see if we can make some sense out of what's going on."

"No," I said, looking at the others at the table. "The article asked what led up to the disappearance, but there's nobody who would know."

I waited, hoping someone would take up my train of thought. All I got was a series of blank stares.

"We know people who would have seen any changes, and been able to track subtle alterations in the Pouakai's behavior."

Another moment of silence passed, until Colin's eyes brightened. "Nanumea!"

"Yes. Nanumea."

"Of course," Alan said, with a grin. "They've been living with the Pouakai. They would have noticed any changes with them."

"Exactly," I replied. "We should head down that way and talk to the Chief."

Alan's mouth clamped into a tight line.

"You don't think we should do that?" Colin asked.

"I do, but I was hoping we could hang around here a little longer, just to see if we could catch more Pouakai."

"In an ideal world, we would, Alan. We need to get moving if we want to keep up with the changes though."

"Yeah, yeah, I know. Shit. I'll head up to the control room, and let Steve know."

"I guess we should get ready to go. Do you have anything to add Mina?" Colin said.

She shook her head demurely.

"Then let's tell Captain Baker about the new plan."

It was hard to tell if the Captain was happy or not. First, he had to relay our plan back to his headquarters in Hawaii and wait for a reply. Colin did the same with the university, although that was more of a formality. I found out that by his orders, Captain Baker had to do whatever Colin wanted, and couldn't say no unless it put the sub and her crew in immediate danger. Both replies came back within a few minutes of each other: Proceed.

Alan shut down the trap remotely, leaving it tied up to the dock at Palmyra. Eventually, someone would come by to retrieve it. Either that, or it would slowly rust away like everything does in the tropics, and sink to the bottom of the lagoon.

An hour after receiving the go ahead for our plan, the last man came down from the sail, and closed the hatch behind him. One of the men on the inflatable boat had told me it was now called the 'fairweather', but after a lifetime of watching submarine movies, I couldn't call it anything but a sail. The Captain gruffly invited Colin and me up to the control room as they readied to dive.

Unlike an airplane pilot, the Captain didn't actually steer this beast. He stood at the back of the room, watching the organized mayhem. Orders were barked out by another officer to those in the room, and over an intercom system to the engineering officers. It wasn't like those movies where they immediately dive, either. The officer kept asking about depth as we moved away from Palmyra, waiting, I guess, for it to be deep enough for him to order us to dive.

The ride felt disorienting. I was used to knowing exactly where I was in relation to the outside world while flying, either through the window or from my instruments. Here though, I couldn't make out anything like a map, compass, or anything else that would give me our location or the direction we were moving in. The sub bucked and rolled strongly as we moved out from the lee side of the island into open water, but otherwise it felt about the same as it had the last several days.

Captain Baker kept quiet. He peered over his half-glasses, looking for signs of anything out of order. After witnessing how explosive his temper could be over the last few days, I wasn't surprised at the tension in the control room.

A quiet discussion began between several officers, until one of them barked an order that I didn't catch. The *ah-oogah* horn sounded, just like it did in those old movies, and someone in front of us shouted, "Dive, dive, dive." A great rushing sound roared through the sub, and gently, the floor started tipping downward. I wasn't expecting that, or for the angle to keep increasing until I had to hold on to a railing behind me. The roaring sound faded away, replaced a few minutes later by unsettling pops and creaks from the hull.

"Test depth," someone called out, as the deck leveled out. More orders were given, and then a quiet settled on the room. Everyone seemed to be holding their breath. I glanced at Colin, but he just looked at the Captain, back at me, and shook his head.

The officer in charge asked for a sonar report. Another crewman rattled of a bunch of numbers and words like target, range, and delta. I got the impression they were tracking another submarine, possibly one of the foreign ones Lieutenant Hanson had mentioned a few days earlier.

Then the officer started turning us left and right, and going up and down a little. The deck pitched with each of these maneuvers, but not as sharply as the first dive. At least I understood some of what he said this time, as the language of heading, bearing, rise and dive made some sense.

We stood next to the Captain for nearly two hours, until the sonar officer stated that contact was lost. Several of the men in the room gave each other pats on the back, and the tension eased measurably. Captain Baker stood up. "Come with me."

Colin and I followed the Captain forward, past the communications room and into a tiny stateroom, smaller than the Amtrak stateroom Jennifer and I had used on our cross-country vacation last year. Despite the size, it was the biggest sleeping quarters I'd seen onboard the *Ohio*.

"Sit down."

We complied, feeling like we were being shown into the Principal's office.

Captain Baker sat down behind a tiny desk and, surprisingly, took a deep breath and sighed. "We're clear for now," he said.

"That's good," Colin replied. "What was all that about for the last couple of hours?"

"We're under way, and gave the other subs the slip."

"Someone was after us?"

"There's always someone looking for us. It's what we do. A Russian Akula and a Chinese Shang have been watching us since we arrived at Palmyra."

I nodded. "I heard something about that from the crew."

"Whatever you heard, it wasn't complete," Baker said sharply. Then he took a breath and softened his tone. "Shipboard rumors are always making the rounds, and they're almost never accurate. The two other subs arrived at Palmyra about the same time we did. Obviously, their satellite observations saw us escorting the *Kilo Moana* down here, and their Pacific Fleet commanders sent them to investigate."

"So there wasn't any danger from them?"

"There's always danger, Major Boone. I don't know what their orders are, and my number one job is the safety of this boat and her crew. Leaving ourselves exposed on the surface for so long, where the others can take their time gathering data about us, compromises that safety."

"They won't find us now?"

"I don't think so. We're heading toward California…"

"Wait a minute…" Colin objected.

"Keep your voice down," Baker said quietly, but sternly. "If you're going to stay on this boat, you must remember your training, and stay quiet. We're heading toward California right now to give a false lead in case they are still tracking us. Once we are sure we're not being tracked, we'll turn south, loop around Palmyra, and head for Nanumea."

"Okay. Sorry."

"Good. Now get some rest, and stay quiet. We should be at Nanumea in about three and a half days, depending on when we can turn south."

We left the Captain's quarters, and walked back to our table in the mess. The others were there, but without an internet connection, we didn't have much to do. We ate with a few of the other crewmen, until we went to our bunks to read.

The crew had set up our temporary quarters in the forward torpedo room, since they didn't have spare rooms for guests. My cot straddled a torpedo, against the port side of the sub. The first night aboard I'd barely slept, thinking about the five hundred pounds of high explosives a few inches from my head. Now, I simply lay back, and resigned myself to boredom, and frequent emergency drills, as we slipped through the deep black ocean.

8

After four days underwater, we approached Nanumea. Captain Baker had been extra cautious about losing our tail, so we'd sailed the wrong way for half a day before turning back southwest. Once we reached Nanumea, he had us sit still for six hours, listening for any other subs in the area. My patience with this cat-and-mouse game had worn thin. We had a job to do too.

We surfaced two hours before sunrise. The Captain hadn't detected any other subs in the area, but he didn't want to be on the surface during daylight either. He would drop us off, and then stay submerged until after sunset, when he'd send the inflatable to get us.

When we popped above the surface, we had a few minutes to check the web while the sailors got the inflatable ready. All over the world, mass die-offs of the Roc had sent people into a frenzy of both happiness and worry. The news sites had reached a fever pitch; one side screaming that the Rocs were dead while saner heads said it was too early to know, but they were drowned out by the near-hysteria of relief.

Cloud cover had prevented the satellites from taking any survey photos of Nanumea. The Captain would let us go ashore, but he'd only risk his inflatables in the early morning hours, since we couldn't be sure if the Pouakai were here or not.

Colin brought his satellite phone with him, along with a laptop, so he could continue the email discussion with colleagues around the world. The five of us, plus two sailors, slid down the side of the sub in the pre-dawn darkness, and into the inflatable boat. I stumbled on the way down, almost ending up in the ocean. Without even a cup of coffee at this early hour, I really dragged.

"How can he see where we're going?" Steve asked in a whisper, nodding toward the sailor steering the inflatable. I shrugged. Then the sailor put on a pair of night-vision goggles, and we started on our way.

A second inflatable was tied up to the sub too. I made out the shapes of more men on the deck of the sub, lowering gear into the boat.

"What's up with that?" I asked Colin, while pointing at the other inflatable.

"The SEALs are coming too. For our protection," he added, rolling his eyes.

"Baker's idea?"

"Yep."

The sea felt calm in the pre-dawn darkness, the island a black line in the faint starlight. A quiet rush of the sea as small swells broke on the reef. The sound got louder as we passed into the narrow cut in the reef and motored into the lagoon. We pulled up to the beach behind the village a few minutes later. Somewhere to the left, invisible in the darkness, lay the wreckage of my plane, probably now corroding away in the saltwater of the Pacific.

As soon as we got ourselves and our gear out of the inflatable, it pulled back into the lagoon, headed for the *Ohio*. The other inflatable arrived and the SEALs slipped onto the shore, all black shadows and silent movement.

"Split up into small groups," Colin told everyone, once we'd gathered on the beach. "Remember how we did it when we were here before. No more than four people together, and walk slowly, keep quiet. If you see a Pouakai, just sit quietly and wait for it to go away."

"Should we go into the village now?" Alan asked.

"No. Spread out along the beach, and wait for first light. When I stand up, you can follow, but try to keep each group separated. Don't form a big mass of people."

Colin motioned to me, and to Lieutenant Hanson. We sat down next to the path leading to the village. The others broke into small groups, with at least one SEAL in each group.

We sat in the cool, damp sand waiting. Sooner than I expected, the first tinge of violet rose in the eastern sky, and the rapid tropical dawn rolled toward us. Within minutes I could make out the tail of my wrecked 767, jutting into the air above the lagoon. It still looked clean, with the airline's logo untouched. I fought back a wave of sadness about everything that had changed since that day.

As the violet sky turned to deep red and orange, Colin stood up.

"Let's go." He waved to the other groups scattered along the beach, and we began to walk inland.

The silence struck me first. When we'd been there earlier in the year, you would hear roosters crowing and people moving about by this time of the morning. Today though, it was deathly still. It didn't feel right. We walked slowly along the path, trying to be as quiet as possible. A bird fluttered overhead, and we stopped for a moment, until we were sure it wasn't a Pouakai. We passed several small homes, all empty.

Colin reached back and adjusted a plastic bag strapped to his backpack.

"What's that?" I whispered.

"A makana for the Chief. I got some fresh pineapple and canned ham from the sub's galley."

I couldn't help smiling. Even out here, he was a model of politeness.

Lieutenant Hanson put his hand on Colin's shoulder, making him jump.

"Sorry," Hanson whispered. He motioned for us to stand behind him, and he continued forward, silently unslinging his rifle. We followed, not quite so silently, behind him.

The Lieutenant stopped moving a few hundred yards from the center of the village, as we entered the same clearing where Brett had been sliced up by the Pouakai the day we'd arrived. The Lieutenant leveled his rifle and dropped to one knee. Colin stopped and knelt. I couldn't see past the Lieutenant and Colin, but knelt down too.

After a few seconds, the Lieutenant stood up, and we followed him into the clearing. At least a hundred freshly dug mounds of dirty sand covered the area. Graves. Rough crosses stood at one end of each mound.

"What happened?" I whispered, aghast at the evidence of carnage.

The Lieutenant didn't respond as he swept the area with the muzzle of his rifle. Nothing moved. We turned onto the road toward the Quonset hut, slowing as we approached. My heart beat faster. What had happened? They couldn't have all died, since someone had to dig those graves.

The metal grate barred the entrance to the hut, and a large piece of cloth covered the inside of the doorway, so we couldn't see in. Lieutenant Hanson looked back at Colin, tilting his head toward the door. Colin nodded, and stepped up to the grate.

"Hello? Anyone there?"

After a moment's silence, footsteps, and then the cloth moved aside. A local looked at us, wide-eyed, and unlocked the grate.

The Quonset hut was filled with people, huddling together on the floor. There were several times as many people crammed into the hut as there had been when my crew and passengers were there. With barely any room to walk around, we stood at the entrance, gasping at the stench of all these people in such a small space.

"Where is the Chief?" I asked the local who let us in.

He looked at us, puzzled, and shook his head. He didn't understand English. Then he looked at Colin and me again, closer, and nodded. He waved at someone, who stood and approached us.

"Captain Boonie, it is good to see you," the new arrival said. I recognized Fatakolonga, who had gone fishing with me several times.

"It's good to see you too, Fata, but what happened? Where is the Chief?"

He led us to the back corner of the hut. Chief Kalahamotu lay on the ground, a bad gash across his stomach. A few tattered rags lay over the wound.

"Chief," Fatakolonga said, "Captain Boonie is here."

The Chief raised his head, and looked at me and then at Colin, before lying back on the ground. I knelt beside him.

"Chief, we came back to see how you are doing, but didn't expect this. What happened?"

"The Pouakai changed," he said in a whisper. "They attacked us."

"When?" Colin asked.

"Ten days ago, I think. I do not know what day it is now."

Fatakolonga nodded. "Yes, it was ten days ago when the change happened."

"What did the Pouakai do?"

The Chief raised his head again, but Fatakolonga put a hand on his shoulder, and continued the story. "The Pouakai came in a thick cloud. Angry. They attacked everything, even people standing still. The Pouakai were not right in their head. They were crazy. They attacked people, buildings, animals, trees. Then they died."

"All at once?"

"No, it took a few days. The Pouakai did not leave Nanumea. They stayed on the ground and water, but did not fly. Some would start shaking, and even attacking other Pouakai. Then they would lie on the ground and stop moving. After that they would die. By the time two days were gone, all the Pouakai were dead."

"You came in here for safety?" I asked.

"Yes, but there were many of our people dead outside. After the Pouakai had died, a few went out to bury our people, then came back here."

"Why come back to the hut?"

"There were more Pouakai in the next few days. Only one or two at a time, but they were crazy too. It was not safe outside. It has been five days since the last one. We don't know if the Pouakai are coming back. Except for when we buried our people, we stay here. If they did come back when we were outside, we could be killed too."

I looked around the shelter. There wasn't much food on the table, and no water. Something would have to give, and soon.

"The Pouakai are dying everywhere," Colin said to Fatakolonga. "All around the world, at about the same time as yours here."

"Why?"

"We don't know. It's all very sudden, and we're trying to figure it out."

"There will be more," the Chief whispered from the ground. We knelt next to him.

"Why do you say that?" Colin asked.

"The Pouakai finished their job. Something else is coming now."

"How do you know?"

"It is what we have done for three years, watch the Pouakai. We watched them, and learned from them. They were here for a reason. One I do not know yet. They would not go away unless their reason for being here is done."

Colin looked at me with a small shrug.

"Chief," I said. "How did you get hurt?"

"My wife was killed by a Pouakai. I went to get her. A Pouakai was on the ground next to her. I thought it was dead, but when I got there it started shaking again. I was too close, and its spear hit me."

"I'm sorry Chief. About your wife, and your injury."

The Chief nodded, laying his head back on the ground.

We stood up, and returned to the entrance. The rest of our group and the SEALs stood just outside, waiting. We explained what we found, and then Colin turned to Fatakolonga.

"Fata, we think the danger from the Pouakai is over."

"It may be, but we have to stay safe. The Chief will tell us when we can go out again."

"I understand. Would you mind if we walked around the island, and checked it out ourselves? We could let you know if there are any Pouakai in the area."

Fata glanced back at the hut, before nodding.

"Okay everyone," Colin said. "Just like we did at Palmyra. I want a good survey of what's here, and how many Pouakai remains you find. Report back here in four hours. That's 1pm, Hawaii time."

We broke into small groups and agreed on which areas to cover. As we turned to leave, an electronic chirping noise sounded. We stopped and looked around, puzzled, except for Colin, who extracted the satellite phone from his backpack.

"Hello?"

I had an odd feeling, watching Colin talk calmly on the phone while standing on a remote island in the South Pacific. For a moment, I wished he'd had that phone when we were here the first time.

"Wait a minute," he said, "I'm going to put this on the speaker. I want everyone to hear."

He laid the phone on a stump of a coconut tree and turned up the volume.

"Go ahead Matt. My team is listening."

A tinny voice emitted from the phone speaker. "Hello everyone. This is Matt Barrow, Colin's assistant here in Honolulu. I called because things have really gotten crazy in the last couple of hours, and we think we may have found Pouakai signatures in new satellite photos."

"Where?" Colin asked.

"How?" Alan asked at the same time.

"I just got the call from the NRO about ten minutes ago. They sent the photos, and I forwarded them on to your email, Colin."

"Why didn't they see the signatures before? I thought all traces of the Pouakai had disappeared a few days ago."

"They had, but the NRO has been retuning the satellites, to see if there were Pouakai signatures at different frequencies of the spectrum. They caught these late yesterday, your time, and sent them on to me."

"I don't get it," Alan said.

"The frequencies that allowed the satellites to identify the Pouakai now show nothing, as if there's no Pouakai left."

"That's what we found out here," Colin said. "The Pouakai are all gone."

"Yes, but the NRO has been scanning up and down the frequency range, looking for other signatures, and found these new ones. The good news is that it's only in two tiny clusters, southwest from your position on Nanumea."

"They think it's Pouakai?"

"It's not anything they've encountered before They said it strongly resembles the signature of the Pouakai, just at a slightly different frequency, as if the color they were looking for had changed."

"Where are these signatures?"

"One cluster is on Anuta island, about six hundred miles southwest of Nanumea. That's at the far east end of the Solomon Islands. The other cluster is over the ocean, about thirty miles south of Anuta."

"That all?"

"So far, yes, but those may be the only photos we get."

"Why?"

"After the satellite sent the pictures to the NRO office, it stopped working."

"The satellite broke?"

"Yes. That's what's really causing the uproar here. The satellite was hit by unidentified fire, followed by the downing of more satellites. They are being targeted with a high-powered energy beam, taking them out."

"Holy shit," Lieutenant Hanson said. "Where from?"

"They don't know. The Russians have lost satellites too, as well as the Chinese, Koreans, Japanese, and European Space Agency. Any satellite capable of imaging the Earth has been hit. It's ratcheting up the global tension. Every country is blaming another for the attacks. It's getting ugly really quickly."

"Is there any pattern to which satellites were hit?"

"They've all been on one hemisphere of the world when hit, roughly centered on the southwest Pacific basin. That's all the NRO would tell me though. Hang on, something is flashing on the news."

We waited for Matt to continue. The morning sun slanted through the coconut palms, and I could tell it was going to be a scorcher of a day. The wind drifted around us lightly, the sky a clear blue infinity.

"They got the international space station," he finally said. We gasped.

"They're saying they got a few seconds of garbled transmission from the astronauts aboard, before all communication quit. An Air Force tracking station in Hawaii says there's multiple targets now where the station should be. I think whatever it is just killed our people up there."

Colin dropped to his knees, and plugged his laptop into the data port on the phone. "Matt, did you already email me those photos?"

"Yes, you should have them in your inbox."

Colin tapped on the laptop, and a few moments later, a photo showed up on the screen. We clustered around him to see the photo, while the SEALs conferred a few feet away. The photo showed a small circular island, in the same false-color I'd seen in the other satellite images. A group of greenish dots were at the center of the island. Colin brought up a second photo, which showed the same island, but with a much larger scale. Below the island, in the middle of the ocean, was another spot of green.

"I have the photos Matt. Is there anything else you can send?"

"Not at the moment. I'm trying to get through to Washington, but there's been trouble with the phone systems since…"

A burst of static sounded and we all jumped.

"Matt?" Colin unplugged his laptop, picked up the phone, and then handed it to me. The display said 'Searching for signal'. I couldn't get anything out of it either. I looked at Colin, and shook my head.

"What happened?" Mina asked.

"I don't know," I said. "The signal from the phone just died. It's trying to find another satellite to lock onto, but nothing's there."

"Whoever is knocking down the surveillance satellites must have taken out the phone sats too," Lieutenant Hanson said, as he joined our group.

"Why?"

"That's how it's done in war. If you take out the enemy's ability to communicate, they can't mount an effective defense against you."

"Who are we fighting against? Who declared war on us, and why now?"

"It could be anyone. The Russians, Chinese, North Koreans."

"Or the Pouakai," Colin said quietly.

The Lieutenant shook his head. "That's a stretch. You said yourself the Pouakai are all gone. So there aren't any Pouakai left down here, and we've never seen anything resembling technology related to them anyway. They are just animals. It would make sense for one of those other countries to take advantage of the confusion of the Pouakai disappearance to mount an attack like this."

"Lieutenant," Colin said. "You may honestly believe that, but I don't. Matt said that all those countries reported their own satellites had been hit too. It has to be more than other countries gunning for war."

"They could be lying, distracting us from the truth."

"To what end? What could they gain from this?"

"Power, domination of this part of the world."

I snorted, and everyone looked at me. "Sorry Lieutenant," I said, "but there's nothing down here that I'd give a nickel for, and neither would any of those other countries. Colin, I understand where the Lieutenant is coming from. I've been part of that military mind myself. Today, Lieutenant, I think you're wrong. Look at the timeline. We take a photo of a possible new flock of Pouakai, our ability to track them is removed. After that, communications are destroyed; if it's true that the phone sats have been shot down too."

"You think all these satellites were deliberately shot down?" Mina asked.

"Yes. Someone, or something, is removing our capability to find these new Pouakai, if that's what they are. Colin, do you agree?"

Colin stared at the ground, lost in thought.

"Colin?"

"Sorry. Yes, I agree. There's an intelligence and technology involved that we aren't aware of yet."

We all stood silently, lost in the enormity of what was happening.

"We need to get back to the sub," Colin finally said. "We have to use their communications equipment to see what else is going on. Lieutenant, can you call the sub to pick us up?"

Hanson shook his head. "I could call, but the Captain wouldn't send the inflatables for us. Not now, especially. I'm sure he's thinking like I am, that it's a foreign power's attempt to knock us out. That means he'll be more protective than ever with the *Ohio*. There's no way he'll surface until after dark. I'll let him know what's happened, and that we need retrieval as soon as possible, but he won't answer back unless something changes. We'll get back tonight, after dark."

I sat down in the sand, and pulled out a bottle of water and a granola bar. Colin looked at the Lieutenant, shrugged, and joined me on the ground for a snack. Sometimes, even in the middle of a crisis, there's nothing you can do but wait.

9

"I'm sorry Brett." I reached down and placed a photograph of my former co-pilot's family on the mound of dirt and sand where we'd buried him. Brett's grave was in a corner of the open area where he'd been killed. He had a view of the sky and ocean. It was beautiful and peaceful.

"This photo is for you. They miss you. We all do. You should see Rachael. She's growing like crazy." In the photo, his wife, Emma, had a sad smile on her face, and daughter Rachael was reaching for the camera, a big grin on hers.

"I wish I could have done more for you. I wish I would have seen that Pouakai coming, or pushed you away, or something. You don't deserve to be here. Nobody does." I took a breath, and let it out slowly. "Jennifer is gone too. It was the Pouakai, just like you. I don't know how life is supposed to work, but this isn't what I expected. You are both supposed to be here. We should all be flying, fishing, and eating dinner together. But we're stuck with the Pouakai, and now we're trying to do something about them. That's why I'm here, with Colin and Alan again. Remember them from our flight here? I quit the airline too. What do you think about that? I was going to go to Colorado with Jennifer, but after what happened to her…"

I knelt down next to the grave, and rearranged the small pieces of white coral that spelled his name. Time, wind, and fallen palm fronds had knocked a few of the pieces out of order.

"We're trying to get a handle on what's happening out here. The Pouakai have died, or at least, a lot of them have. We haven't seen any for over a week now, but Colin and Alan seem to think there's something else going on. So does the Chief. I don't know what to think, myself. A bunch of satellites have been knocked out. There's a lot of finger pointing going on over that too. You know me; I don't believe in coincidence that much. The satellites have all been shot at when they were over this end of the Pacific, and this is where Colin thinks the Pouakai first came from. There's a connection there."

"Anyway, that's why I'm here again, and Emma gave me this photo to give to you, in case I made it back."

I stopped, feeling the tears welling up again. It was odd, talking to a grave like this, but it felt good. After a deep breath, and a look up at the blue sky, I continued. "Rachael is crawling almost as fast as Emma can walk now. She's got your energy, and your smile too."

I arranged a few more pieces of coral on the grave, before standing up.

"I just wanted to talk. Without you around, I don't have any tree-hugging liberals to argue with." I smiled. "So I guess I'll be going now. I'll tell Emma you're doing fine here." I choked up for a moment. "She misses you Brett. We all do. God bless."

The sun almost touching the horizon, I walked back to the lagoon, where the rest of our team waited for the sub crew to pick us up. Fatakolonga stood there too, talking quietly with Colin and Lieutenant Hanson. The Lieutenant looked relaxed, his rifle slung over a shoulder and a banana in hand. He nodded as I walked up.

"Captain Boonie," Fata said. "Anything found?"

"No, nothing out there. I was just saying goodbye to my friend."

"The Chief would like you to come back someday."

"I would like that Fata. Maybe one day when this is all over, I will come back. We can fish, and talk about how much better it will be then. Will you all be okay for now?"

"Yes, we will survive. That is what we do."

"Good luck. Tell the Chief I will do whatever I can for you."

"Thank you, Captain Boonie."

We shook hands, then he walked into the jungle.

"What do we do now?" I asked Colin. He shrugged.

"I'll have to find out what other news there is from my colleagues, and if there were any other satellite photos taken of this area before they were knocked out. I've had some sporadic contact through the sat phone, but I really need the secure comm equipment on the sub. My first choice is to head out to Anuta and track down those Pouakai signatures in the photos."

"I don't know if the Captain will go for that," the Lieutenant said. "If things have gotten as dicey as it sounds, he may want to go back to Hawaii and prep for a fight. Or he may be ordered to do that anyway."

"I hope not. We still need to stay focused on the Pouakai. I believe they are the underlying reason for all this trouble in the first place."

"But if they're gone…"

"I don't think that they are. We've got the photos that show the objects on Anuta. That's why we need to be out here looking."

"It is up to the Captain, and the commanders back in Hawaii too. They get the final word on what we do, and where we go."

"I hope they realize how important our mission is," Colin said passionately.

"So is the security of the U.S."

"Guys," I said. "This won't get us anywhere. One step at a time. Which means getting back to the sub first, and finding out what's going on, before making an intelligent decision."

Hanson grinned. "How is it that you Air Guard pukes are so level-headed?"

"Years of keeping you Navy guys safe from yourselves."

Twilight fell on the island, the winds gentler than usual. Just a few clouds drifted overhead, shifting from orange to red to purple. The rapid tropical night dropped like a blanket over Nanumea, and as the first stars stole into view, two inflatables skimmed into the lagoon, heading toward our beach.

10

"Somehow I knew you'd want to keep going," Captain Baker said, with a shake of his head.

"There's no question," Colin insisted. "We're here to search for Pouakai. We have photographic evidence of more of them out in the Solomons. We have to find out what it means."

Baker glared at me. "I suppose you feel the same way, Major?"

"Honestly, I don't know. I can see both sides, but I don't know which option is the right one."

"You're supposed to be an airline captain, Major. A decision maker. What if you were in charge here?"

I shrugged, and glanced around the control room of the *Ohio*. We were bathed in the deep red glow of night operations, so anyone heading up the fairweather to the bridge wouldn't be night-blind.

"You've reminded us many times that we're not in command."

A trace of a smile curled at the Captain's mouth. "At least you remembered that. And you are right; it's not your decision. I'm just waiting for orders from SUBCOMPAC to head back to Hawaii."

"Then I'm glad I got a few messages back to my office," Colin said. "This is too important to ignore. We have evidence of more Pouakai, possibly unlike the ones we know about now and you want to ignore that? Don't you see the connection between these new signatures and the loss of our satellites?"

"It is a possibility, although a remote one. We haven't seen any hint of technology from them, especially enough to shoot down multiple satellites, as well as the space station. Right now though, we are on the brink of a shooting war, and I don't want to be stuck in a far corner of the ocean when we're needed back home."

"You don't think that finding the root of all this trouble is more important?"

"I deal in realities, Professor Benoit. The reality is that we may be under attack right now. My number one duty is to protect the United States of America. That is what I get paid to do, and what I'm trained to do. That job will be better done by heading back to Hawaii than hunting Pouakai."

"We disagree then."

"We do. The final decision isn't either of ours. We just have to wait until our orders come through."

Colin's face shined beet red. He did a good job controlling his anger, managing to avoid knocking the Captain to the deck.

"When will we hear something?" I asked.

"Any time now, I'm sure."

"Then we'll wait. Maybe get some dinner too. Let us know when the message gets here."

"Of course." The Captain turned to talk to his executive officer, pointedly ignoring us, even though we were standing right next to him. Eventually I caught Colin's eye, and cocked my head toward the rear of the sub. Dinner-time.

He didn't say a word as we walked the cramped corridors toward the mess. He kept quiet through the entire meal, too. Alan, Steve and Mina were already there, digging into trays piled high with steak and mashed potatoes. The rest of us made small talk, ignoring Colin, who ate slowly.

Eventually, the others drifted away, tired after our long day on Nanumea. I stayed to keep Colin company, even though he wasn't talking. He just stared into space, as if listening to a sound nobody else could hear. Weary, and unable to keep my eyes open after sitting for half an hour, I stood up.

"Good night Colin. I'm heading to bed."

I'd taken two steps when he spoke up.

"You didn't support me, Boonie."

"What?"

"You didn't come to my side, when we were talking to the Captain."

"I didn't say anything against you."

"But you didn't support my side."

I sat down again, and folded my arms on the table. "Colin, I didn't support the Captain's side either. There are two sides to this argument, just like any other argument. Look, I've been in the military, so I know where their priorities lie. It's their job to protect the country. They're wired to think that way; so was I once. I understand them, but I'm not one of them. I understand you too, even though I'm not a scientist. You have some good points, and it's your job to defend them."

He glared at me, but I continued. "In the end, it's not my place to make a decision. If I were Captain of this sub, and unable to communicate with my commanders, I'd make a decision based on my tactical experience. However, I'm not the Captain here. You have to realize that you're not in a position to make that final decision either. That should be left up to those actually in charge. It's kind of like politics. Everyone has an opinion, but someone has to make the final decision. If everyone kept yelling, and insisting that it absolutely had to go their way, nothing would get accomplished. It's what you learn when put into a position of command. If you are the decision maker, you gather your information, and make the decision. If you let those around you make the choices, something bad usually happens. We are the voices of information here, not the decision makers."

After remaining quiet for almost a minute, he finally looked at me, and spoke. "This is a hell of a time to start playing politics." I caught the first hint of a smile on his face. "Asshole," he added. "I told you not to take that Political Science class."

"I had to. It's what Jennifer took that semester, and I wanted to be around her more."

We both leaned back in our chairs, and relaxed.

"Science team, report to the control room," came a voice from the speaker.

"It's showtime," I said.

We met Alan, Steve and Mina as they entered the control room from the opposite direction, all three looking like they'd just been rousted out of bed. Captain Baker stood at the back wall again, a single sheet of paper in hand. He looked at us over his half-glasses, but I couldn't make out any emotion on his face. I still didn't know which way we'd be going.

"This just came in from SUBCOMPAC. We are…" he paused, and cleared his throat. "I'll read the orders. To Baker, Riley, Captain, *USS Ohio*, from SUBCOMPAC. You are to proceed as directed by Professor Benoit to identify, and classify if possible, the signatures seen in the recent photographs of the Solomon Islands. Every attempt will be made to ascertain the location and origin of any and all creatures known as Rocs, or Pouakai."

He had an odd look on his face, his mouth drawn in a tight line. It took a few seconds for him to continue. "Until further notice, you will take all direction from Benoit, Colin, Professor of Astrophysics and Astrobiology, University of Hawaii at Manoa. He will direct your course and plan any explorations you make on Anuta, or other islands as seen fit. You will also use all means possible to avoid detection by other naval operations, and avoid contact with them. Defense is allowed only if in immediate danger. These orders come from the highest sources. End. Signed, Bianchi, Arben, Admiral, COMPACFLT."

The captain put the paper down, and looked over his glasses again at Colin. The two stared at each other for a few seconds. To Colin's credit, he didn't smile.

"Where are we going, Professor?"

"Anuta."

The Captain turned, stone faced, and pulled down a microphone.

"Nav, Control."

"Nav aye sir."

"New course. Anuta Island."

"Stand by, sir." The sound of typing on a keyboard came over the speaker. "Got it, sir. Eleven, thirty-six point six south, one sixty-nine, fifty-one east. That's five hundred twenty miles west southwest. Bearing two two five point five."

"Plot it, Nav. Conn, prepare to dive. Course two-two-five-point-five."

"Two-two-five-point-five, aye sir."

The Captain ignored us again, so we returned to our cots, straddling the torpedoes at the front of the sub. I sat down and looked at Colin. A definite smirk crossed his face now.

"What's that for?"

"What?"

"That look you've got. Catch a canary lately?"

"No, nothing like that."

"Then what is it?"

He looked around and then walked over to me. He leaned in, speaking quietly.

"That line in the message to the Captain. Remember? It said 'These orders come from the highest sources'."

"Yeah, so?"

"It's a kind of code phrase. One of the messages I sent this afternoon, I think did the job."

"Colin, who did you write to?"

He grabbed a toothbrush from his duffle, and walked toward the head. He stopped in the doorway, a big grin on his face.

"You're not the only one who can play politics, you know."

"You knew all along this would happen!"

He shrugged, and then disappeared down the corridor, a big grin still on his face.

PART 4
SOLOMON ISLANDS

1

There wasn't room for another person in the mess. Every SEAL was jammed in there, along with Colin and our team, plus most of the command crew of the *Ohio*.

No more photos had been taken of Anuta, because all the satellites that could do it no longer existed. Most of the communications birds had been taken out too, including all the geostationary satellites within view of our location. The best we could do while submerged was the very low frequency radio. But that had a data rate so slow it was useless for anything except the simplest messages. About all we got was a daily note that said, 'continue'.

We were on our own.

We'd left Nanumea two days earlier, and slipped as quietly as possible toward Anuta. Now we were about to go ashore, looking for…what? I had no idea, and that scared the hell out of me. The photos weren't detailed enough to show us anything other than the presence of altered Pouakai signatures. Beyond that, we were groping in the dark.

We started our day at Anuta with a four a.m. briefing, local time. Colin and Lieutenant Hanson stood at a whiteboard they'd propped up on one wall. Someone had pasted an enlargement of the photograph of Anuta there, a beautiful blue and green oval, creating a vibrant splash of color against the drab steel and worn linoleum of the mess. Colin tapped a pointer on the wall, and the talking quieted.

"Here's what we know," Colin said.

"Speak up," someone in the crowd shouted.

"Sorry. Here's what we know. This is the only image we received of Anuta before the satellites started getting shot at. These spots here," Colin circled the highlighted clusters with his pointer, "are very similar in signature to those we got of the Pouakai, before most of them disappeared."

"How many spots are there?"

"We don't know for sure, the resolution wasn't good enough. They're all in a cluster, here in what we think is a clearing, on the northern part of the island, below the top of this hill."

Lieutenant Hanson stepped up to the board, and pointed.

"The island itself is pretty small. Oval shaped, about half a mile north to south, and a third of a mile east and west. Unlike Palmyra or Nanumea, it has some elevation to it. The center hill goes up a couple of hundred feet. The targets in the photo are on the north slope of that hill. The image was taken three days ago, so on an island that small they could be anywhere by now. Or they could have flown off, and we'll find nothing. For planning purposes however, we will proceed based on the likelihood of Pouakai being there."

"The Lieutenant and I have talked a lot about this over the last two days," Colin said. "If these are Pouakai, we may be safe, if we follow the Nanumea protocol of travelling slowly and in small groups, and keeping quiet. If they've changed behavior though, like the ones that attacked Nanumea recently, they could be very dangerous. That's why we have all of you with us. Those of us on the science team will split into groups of one or two, with at least one SEAL in each group. We will proceed as slowly and carefully as possible."

Hanson pointed at the map. "Squad A will accompany the scientists, split into three groups. We plan on converging on the target location from different directions. Squads B and C will be independent, with C concentrating on the village at the south end of the island, and B approaching the center of the island from the side opposite of squad A."

Captain Baker strode into the mess.

"Captain on deck." People stood up, making a path for him to the front of the room. Without acknowledging Colin or Lieutenant Hanson, he turned to address the crowd.

"We are tracking a Russian sub, fifty-five miles to the northeast." A quiet murmur ran through the room, which the Captain quashed with a glare. "There is also a French sub in the same vicinity. We don't know if they're both tracking us, or if they're tracking each other and happen to be in the neighborhood. We also thought we heard a trace of a Chinese sub on the way down here, but the signal didn't reappear. That being said, it is possible we're being tracked. It would be a first if they could find us, but we can't take anything for granted. It's also possible that with the amount of communications traffic we've generated, someone has leaked our intentions. Those subs may not see us yet, but they're expecting us to be here."

For the first time since entering the room, he turned to Colin and Lieutenant Hanson. "Our plan to drop you on Anuta is unchanged. However, after you are ashore, we will be going deep and listening for approaching targets. If anyone is nearby, you will have to wait until they are gone before you are extracted. You will maintain radio silence, except for assigned contact times."

The Captain pivoted and left the mess, and the mood in the room relaxed perceptibly.

"That is all we have," Colin said, looking at the clock on the wall. "We'll surface in ninety minutes. Good luck."

Most people stayed where they were, talking quietly with their neighbors. Colin sat down at our table.

Alan studied the original photos of Anuta, while Steve rested his head on top of his folded arms, snoring quietly. Mina sat still, hands in her lap, and Colin looked at me with a slight shrug as if to say, here we go again. I felt tired, scared, and had an odd, empty feeling in my heart. Nothing seemed to make me happy any more.

Last night, lying on my cot with my head just inches from a torpedo warhead, I tried to sort through what had happened so far. Almost everything that had happened over the course of this year had been out of my control. What I needed was to make some sort of contribution to this mission, instead of letting events simply happen to me. That's why I'd volunteered for this trip as soon as Colin and Anna had suggested it, even if I didn't know it at the time. So far though, I felt more like an observer than a participant in this mission.

If I wanted to make a difference, what should I do? I guess I'd already made that decision. I was heading into the unknown with an uncertain plan and no clear objectives. I had to go forward with the mission, whatever direction that took. Though lately, it felt like someone had hit the accelerator, and we didn't have any brakes.

"You still with us Boonie?" Colin asked. He'd been talking for a few moments, but I'd been lost in thought.

"Sorry. Still here. You were saying?'

"Did you want to carry my gun?"

"You don't want it?"

"The Lieutenant showed me how it works, but I still think I'd be more of a danger to all you than to the Pouakai."

"Take it with you Colin. You never know if you'll need it."

He hefted the dark .45 automatic and belt holster that he was supposed to wear on Anuta. The SEALs had provided each of our group with a sidearm and ammunition. I was the only one of our group who knew how to shoot a gun, however. I worried about Mina who would probably be knocked back a dozen feet by the recoil, if she even had the strength to hold it steady long enough to take aim .

"What are we looking for when we get there?" I asked.

"Whatever we can find. That photo showed Pouakai-like signatures on the island, and another group, likely in flight, south of the island, over the ocean. That's how it works. We find clues, and go to look. We do this one step at a time, stay flexible, and adapt to changes. If we don't look, nobody else will."

I stared at the large photo still on the wall, our approach marked with red arrows. "This is sounding more like a military mission every day. How is it that it's being run by a scientist?"

Colin smiled. "We do what we have to do. The Pouakai have changed since we left Honolulu. We have to change too, or we won't be able to finish the job we came here for."

An hour and ten minutes to go. We woke up Steve, and then I went through the steps on safely using the .45 again.

2

At least the Captain didn't have to worry about spy satellites tagging our location. We piled into the inflatables, and motored toward the island. I realized how small it was as we approached, in the deep violet and orange light of dawn. It only took us a few minutes to completely circle the island. After the other squads were in position, we approached the beach on the east side. No Pouakai flew overhead.

Unlike Nanumea or Palmyra, there wasn't a man-made cut through the reef. The surf ran low though, and we bounced over the waves breaking on the coral reef. The kid driving the inflatable had obviously had practice. He timed it so we caught the lip of a rising wave, and surfed over on the breakers. The eastside beach of Anuta lay ahead, palm trees hanging listlessly in the morning calm. The island looked different from Nanumea or Palmyra, with a substantial hill rising at the center.

"Keep an eye out," Lieutenant Hanson said above the roar of the surf. "If you see anything, don't shout, but get our attention and point it out."

We all nodded solemnly, and instinctively looked upward. Still no sign of Pouakai.

The boat grated to a stop on the coarse sand beach, and we all piled out. These guys definitely had their act together; we all landed within thirty seconds of each other, and in another fifteen seconds we'd bailed out of the inflatables. The boats left, on their way back to the sub, to keep them safe from a possible Pouakai attack.

Colin and I stuck with the Lieutenant, while Alan went left with one SEAL, and Steve and Mina took off to the right with two others. We'd been fitted with earpiece radios, so we could keep in contact with the other groups. The SEALs didn't want us talking except in an emergency though, so all we heard was an occasional word from the squad leaders.

Cool morning air flowed gently from the hill above, and the raucous calls of birds echoed from the jungle.

The plan had us converging on the center of the island from east and west, checking for signs of Pouakai. It was an easy strategy to remember, so what occupied my mind was fear. If we were approaching some sort of nest, or birthing ground, who knows what we'd find. As far as we knew, the only Pouakai signs visible in the Pacific when the photos were taken were on this island. On the other hand, there are always large areas of the ocean covered in cloud that can't be imaged. The satellite could have missed a lot. It seemed like we were taking a big risk, but Colin, Lieutenant Hanson and I all thought it was our best chance of finding evidence to help solve the mystery of the Pouakai. Because, if so many had died in the last week, yet there were Pouakai still on Anuta, there had to be something special about this place.

Lieutenant Hanson waved the muzzle of his rifle toward a path that led up the hill. The other two groups from our boat separated, walking a few hundred feet in opposite directions, looking for other ways off the beach. We walked carefully up the path, the jungle close on both sides.

"Team C here," came a voice over the radio. "We've got boats down at the village." The Lieutenant stopped, and dropped to one knee.

"Identification?" he asked.

"Unknown. I've never seen anything like them. They look primitive, but huge, and crudely made. There's no way one person could lift them, or even half a dozen people."

"How big?"

"Maybe fifty feet long, fifteen wide. Made from split portions of logs lashed together, and bent into shape. There's a resin, or something like it, filling the gaps."

The Lieutenant looked at Colin. "Sound like anything the locals would have built?"

"No."

Hanson spoke into the microphone again. "Anything inside the boats to identify whose they are?"

"No, sir."

"Any other activity around there?"

"Negative. It's quiet here. No villagers. No bodies. Nothing moving."

Hanson paused a moment, and looked around the canopy of the jungle. Small birds flitted back and forth, squawking noisily. "Continue your survey of the village. Team B, status?"

"Enroute, as planned."

"Continue."

The trail proved difficult to hike up, muddy and overgrown, and tough to get past in places. Either this trail wasn't being used much, or there wasn't anyone around to use it. We passed through a small clearing, with a few good-sized boulders, mostly covered in vines. As we were about to re-enter the jungle, I looked back at the clearing, and got a jolt.

"Lieutenant," I said, as loud as I dared.

I pointed to the rear of one of the boulders. A human skeleton lay there, the flesh gone. The Lieutenant walked down to the boulder, and carefully poked at the skeleton with his survival knife. He looked skyward for a moment, before rejoining us. We continued up the trail until we were well into the jungle again.

"It's likely been there for at least a couple of years," the Lieutenant said. "Probably killed by Pouakai."

"Polynesians will bury their dead, if possible," Colin said. "That tells me there isn't anyone left living on the island."

"Then whose boats are down by the village?" I asked.

The three of us just looked at each other for a moment, and then continued up the trail. It ran only three hundred yards from the beach to the center of the island, but the overgrown trail made it difficult going. Once we'd climbed further up the slope, the land leveled, and the trees thinned out, leaving mostly tall grass and shrubs on either side of us. This was the grassy area where the signatures showed up on the photo. The grass grew so tall in places however, that we couldn't see more than a few feet ahead of us.

The Lieutenant stopped. "Squad B, location," he whispered.

"Grass field, west side," came the reply.

"Squad A two, A three, location."

"A two, jungle, below the peak."

Hanson pointed off to our left. That was Alan, and his SEAL escort.

"A three, grass field, northeast slope."

He pointed to our right, where Steve, Mina, and their SEALs were. We were still converging on the same spot.

The Lieutenant stood up again, and moved forward carefully. He pushed aside tall clumps of grass with the muzzle of his rifle, peered ahead, before waving us forward to the next clump. I kept my ears open for the high-pitched whistle of the Pouakai, but the only sounds were the surf behind us, the birds around us, and the wind overhead.

Then a different sound rumbled through the background of island noise. A deep grunting sounded at irregular intervals from up ahead. We stopped, and the hairs on the back of my neck stood up. Hanson looked at Colin, who shook his head.

"Sound ahead. Animal-like," came the voice from Squad B.

"Copy," Hanson replied. "Hold your position, we'll take a look." He motioned to Colin and me, and we moved forward, one slow step at a time.

I reached for my .45, pulled it out, and slid the safety off. I tapped Colin on his arm, and showed him the weapon. He shook his head.

The grunting grew louder as we reached the crest of the hill. The ground was mostly level ahead. To our left rose the gentle slope to the island's peak, and to our right, the grass rolled down toward the rocks at the north end of Anuta. The tops of the grass in front of us waved in the breeze, well over our heads. We couldn't see more than a couple of feet forward.

The Lieutenant looked at Colin, and then at me. He cocked his head toward the sound, with a puzzled look on his face. I pictured a large boar, or maybe some other big animal that had been running loose on the island for three years. What kind of animals did the islanders keep?

My arms tingled, and I felt jumpy. My heart pounded hard, my breathing ragged. I didn't want to make a mistake with the .45, so I slid the safety back on, until I thought about what might lie ahead, and slid it off again.

The Lieutenant pointed the muzzle of his rifle into the tall grass, and gently moved it to one side. A clearing appeared ahead, filled with horrors.

A group of black monsters stood in a tight cluster in the clearing, huge and humanoid, with the shiny black skin of the Pouakai. They had long legs—longer than looked right—bent at the knees as they stood. Shiny, domed heads with no neck topped a humpbacked torso, with arms lower down the torso than a human's. An appendage grew on their backs too, like an odd set of wings that looked too small to fly with.

A loud grunt echoed through the grass, as the entire group whipped their heads around in an instant. Huge iridescent blue eyes glared at us from the front of their domed heads. For an agonizing moment, nothing in the world moved.

The monsters screamed, the whistle of a Pouakai amplified a thousand times. I jumped back in shock. Time seemed to slow down as one of the creatures leapt toward us. Its long legs extending like a frog's, it covered the twenty feet in a flash. The wings on its back spread out, helping control its flight through the air.

The Lieutenant brought his rifle up, and fired two rounds before the creature crashed down on top of him. More inhuman shrieks echoed through the grass, and the creatures leapt in all directions. Then an explosion of rifle fire came from all directions.

"What the fuck is that?" Someone shouted into their mic.

"RUN!" I screamed at Colin, who stood still as a statue. I hit him in the shoulder and turned to run, but he stood rooted to the spot.

I grabbed his arm and pulled him away from the clearing. "MOVE IT!" I yelled. He followed, still sluggish and disoriented. We got about twenty feet away when he looked at me.

"What the hell—" he started to say. Another monster ran through the grass toward us, screaming. I turned as it crouched to leap, and raised my .45. My fingers were leaden, slow to move, and the creature jumped too fast. Then the gun kicked hard, and I pulled the trigger again and again. The thing had jumped, but at an angle. I'd hit it in the leg. It crashed into the grass next to us, twitching like mad.

I looked toward the clearing. The first creature that had jumped toward us moved. Then I realized it was the Lieutenant, trying to push the bulk of the creature off of his legs.

"Colin, go!" I pointed at the Lieutenant, and covered the two of them, aiming my pistol toward the clearing. Colin understood, and ran toward the downed SEAL. He pushed on the body and rolled it off of the Lieutenant's legs.

"Come on!" I shouted.

"Legs broken," Hanson growled. "Go."

"We can't leave you."

"Go! I can't walk. Get help."

I took a deep breath. He was right. We had no way to move him out of the area.

I screamed "Colin, move!" as another creature looked at us from the clearing, not fifteen feet away. I pulled the trigger again, without even thinking about how I aimed. The bullets hit the ground in front of the thing, spraying dirt in all directions. The creature leapt fast, going the other way.

"I've got my rifle," Hanson said. "Get the hell out of here. Regroup at the beach."

The creature at Hanson's feet moved, and both Colin and I instinctively jumped back. Hanson pointed his rifle at the monster's belly and fired twice. Pale yellow fluid sprayed everywhere, and then it lay still again. Colin ran up to the creature.

"What the hell are you doing?" Hanson snapped, grimacing in pain.

"I've got to see what it is."

"Later. If these things kill you, you won't be any use to us. Go! Get the fuck away from these things, now."

I looked around. There weren't any of the creatures in the clearing. One carcass lay at the Lieutenant's feet, the other a few yards away. The second body twitched. Without a moment's thought, I walked up to it and put two more slugs into its chest. It lay still.

"Squad A under attack," the Lieutenant said into his radio. "Large creatures, seven to nine feet tall. Humanoid. Black in color. They can jump a dozen yards in one leap. Shoot on sight."

"Colin, move," I said, breathing heavily.

Reluctantly, he stood up, and we ran down the hill toward the beach.

"Squad B has taken casualties," came a voice in my ear. "Retreating to the beach."

I pushed the microphone button on my belt. "The Lieutenant is hurt too. He's at the clearing, east side. Broken legs."

"Copy. We'll send the medic."

"Cancel that order," I heard Hanson say. "I'm okay for now. Regroup and assess."

"Roger."

Slipping and stumbling, we ran down the path to the beach. We went a lot faster downhill, and a few minutes later spilled onto the beach where we'd begun the climb. Moments after we rolled onto the beach, the other two teams from our squad appeared, and ran toward us. Alan and his SEAL came in on one side, Steve and Mina with their escorts on the other. I breathed a sigh of relief, and silently said thanks that they were all still in one piece.

"Oh my god, oh my god," Mina panted, as she dashed up to us. She ran right into me, nearly knocking me down.

"We heard the shooting," Alan said, puffing hard. "What was it?"

"I have no idea," I replied. "You didn't see the things?"

He shook his head.

"We saw it," Steve said, out of breath. "We saw one go by, running. So fast. So awful…"

"The Lieutenant," one of the SEALs asked. "Where is he, and how's he doing?"

"He's up the hill, where we found those things. One jumped on him, and broke his leg before he killed it. He told us to go, said he'd use his rifle if necessary."

Several people were talking at once on the radio, so I pulled out my earpiece to avoid the chatter and concentrate on the people in front of me.

"Colin," Alan asked, "could you see what it was?"

"Not it. They. There were a lot of them."

"Pouakai?"

"No, but I think they're related. Same skin, same blood."

"What?"

"I got a quick look at the one the Lieutenant shot. Same fluid in the body, and it looked like the same general type of internal organ design."

One of the SEALs spoke up. "I don't care what they are. They tried to kill us, and they got some of Squad B."

The other SEALs had taken positions around our group, aiming their rifles across the wide beach, toward the tree line.

"Are we safe here?" Mina asked, crying. "Are they going to get us?"

"I don't know," the SEAL said. "We're trying to figure out where everyone is, and then we'll regroup."

The SEAL that had been talking on the radio walked up to us. "You," he said, pointing at me. "How many of those things were there?"

"At least a dozen, probably more. I didn't get a good look before they jumped."

He paused, listening to the radio. I put my earpiece back in.

"…three lost. On the west beach now."

"Copy," said the SEAL next to me. "Team C, report."

"Secure. No activity in the village."

"Good. Standby." He pulled out a copy of the photograph of the island. "The beach is continuous on both sides of the island down to the village. Team B, move south to join team C. We will do the same on this side. Keep an eye out for the creatures."

He looked at all of us. "Let's move."

We walked along the beach toward the village at the south end of the island. Every little crack or pop from the jungle made us jump. The SEALs kept their rifles ready, pointed into the trees. We walked quietly, terrified of what stalked the island, nearby but out of view. They weren't Pouakai, but there was a connection; there had to be.

My stomach churned from the fear that those things were here, somewhere nearby. My hands shook too. I tried to get them to stop, but they wouldn't obey. They had a mind of their own. Finally, I shoved them into my pockets, just to have a place to put them.

We were stuck on this tiny island until tonight, with an unknown number of those creatures on it.

It only took five minutes to get to the village, but it seemed like an eternity.

3

The south end of the island had a series of dilapidated huts strung along the beach. We could see right away that nobody had lived here for years. The two huge boats the SEALs had mentioned sat fifty feet apart on the beach, listing to one side, creating an overhang between the outer hull and the sand. Their bows pointed up the gently-sloping beach, the aft ends still touched the water. I'd never seen anything like them. The logs were roughly hewn in half, the cut face on the inside of the boat, lashed together with vines. They'd been bent with a lot of force, bringing them together at the bow and stern. Between the logs was a hard, whitish resin, which felt like epoxy. The vines holding the things together were soft and green. The boats had been recently built.

The SEALs formed a perimeter around three of the largest huts, protecting us from whatever roamed the island. Colin and the rest of our group stood with me on the beach in front of the huts.

"Ever see boats like that?" Colin asked Steve.

"Nope," Steve replied. Our resident expert on Polynesia, he'd been an anthropology major before coming over to Colin's department. "Never seen anything like that in Polynesia, Micronesia, Melanesia, or anywhere else, for that matter." He ran his fingers through his bushy red beard, as he studied the boats.

"Do you think those creatures we saw built them?" I asked.

"I'd say that is our best bet for now," Colin said.

I sat down in the sand, in the shade of an overhanging palm tree, and opened a water bottle. The rest of the team followed suit. I was still shaky, but it felt safer here, with the SEALs between us and the jungle. Mina pulled a big camera out of her backpack, and started pushing buttons on its control panel.

"Where could these things come from?" I asked Colin. "What the hell are they?"

"I don't know Boonie, I just don't know. I was expecting Pouakai, not these monsters."

"Are they related?"

"Just a guess, but I'd say yes. They have the same skin, and the brief look I got at the internals seemed to match what we saw inside the Pouakai, but the relation between the two? I have no idea."

Mina leaned over, and offered her camera to Colin. The display screen showed a perfectly framed image of one of the creatures, bounding past the camera, not a dozen feet away.

"Holy shit," Colin said. "Mina, how did you get this?"

"I took picture. I thought you would want one."

The four men in our group stared at tiny Mina. I remembered my scream of terror, trying to get Colin to move, tangible fear of the creatures present in my gut. Yet Mina had had enough cool composure that, even with these unknown monsters running past her, she grabbed her camera, framed them, and took a photo.

"There are more," she said.

Colin scrolled through the photos. Mina had put the camera into rapid shutter mode, so she caught the monster bounding toward, and then past, her group.

"Incredible," Colin said, quietly. "Look at that leg motion, that extension. They must have one hell of a set of muscles there."

"Sir," one of the SEALs said, walking up to Colin. "We have established a perimeter defense. Do you have instructions for us?"

"You are…?"

"Petty Officer Gunderson, sir"

"Any word from the Lieutenant?"

"He pinged us over the radio, meaning he is okay, but doesn't want to talk."

"So you're in charge here?"

"For now, sir, until the Lieutenant gets back."

"What do you suggest?"

The young SEAL paused. He had closely cropped blonde hair, and pale blue eyes. He looked about sixteen, but had to be at least twenty. Like all the SEALs, he was in far better shape than I ever had been, or would be.

"We should probably wait here until nightfall," Gunderson said. "Then we'll call the *Ohio*, and arrange for our pickup."

"What about the Lieutenant?"

"We'll send out a rescue team soon, once we are sure you'll be secure here. It should only take…"

A brief whistle rose, then a loud *thunk*. Gunderson's chest exploded in a spray of red. Mina screamed. A thick length of bamboo, its tip sharpened into a spear, protruded from Gunderson's chest, and he collapsed to the ground in a heap.

"Move! Move! Move! Get to cover!" the SEALs shouted from their position on the other side of the huts. More bamboo spears filled the air, several landing in the sand around us.

"Under the boats!" I shouted. The overhang from the listing boats provided a little shelter, but not much. A blast of rifle fire sounded; the SEALs on the perimeter fired into the jungle.

Thunk. Thunk. More spears filled the air, landing in the sand around us. Someone was throwing them at us from the hillside above the village, their position well hidden in the jungle.

Another whistle and *thunk*, and Steve yelled, "Son of a bitch!" A spear had bounced off his ankle. "Oh shit, oh shit," he grunted, as he rolled in closer to us.

"Under here." Colin pulled Steve further under the overhanging boat.

I helped pull Steve in closer. Right in front of me, blood poured from the wound in his leg. Mina, down by my feet, handed me a T-shirt from her backpack. I wrapped it around the wound, and held it to try and stop the bleeding. The spear had glanced off of Steve's leg, and lay in the sand next to us.

Thunk. Another spear landed in the sand, just feet away. Steve moaned, and tried to roll over.

"Don't move," Colin said sharply.

"Science team, are you still with us?" came a voice in my earpiece.

I pushed the microphone button on my belt. "We're here, under the big boats."

"Roger. Squad A, fall back, and cover the science team."

"We've got one injured," I said, "and Gunderson is gone."

"Understood. Lee, stay with squad A, and take care of the injured."

"Copy," said a new voice.

The original voice continued. "Squads B and C, line abreast, stay low. We'll move up the hill. It looked like the spears came from about thirty yards into the jungle. Squads ready?"

A quick reply came from several SEALs, before a silence fell. Four of the SEALs moved rapidly toward the boats. They crouched in with us under the overhang. One of them peeked out, ducking back as another spear went *thunk* into the sand near us.

"This isn't protected enough," he said.

"What about there?" I pointed to a big rock, a short distance away. It sat ten feet from the edge of the water, tall and wide, with a vertical side facing the ocean. We could all fit behind it. The rock would provide better protection from incoming spears, but how would we get over there without being hit?

The SEAL next to me looked where I pointed, and nodded. "Chang, you in the jungle yet?" he radioed.

"Negative."

"We're moving the science team to a safer position. I'll lay down cover fire into the jungle as we make a run for it, so stay low for now. I'll radio when we're in position."

"Roger."

He whispered something to the other SEALs, Alan and Colin. Then he turned to Mina and me.

"When I say 'go', make a run for the rock. We'll fire into the jungle, and hopefully make those creatures duck long enough for us to get over there."

"What about Steve?" I asked.

"I'll carry him."

The SEAL moved up next to Steve. "Ready?" Steve just moaned.

With a nod to the other soldiers, he stepped out just far enough to get his muscular arms under Steve. At the same time the three other SEALs moved out from under the boat, and fired their rifles into the jungle.

"Go!"

I dashed across the sand, a furious volley of rifle fire echoing across the beach. Mina ran ahead of me, dodging around Gunderson's body. In seconds we made it to the shelter of the rock. The SEAL carrying Steve moved as fast as I did, even with the load in his arms. Steve screamed as his legs bounced up and down. Colin dove behind the rock next, until finally Alan fell down in the sand with us, puffing hard. The three SEALs firing the rifles were moving sideways, still shooting, until they were behind the rock, all safe. A thick cloud of smoke rolled past us, the sharp smell of gunpowder in the air.

"We're clear," the leader radioed.

"Roger. Keep an eye out for these things, especially from the sides if they circle around us."

"Will do."

An occasional weak wave washed up within a few feet of us, but we didn't get wet. The bulk of the rock lay between us and the jungle.

The SEAL carrying Steve set him down in the damp sand; Steve had passed out. He dropped a backpack to the sand. Inside was a mass of medical gear.

"Petty Officer Brayden Lee," he said, offering me his hand.

"Mark Boone. Everyone calls me Boonie," I said, returning the handshake. "You're the medic?"

Lee nodded, and got to work on Steve's wound. Several rifle shots sounded through the nearby jungle, followed by two distant shots echoing over the island.

"The Lieutenant?" I asked. Lee nodded, and continued cleaning Steve's leg. I hoped Lieutenant Hanson was okay. The radio remained silent.

There were still twelve hours until we could contact the *Ohio* again. Twelve hours on this tiny rock, surrounded by God-knows-what. The other three SEALs positioned themselves so they could see both up and down the beach. They peeked irregularly over the rock toward the jungle, just to make sure nothing snuck up on us. I crouched with one of the SEALs, pistol in hand, scanning the beach. Every little sound made me jump. After fifteen minutes, I was so exhausted that I sat down in the sand next to Colin, my back against the rock. I closed my eyes for a moment, and took a long, deep breath.

This expedition had gone far beyond what I'd expected when I agreed to come along. It felt like a lifetime ago that we'd left Honolulu. There was no way out of it now. Whatever happened, I was along for the ride. I'd started the morning feeling scared, but oddly, the encounter with the creatures had left me maddened more than scared. Those monsters didn't belong and that set off a wave of anger in me. The mood crept up on me, and kept me from dwelling on what I had lost.

Sitting next to me in the sand, Colin stared off into the distance.

He slowly shook his head, staring at the horizon. "Why would they be here? Those creatures don't make sense."

"Yeah, I've never seen anything like them either."

"I don't mean it that way. They're obviously related to the Pouakai, but different. Too different."

He asked Mina for the camera again, and turned on the display. That amazing photo of the monster came up again, running past the camera.

"What do you see?" Colin asked.

"The monsters that attacked us."

"Look closely. Like a scientist. They're humanoid. Legs, arms, torso, head."

I studied the photo. "The legs are too long, the arms too low. There's this small fan or wing thing on their back too, and the head's all wrong. Doesn't look too human to me."

"I said humanoid, not human. Compare these things to the Pouakai. These creatures are closer to us in design than to the Pouakai."

"What's your point?"

"In any organism, evolution moves slowly, relatively speaking. It took millions of years for the shrew-like ancestor of mammals to differentiate into cats, elephants, and humans. I think the Pouakai share an evolutionary past with these creatures, but in biological terms there's no way one evolved directly from the other."

"Okay, so these things didn't evolve from the Pouakai, but they're still related," I said wearily. "Why is that a problem?"

Colin turned to me, his voice intense. "Because if these creatures didn't evolve from the Pouakai, or even the other way around, then we still haven't found the source! We're still left with the same question we started with: where did they come from? Only now we have the added complication of having to explain the origin of two different species."

I put my head back against the rock, and stared at the edge of the sharp blue horizon, dividing ocean from sky. The mid-morning sun beat down on us hard, and it was getting hot.

"Then there's other questions too," Colin continued. "Like, why haven't we seen these creatures before? Why here, and why only after the Pouakai seem to have died off? These are the questions we have to find answers to."

"Aw crap," I said with a smile. "Only you could have come up with more questions than answers."

Petty Officer Lee had finished bandaging the wound on Steve's leg and packed his first aid gear away. He sat down in the sand, his rifle held upright.

"Movement," one of the SEALs to my right said quietly. In one fluid motion, Lee stood, and came up behind the two SEALs.

"Movement here too," said the SEAL to the left. "At the tree line, about fifty yards away."

There were three SEALs with rifles on the right side, so I pulled out my .45, and knelt down next the one on the left.

"Get down," Lee said to us. "Stay as low as you can, and listen for orders."

The rest of our group hunkered against the rock, while I kept an eye open for anything moving in the distance. Colin, Alan, and Mina all had their pistols out and ready. That scared me almost as much as the possibility of seeing those creatures again.

More than anything, I wanted answers about the Pouakai and these new monsters; about what they were and where they came from. And I wanted to go wherever I could find those answers. As I looked down the beach from our tiny shelter behind the rock however, I realized that of all the places I wanted to be right now, this beach not very high on my list.

4

"Squad A has movement on the beach," Petty Officer Lee radioed.

"Have they attacked yet?"

"No, just a quick view, both directions down the beach. About fifty yards away, east and west, at the tree line."

"We're approaching the center of the island, nothing in sight yet. I'll send squad B as backup, but it will be at least five minutes. We'll get the Lieutenant, and then come back along the east beach."

"Roger."

I looked down the beach to the east. For a few minutes, nothing moved. Then something shifted behind the first row of trees; a hopping motion, and a glint of sunlight on shiny black skin.

Crack. A bamboo spear bounced off the top of the rock, and splashed into the shallow water in front of us.

"Stay low," Lee said. "Don't stick your head up over the rock, and keep an eye out along the beach."

Nothing moved toward the east, and the guys behind me, looking west, were silent. Then a blur of movement in the trees, and something whistled toward us.

"Incoming!" the SEAL next to me shouted. He pushed me back from our vantage point, and rolled out of the way. The spear jabbed into the sand right where we had been crouching.

"On my mark," Lee said, "heavy fire into the jungle." The rest of the SEALs nodded.

Before he gave the order though, that horrible scream came from the jungle, and a horde of creatures poured out from behind the trees.

"Fire!" Lee shouted.

The noise was incredible and painful. Alan, Mina and Steve crouched down, hiding behind the rock. Colin and I stood behind the SEALs, watching through the cloud of smoke. We had the advantage of being behind the rock, and the creatures didn't. Maybe they didn't understand the way rifles worked, but the SEALs mowed them down long before they made it to our rock. One spear whistled overhead, coming from behind the rock. Lee stood up and fired several dozen rounds that way, and then crouched down again. At least a dozen creatures lay in the sand between us and the jungle, a few still twitching. The rapid pace of firing slowed, until it was down to a couple of sporadic shots. Then silence.

"Squad A, status," came the voice over the radio.

"We came under attack and returned fire. We're secure. No injuries." Lee stood up, and quickly surveyed the scene. "About two dozen creatures dead," he said as he crouched again. "No movement now."

"Copy. We are one minute away, above the tree line to your east. No sign of creatures here. Wait, got one on the ground. Good shot. Stand by, and don't fire this direction."

We waited as Squad B made its way toward us. Within a minute, birds started chirping again.

"Squad B is moving out to the beach," came the voice in my earpiece. "Hold fire." Seconds later, four SEALs moved smoothly onto the beach, covering the jungle with their rifles. They jogged toward us, stepping over the fallen monsters. There really wasn't enough room behind the rock to provide protection for everyone, but when they reached us, they crouched for a minute.

"How many of those things do you think there are?" Lee asked Colin.

"I don't know," he said with a shrug. "If those boats are what brought them here, probably no more than a couple of dozen. But if they've been here a long time, there could be hundreds holed up in a cave somewhere. There's no way to tell since we don't have access to older satellite photos. That may have told us how thickly populated the island was."

I crouched down, waiting. Mina sat in a tiny ball, knees pulled up under her chin, shaking badly. I took the water bottle from her backpack and gave it to her. She took a sip but didn't look at me or say anything. It was shock, of course, from the noise and violence of the attacks. I sat next to her, and put my arm around her shoulder. I hoped a warm, quiet presence would help. She didn't move, but she did relax.

"Squad C entering the beach, east of your position," squawked the radio. "Lee, we have the Lieutenant. Meet you at the rock."

A team of SEALs appeared to the east, carrying a hastily made stretcher—two bamboo poles lashed together with vines—with Lieutenant Hanson. His backpack and rifle bounced on his stomach as the other SEALs carried him toward us. Petty Officer Lee opened his medical pack as the others set the Lieutenant down on the sand. Hanson's left pant leg was stained dark red with blood, his face pale and sweaty. Lee cut away the bloody pants, and started to work on the Lieutenant's leg. Hanson laid his pack in the sand next to him.

"Squad A, stay here with the science team," the Lieutenant said, his voice rough. "Squads B and C, sweep the island. I didn't see very many of those things after the first attack. There can't be that many more left on the island, and I want them gone. Sweep the island clean."

The other squads took off into the jungle, leaving us with our original protectors.

Drained, I sat on the sand between Mina and Colin. Lee had said that Steve would be out for a while because of the drugs he'd given him. Alan stared into the distance, probably also in shock.

The merciless sun scorched us, but we needed the protection of that rock more than the shade of a tree. Every few minutes we'd get an update from the SEALs. So far, nothing. Fifteen minutes after the others had left, Colin stood up.

"I need to look at one of those things," he said to the Lieutenant.

"Not a chance. You're gonna stay here."

"Lieutenant, this is why we're here, to learn about these things. Remember?"

The Lieutenant sighed, grimacing as the medic pulled another stitch tight.

"Fine. Moss, Jackson, provide cover. These guys are going out to check on one of the creatures. But," he said to Colin, "if these guys say get back to this rock, do it. No questions, no delay. Got it?"

"Got it."

Two of the SEALs moved out from behind the rock and up the beach. Colin motioned for me to follow, and I nodded, glad to have something to do. We stayed behind the SEALs, watching for any creatures. Nothing moved in the jungle. Colin knelt next to the nearest creature, dead on the sand, and pulled the case of surgical tools from his backpack.

"They're not melting," I said, kneeling next to Colin.

"No. Not like the Pouakai."

This creature had a large wound in the center of its head, and Colin poked around in the hole for a moment. The skin was gone, but the skull remained intact. One iridescent blue eye stared at me, the other blown away by the bullet that had smashed into the creature.

"I'll need to find one that isn't hit in the head after this."

"Whatever you say, doc," one of the SEALs said.

Colin took a scalpel, and slit the creature's torso open, starting at the neck. A flood of pale yellow, watery liquid poured out for a moment, and then slowed. Two more quick incisions across its chest, and Colin opened up the torso like a pair of saloon doors. There weren't any ribs, just a mass of the same white fibers I'd seen in the Pouakai.

"Colin, should I get Alan?"

"No, he's in shock. He wouldn't be much help right now." He didn't even look up. "Go grab Mina's camera."

I ran back with the camera, and took pictures where Colin directed.

"It's got bones," he said, pointing, as I snapped a photo. "Or, at least I think they are. More like a mix of bones, and the fiber stuff the Pouakai have. "

They didn't look like any bones I'd seen before. Metallic gray in color, a pair of rods ran parallel to each other up the center of its body. The guts looked like the Pouakai's, all whitish fibers and yellow fluid. A few larger white bags and bulges sat low in the opening. Colin sliced into the thing's legs next, and found more fibers surrounding a single thick bone. Its arms looked about the same, on a smaller scale. After ten minutes of probing, Colin wanted to move on. He found another without a head wound, and carefully sliced away the skin on its huge domed head.

It was too odd to be repulsive. I wanted to see more. I wanted to watch Colin peel the skin from these things, see them broken. Even though part of me wanted to see what they were made of, part of me wanted to hurt them. Badly.

Was that really why I'd come all this way?

"Boonie, here, please?"

Colin had been calling me, but I hadn't heard him. I snapped several shots of the partially exposed skull, and eye. It wasn't an eyeball like ours, but a thin, flat area on the creature's face, harder than the surrounding skin. It almost looked like a sensor, or even a reflector, glued to its skin. Colin carefully cut around an eye, and peered underneath.

"Hmmm. Interesting," he mumbled.

"Yes?"

"I don't see any connections under this eye. There are no nerves going into the skull."

I looked where Colin had pulled up the skin, and took a picture of it.

"Maybe the nerves are in the skin, and go into the skull somewhere else," I said. "Or maybe it uses Bluetooth. Blue-eye."

"Could be," he said blandly, not getting the joke.

He sat back and looked at the skull for a moment.

"Where is the mouth?" I asked.

"Doesn't have one."

"How does it eat?" I asked, and then stopped. "Oh, solar power, like the Pouakai?"

Colin nodded. "Probably."

"I wonder how it makes the grunting noise, or that scream."

He reached into the tool kit, and took out a shiny steel saw. The wickedly sharp teeth glinted in the sunlight.

"Let's see what's inside the noggin here…"

He placed the saw on an exposed area of the skull, and gently pushed forward. Nothing happened to the skull, so he placed it on the same spot and repeated the motion, pushing harder. Still nothing.

"Come on…" he grunted, and bore down hard as he pushed the saw. With a staccato ping, the saw zipped across the skull, sending little bits of metal flying in all directions. The teeth had ripped right off the bone saw. Not a mark showed on the skull.

"Well," I said. "That's nice."

"We'll need to find out what these bones are made from." Colin stood up. "Not a lot of time here to be subtle, so..."

He pulled the .45 from his holster, and aimed at the creature's head.

"Colin, I don't think you should…"

Blam. The bullet ricocheted off the skull, and into the jungle. I'd never seen two people move faster than our SEALs did, diving to the ground and covering us with their rifles.

"Sir-drop-your-weapon!" The blood drained from Colin's face, and he dropped his gun, knees shaking, sinking to the sand.

"Colin, it's okay," I said. "You didn't know that would happen." I stepped over and picked up his gun. "It's okay guys, I've put the safety on."

"Sorry," Colin whispered, still shaking. "I didn't know it would do that."

"I understand sir," one SEAL said, standing up and aiming his rifle skyward. "Next time, let us know if you're going to do that. Maybe have us do the shooting too. We're the experts here, you know." A grin crossed his face, the first I'd seen all day.

"Yeah, right," Colin said weakly. "Your turn next."

I helped Colin stand, and felt a smile cross my face too.

We looked at the creature. "Son of a bitch," Colin said softly, as he reached down to touch the bone. There wasn't a mark on it.

"There's one headed your way," the radio blared, just as a loud crashing sound came from the jungle down the beach. Several rifle shots echoed across the island, and one of the creatures bounded over the last row of trees and out onto the beach, a hundred yards away. Both SEALs dropped to one knee and took aim. Another group of SEALs appeared out of the jungle, behind the creature, so our guys held their fire.

"Take cover!" someone shouted, and I heard the rest of our group running toward the rock.

The monster moved a little like a frog, but more fluidly. It didn't have a spear in its hand, but that wouldn't stop it from hurting whoever it ran into. Who knew what other protection might have; poisonous fangs? Laser vision?

Another group of SEALs poured out of the jungle, just ahead of the first group. They pounded down the beach, their rifles aimed our direction.

"Don't fire," Petty Officer Lee said into the radio. "We're in your line of fire. We'll send up a warning shot, try to stop it." Our SEALs aimed their rifles skyward. The creature jumped closer, covering twenty to thirty feet with each soaring leap.

I gripped my pistol, heart pounding. The creature was fifty feet away, bounding right toward us.

"Fire." The SEALs fired skyward. A huge crack echoed across the beach, and the creature skidded to a stop, frozen in place at the edge of the water. The SEALs behind it caught up and stopped, fifty feet behind the monster. Some of the soldiers moved closer to the jungle, cutting off its access inland. Surrounded, its back to the water, it didn't move an inch.

"What's it going to do?" I whispered to Colin.

"I don't have a fucking clue."

Petty Officer Lee looked over his shoulder at the Lieutenant, still in the sand, leaning against the rock. "Sir?"

"Hold your position," Hanson said, over the sound of the surf. "Wait and see what it does."

It wasn't doing anything. Stock still, it stared into the jungle. The SEALs were puffing hard after the chase down the beach, but this creature didn't appear to breathe.

The standoff held, motionless for nearly a minute, a dozen rifles aimed at the creature. How much longer would it remain there?

Without realizing what I was doing, I stood up, and walked toward the ebon monster with my .45 in hand, pointed down toward the sand.

"Boonie, what the hell…" Colin yelled.

"Sir, get back!" A couple of SEALs shouted at the same time.

The sand felt soft beneath my feet, the sun an intense heat on my head, and the ocean a roar in the distance. All I could see though was this monster. It finally moved, rolling its big domed head toward me, as if on ball bearings.

"Boonie," Colin hissed again. I ignored him.

From thirty feet away, it tracked my every move with its head. Its skin had the same glossy black sheen as the Pouakai. Was there any sign of intelligence? I slowed, and then stopped, less than twenty feet from the monster. It towered over me, even from that distance.

I took a deep breath. "Why are you here?"

It stared at me with those blue ovals on its head. Would it understand me? Could it even hear me?

Louder now, I repeated, "I said, why are you here?"

There was no movement from it, or the SEALs. I sensed all those rifles pointed so close to me, though. Then the thing's hands moved slowly. Too many long fingers, like a spider's legs. The fingers rolled up and down, as if it were practicing on an imaginary piano.

"Do you understand me? Those soldiers will kill you if you move against me. Is there any way you can communicate with us?"

Its fingers drummed faster, and for a split second it crouched down slightly. I started to raise my pistol, but it leapt too fast. Instantly, the SEALs fired. The concussion hit me from all sides, and the creature plowed into the sand, just a yard from my feet. Pale yellow fluid poured out of multiple holes in its body.

The SEALs dashed up the beach toward me. A couple pulled me away as the rest covered the monster. Lightheaded, I sank to the sand, and started to shake

Colin ran up the beach, and crouched in the sand next to me.

"Boonie," he said quietly, "are you okay? What the hell were you thinking?"

"I had to know," I replied, voice quavering. "There has to be something in there that could give us answers."

"Answers? What was it supposed to do, Boonie? Sit down for a philosophical discussion? It's an animal."

"It made those spears, it could make tools."

"Chimps make tools. If there was real intelligence there, we would have seen something more."

He was right. There hadn't been any sign of intelligence behind those blue ovals. It had been an animal trapped on the beach, and it reacted like any animal backed into a corner would; it lashed out at the nearest object. Me.

"Sorry," I whispered. "I was angry. I thought if I could just find out what made it tick…"

Alan and Mina walked up to us, and stood next to Colin, looking at the dead monster.

"You hurt?" Mina asked.

"No, just…weak."

Colin reached out a hand, and helped me stand.

"What the hell was I thinking?"

"The same thing all of us were," Colin said, "but you weren't just going to wait to find out."

"It may not have been in the most logical way," Alan said, "but you did try communicating."

"Yeah, well, that's why you guys are the brains, and I'm the brawn."

"Did you get anything out of this?" Colin asked.

I shook my head. "No, you're right. It's an animal. We'd backed it into a corner, and it lashed out. It couldn't answer my questions."

There were no answers on that beach. Colin brought out his surgical kit again, but didn't find anything different in this monster than in the others.

We retreated to the protection of the rock while two squads of SEALs swept the island again and again. Eight hours later the sun was setting, and no more creatures had been found alive. There weren't any caves or other hiding places, and by the end of the day we were pretty confident that we'd killed all the creatures on the island. The original nest we'd encountered was just an area of flattened grass. There were no clothes, food, or any other signs that these were anything but animals. The SEALs found the remains of a few people scattered across the island, but they'd been dead for years.

They also found the stand of bamboo where the creatures had made their weapons. The spears were hacked off and sharpened with a few shards of volcanic rock. No other tools were found. There wasn't anything to show they were much further up the evolutionary ladder than chimps. The big questions left were what were they, how had they made the boats, and where had they come from, if not Anuta? Those questions were added to the long list we were already had from the Pouakai, but of course, there were no more answers to be found here.

Colin saved several samples of the creature's tissue, including one eye, in some specimen containers. Hopefully they would reveal something about these creatures that we couldn't find from the Pouakai. The creature's bones didn't yield to any of our tools, so he got a sample by the crude but expedient method of hacking off one of the creature's fingers at a joint, and putting it whole into another jar.

When the inflatables arrived to take us away from this nightmare island, it took longer to get going than when we arrived. Two SEALs carried Steve with his bandaged leg. The Lieutenant, in an inflatable cast, hobbled through the waves and heaved himself into one of the boats. The rest of us piled in, too weary to complain about the cold water.

The SEALs brought their four dead comrades with us, wrapped in plastic body bags. I guess having body bags in your supplies is just part of being a SEAL. Four people dead and all we had to show for the effort was another set of complications to try and sort through.

Anuta faded away in the darkness, like a nightmare slowly disappearing into the mists of sleep.

5

Captain Baker sat at his desk, and calmly listened to our description of the day's events. He'd already debriefed Lieutenant Hanson and the other SEALs.

"What do we do now?" he asked.

"We continue the search," Colin said. "We are almost certain these creatures didn't originate on Anuta, but came here in those boats. We have to go search for where these creatures came from."

Baker rubbed his eyes under his half-glasses. "We don't have any other photos or data showing where, or if, these additional creatures exist, let alone where they came from."

"There's this," Colin said, and pulled out the original satellite photo of Anuta. "This group of signatures southwest of the island. It must have been one of those boats, carrying the creatures to Anuta."

"That doesn't show us where they came from."

"It gives us a direction where they came from. Here, look at this." Colin unfolded a chart on the Captain's desk.

"Who the hell authorized you to have this?" Baker stood up, waving a finger at the chart.

"It doesn't matter…"

"Yes it does, professor. These are classified documents, with sensitive military information on them. We don't just hand them out when asked. Who gave them to you?"

Colin crossed his arms, and didn't reply.

"Okay," the Captain said, sitting back down. "I'll find out one way or another. There are no secrets on this boat. What's so important on the chart?"

Colin shook his head, and then turned the chart toward Baker, and laid the photo of Anuta on top of it. "On this photo, we have signatures of the creatures here on the island, and also here, about ten miles southwest. We think this was the second group of creatures heading toward Anuta in their boat. Alan and I did some quick calculations using the creature's tissue samples before we came in here. The bone density is quite high. If they got in the water, they'd sink."

Baker looked at Colin with his head tilted to one side, as if urging him to continue.

"This tells us the creatures probably aren't aquatic," Colin said, "or even semi-aquatic like the Pouakai. They had to come from land somewhere. Now, those boats they came in were huge, and crude. I doubt they were able to move through the water very fast, even if the creatures had unlimited endurance. With their lack of technology, I don't think they used anything more than paddles to move the boat through the water. They came from somewhere nearby.

"Maybe my people back in Honolulu and D.C. have found something since we lost communication with them, but as far as I know, there weren't any other signs in the area of these creatures. Given the short time they had to move around and not be seen, I think they came to Anuta from somewhere in this general part of the Pacific."

"Actually," the Captain said, "I think I can help you a little here. We have been getting VLF transmissions for you. Just a few words a day, mind you, but the one that came in while you were on the island said, 'nothing new'. I'm assuming that means something to you?"

Colin nodded. "Yes. It means my associates haven't found any other signs of these creatures on older photos. They thought they were looking for Pouakai, but the result is the same. There's nothing showing in the photos from earlier this week, before the satellites were shot down."

"So what are we going to do?"

Colin pointed at the photo. "We backtrack from the location of the creatures in the boat. If they were heading directly for Anuta, we work backwards and find where they came from."

"They may have changed course along the way," the Captain said. "Maybe they just happened to see the island and turned toward it."

"I don't think so," Alan said, speaking up for the first time. "From a boat like that, you can only see the island from a short distance away. Since two boatloads of these monsters arrived at the same spot at different times, they were probably heading there all along."

The Captain studied the photo for a moment. "Okay. Where did they come from?"

Colin pointed at the chart. "Backtracking on the course from the creature's boat to the island, you end up here." He pointed at a speck on the chart, southwest of Anuta. "Tikopia."

We all craned our necks, looking at the chart.

"That's about seventy miles west-southwest," the Captain said quietly. "There's no way these creatures could see Anuta from there. If they did come from Tikopia, how did they know it was there?"

Nobody else spoke, so I did. "Captain, that is what we're out here to discover."

He studied the chart again, unfolding it further. "If they didn't come from Tikopia, the next land is here, the northern islands of Vanuatu."

"They could have come from there," Colin replied, "but those are more than a couple of hundred miles away. I think we need to be thorough, and check out Tikopia first."

The Captain's chair squeaked as he leaned back. He took off his glasses, and rubbed his eyes again. With a tired wave of his hand, he said, "I will consider it. You're dismissed."

We all stood, too weary to complain.

"Except you," he said, pointing at me. I sat down as Colin and Alan squeezed into the tight corridor.

"I heard about your little adventure on the beach," Baker said. "What the hell were you thinking, walking up to one of those creatures? You put everyone in danger with that stunt, including your own team members."

"I'm sorry, Captain. I honestly don't know why I did it, other than I wanted answers."

"Get any?"

"No, sir."

"You won't be doing anything like that again, will you?"

"Not a chance."

He looked directly at me for several seconds.

"Good." Then a tiny, sad smile crossed his face. "Major, I understand your position, and motivation. I lost my wife two years ago when Jakarta was attacked by Pouakai."

"I didn't know that, sir…"

"She worked as a naval attaché at our embassy. Her evacuation was scheduled that day, but she didn't make it to the airport."

"I'm sorry, sir. I had no idea."

"It was a risk we both knew about. She died serving her country, so there's no dishonor in what happened. I think it's the way she wanted to go." He paused, and looked at a photo on the wall. In it, Baker stood next to an attractive, older blonde in a Navy uniform. "We're both military men, Major. We know what it means to follow orders. My orders say to do as the Professor directs. I also have orders to keep this sub safe, and protect the United States. While you were on Anuta, a Russian sub came by, probably looking for us."

"Did he detect the *Ohio*?"

"Not that we could tell. We'd gone deep, as I told you before you left. The French sub we'd detected earlier was tailing the Russian and came through an hour behind. They both left heading southeast.

If the French sub been any later coming through, we wouldn't have been able to come and get you tonight. You would have all spent the night on Anuta."

"That wouldn't have been…desirable," I said, with a small laugh.

He smiled. "No, probably not."

"So are we going to Tikopia?"

"That's what the professor wants, so we go there. We're not completely alone out here though, and everyone is on a hair trigger. We have to be careful. If there's any sign of other subs we'll go quiet, and wait it out."

"How long until we get there?"

"We could be there in a few hours, but first, I wanted to ask you if you think those things really came from Tikopia."

"It's as good a choice as any other. After what we found on Anuta, I don't think they've been here long. Those boats are fairly new looking, recently built. I think they came here from somewhere else, but where that somewhere is, I'm not sure. We have to find them though. If those things are allowed to spread across the Pacific, let alone the world, it could be even more of a disaster than with the Pouakai."

"Why?"

"Because they can live and travel on land. They're tough, aggressive, and apparently fearless. Maybe we could stop them, or maybe not, but it would be bloody. Given how weak so many countries are around the world, the creatures may have the tactical advantage, even if we are technologically superior."

"I wouldn't say they are all that primitive, Major. If they did come from the stars, or were engineered by someone, we could be in for a nasty shock when we reach wherever they come from."

I didn't know what to say, because he had crystallized my fears about the origins of the Pouakai and these new creatures.

"We'll leave at first light," he said. "That way we can keep an eye on the route between Tikopia and Anuta, in case there are any more of those things paddling their way here. Do you think you can convince the Professor it's a good idea to wait until morning?"

"I'll do my best."

"Good. I understand what your team is doing, Major. After hearing the reports from you and Lieutenant Hanson, I believe we are on the right track. I need you to understand that I have other obligations too. This can't be strictly by your rules because I have to protect this sub, my crew, and look out for the defense of our country too. I will do whatever I can to help find the answers you're looking for, but the safety of the *Ohio* comes first."

"I'd say the same thing if this was one of my airplanes."

On my way to the torpedo room and my waiting cot, I couldn't help but feel a shiver of fear. The Captain was right. Wherever these creatures came from, what we were seeking out could easily be beyond humanity's ability to handle.

6

The rest of our group accepted the overnight delay. We were all too exhausted to complain. I think I was nearly asleep before my head touched the pillow. I dreamt of monsters.

Over coffee the next morning, we talked about our nightmarish day on Anuta. Steve hobbled in on crutches, with a big cast and bandage around his leg, and sat down with us. Whatever we were doing at our next landfall, it wouldn't include him.

Alan brought up the question of what to call the new monsters.

"I don't know," Colin said. "The Pouakai name originated with the Nanumeans, and came from Polynesian mythology."

"Whatever they are called," Mina said softly, "they were horrible, frightening."

"Then maybe that is what we should call them," Steve said.

"What?"

"There's a word in the language of Kiribati that roughly means frightful, or terrifying. It varies a little from island to island, but in general, the root word is Kakamaku."

"Kakamaku?" I said. "That's not something that just rolls off the tongue."

"It works," Colin said. "I think I'll use it."

"Can you do that? Just name a creature whatever you want?"

"If you are the first to discover a new species, and publish a paper about it, yes you can. There are more rules involved in giving it an official species name, but I like Kakamaku for public use. Besides, who's going to complain about it? The Kakamaku?"

A quiet chuckle drifted up from everyone at the table.

"Then Kakamaku it is."

Most of our team wandered away after breakfast. I felt the sub start forward, and was happy to be moving away from Anuta. I didn't know what we'd find on Tikopia, but I hoped that after Anuta the change would be welcome. Staring into my empty coffee mug, I heard Colin clear his throat. We were the only ones sitting at the table.

"Want to talk about it?" he asked.

"About what?"

"What happened yesterday, on the beach."

I shrugged my shoulders. A lot of things churned around in my mind, and I wasn't sure I could sort it all out right away. I made a noncommittal sound.

"Boonie, I brought you along because you've always been a rock, and I could count on you when things got rough. What you did on the beach though, scared me."

"Sorry. I don't know why I did that. It's been a tough few weeks."

"I understand," he said, a small smile on his face. "I just want to make sure you're still up to the job here. I don't want to push you into something that would be a problem for you, or for us."

"The last thing I want is to be a problem for all of you."

"You're not a problem. I just want to make sure you're thinking clearly, that's all."

I stared into the depths of the empty mug, trying to pull it all together. Why had I walked out to face the monster—the Kakamaku?

"Colin, have you ever lost something big, something important to you?"

"Not really. Maybe a few little things, but not like you have."

I hesitated, not sure if I wanted to follow this train of thought. If not Colin though, there was nobody else I would talk to.

"I'm not really sure how I should feel, and that's what's bothering me. I've lost Jennifer, my job, and the rest of my world is slipping away too. It's like I'm flailing around in a vacuum, and I don't know where the nearest handhold is. I'm looking for a reason, but there's nothing to hold onto."

"We're all flailing about these days, Boonie. The Pouakai have changed everything. You've just been hit harder than anyone else here."

I took a deep breath. "So what should I do about it?"

"Rely on your friends and family. We're all here. Just try to remember that you're not in this alone."

I forced a smile. "Thanks." He stood up and gave me a pat on the shoulder as he walked away. I didn't feel any better though. Intellectually, I knew he was right. But deep down inside though, that caged animal that's part of all of us thrashed to get out.

If it did, I sincerely hoped nobody else would get hurt.

7

"Take a look," Captain Baker said. I stepped up to the periscope, and peered in. Colin looked through the set of eyepieces on the opposite side of the scope. Over the wavetops stood the outline of Tikopia, another tiny speck of land even more rugged than Anuta, with a high ridge circling a lake in the middle of the island. I couldn't see the lake through the periscope, but it showed on the charts I'd seen of the island. The late afternoon sun blazed down and the island's trees stood out in brilliant green against the deep blue ocean. It had been a quiet trip away from Anuta. We hadn't seen anything on or under the water along the way. Now parked a few miles from the shore of Tikopia, we had to figure out what to do next.

"No signals, sir," came a voice from the forward end of the control room. "No signs of EM emissions at all."

"Thank you, Chief," the Captain said.

I looked at the island for a few moments, before turning to the Captain. "How long do we wait before going ashore?"

"If we don't find any electronic signals from the island, and we don't see any of your Kakamaku, then tomorrow morning should work. I don't want to send you and the SEALs ashore this late in the day."

Colin turned the periscope, looking around the area of the sub. He caught his breath.

"Captain, look at this."

Baker brushed me aside and looked into the periscope.

"Target, bearing three three five. Sonar, any contact?"

"No, sir."

"It looks like one of those big boats you guys found on Anuta," the Captain said quietly.

"Yes, it does," Colin replied.

The Captain flicked a switch, and the image from the periscope appeared on the overhead monitors. In the distance, a big boat slowly moved northeast. The image zoomed in and the grainy picture bobbed on the screen as the sub rolled. It was clearly another boat like the ones from Anuta.

"Got the target," said the sonar operator. "It's faint, no power. Sounds like manual oars. Course agrees, approximately zero-five-six degrees. Sir, they are heading directly away from Tikopia, and toward Anuta."

The Captain peered around the periscope at Colin. "It looks like you were right, professor. What do you want to do now?"

"Could we follow them?"

"Sure, but that would just take us back to Anuta."

"Then we'd be right where we were before," Colin sighed, "with Kakamaku living on Anuta."

"Could you sink the boat, Captain?" I asked.

"Certainly. Using one of our torpedoes is a bit of overkill on a boat that size. Even if one of those things survived the explosion, they'd sink. You said they are too dense to float in the water, right?"

Colin nodded, but remained silent.

"Professor, we should make a decision before we waste the opportunity."

"I know. I'm just not in favor of shooting first."

"If you have any other options, I'd be glad to hear them."

Colin stared through the periscope. I glanced up at the monitor again. The Kakamaku themselves weren't visible from that distance, and only a hint of motion showed they were rowing themselves toward Anuta.

"We have to go ashore on Tikopia," Colin said quietly, "to find out what's going on there."

"I agree," Baker replied.

"Captain, my concern is that if this is the home of the Kakamaku, or the Pouakai, don't you think they would respond with aggression if we destroyed that boat?"

"What are they going to do, Professor? We've never seen evidence of intelligence in those animals, and not a trace of electronics or advanced technology either. Are you expecting them to try and board the *Ohio* like a bunch of pirates?"

Colin shook his head, and looked into the periscope again. "I don't know, Captain. There's just too much we don't understand about them yet."

Another minute of silence passed, as the Captain silently fumed, his face set in a deep scowl. Finally, he said, "Professor, are we going to sink that boat, or not?"

Colin looked at me with indecision on his face. I nodded and he turned back to Baker. "Yes, Captain. I guess we should."

"Weapons control, get a firing solution on the target."

"Already done, sir."

"Good. Weapons officer, load and arm one fish. Proximity fuse."

"Yes sir."

I looked at Colin, who still peered through the periscope, shaking his head.

"Colin," I whispered. "Are you okay?"

"Sure, Boonie. This is just moving too fast for me. I wish we had more time to observe them, to study them."

"I don't think we have the luxury of time."

"I know that but I don't like it."

Red lights came on throughout the control room, and a quiet, persistent chime sounded in the sub.

"The fish is ready in the tube," the weapons officer said. "Firing solution loaded."

"Fire."

The torpedo launch didn't make any noise in the control room, but several lights on the weapons board turned green. Both Colin and the Captain looked into the periscope, while I watched the monitor.

"Time to impact thirty seconds," the weapons officer said. "Twenty, ten, five."

I concentrated on the monitor. Nothing had changed since we'd spotted the boat. They were still rowing, as before, when a huge spout of water obliterated the boat. The scale of the explosion was enormous. Water flew skyward in a massive white mountain, at least a hundred feet high. An instant later a loud hammer sounded through the hull of the *Ohio.*

The mountain of water dropped back to the surface of the ocean, leaving a circle of white bubbles on the surface.

Both Colin and the Captain stood up.

"Good work Lieutenant," the Captain said to the weapons officer. "A nice clean hit. Helm, turn left…"

Slam.

A huge explosion rocked the sub, and I got knocked to the deck as metal clanged above us. Colin and the Captain held on to the periscope.

"Collision alert! Collision alert!" the loudspeakers echoed.

Cold water sprayed down on me from the ceiling. I tasted the ocean.

"Damage team, to the control room," came another voice.

"Report!" the Captain shouted.

"Sir, I got an off-scale electromagnetic pulse as we were hit," the signal detection officer said. "It pegged everything. Now my instruments are dead."

"Communications are out sir," said the comm officer. "Same time as the impact. Nothing is working."

Four men in oxygen packs charged into the control room and up the ladder toward the sail, where the water spilled in. I hauled myself out of the way, as the men scrambled up the ladder. Colin followed me off of the periscope platform, and we stood at the back of the room. It was controlled chaos for a couple of minutes until the damage team sealed off the water from above. Maybe all those drills had helped after all. My heart still pounded, terrified at the thought of being aboard a sinking sub.

"You okay?" I asked Colin.

He nodded. "I was afraid of that."

The Captain turned toward us. "Afraid of what?"

"Provoking a response from these creatures," Colin said.

"They're just animals. What could they have done to us? Something hit us; we just don't know what it was yet."

"Captain, did you see any ships nearby in the periscope? I didn't. You heard the signals officer. There was a huge electromagnetic blast, aimed right at us. Something on that island saw us blow their boat to smithereens, and tried to do the same to us."

"Professor, we haven't seen any signs of technology we can trace to these creatures, or from that island, either. The only thing sticking out of the water was the periscope mast and a couple of antennas. That's a mighty small target to see and hit in such a short time."

"Maybe they'd been watching us all along, but didn't want to attract attention to themselves."

That shut the Captain up. The damage team left the control room a few minutes later, and then a dive crew exited through the SEALs' escape trunk to do an exterior survey while we were still submerged. They came back with photos that even made the Captain raise an eyebrow. The tops of the periscope and antennas looked like they had been melted off. Fortunately we'd been deep enough that whatever hit us couldn't penetrate through the water to the hull of the sub. Otherwise, we'd be dead.

The Captain called a meeting right after he saw those photos. Our team was there as well.

"Anyone care to guess what caused this?" he said, holding up the photo.

"It had to be that EM beam that we detected," Alan Gee said.

"How could it have done that much damage?" one of the powerplant engineers said. "That would require far more energy than we've been able to deliver yet."

"Do you have another explanation?"

"The Russians and the Chinese have been following our development of directed energy weapons. Maybe they've made progress that we haven't matched yet."

"Where did it come from then?" Alan asked. "Were there any other subs in the area? Any aircraft?"

"Not that we heard," replied the sonar officer.

"Gentlemen," the Captain said, "the periscope mast was burned off right at the water level. That means, because of the curvature of the Earth, whatever hit us was either very close or somewhere above us. As far as we know, all satellites that could see us have been destroyed, and we hadn't detected any aircraft in the area at the time of the blast. That leaves us with the most probable location being Tikopia."

We were all silent for a few seconds.

"What should we do?" I asked.

The Captain looked around the room. Nobody else spoke. "Here's our situation," he said. "We've lost meaningful communications with our command headquarters, especially since we are not going to surface. I'm not going to place the *Ohio* in the way of whatever melted the periscope and antennas. We believe that the professor's monsters are coming from Tikopia, and spreading outward. They've gone to Anuta, and maybe other islands too. Right now, they're limited to this corner of the Pacific. If they spread further, because of their ability to move on land, they could pose a grave threat to all of mankind. We have a duty to eliminate those things, and prevent them from multiplying and spreading."

"How do we do that?" Colin asked. "We don't even know what the source is."

"We have several options at our disposal, Professor. Including the nuclear tipped Tomahawks in their launch tubes right back there," Baker said, pointing aft.

"How do we know where to aim? How do we know that it would even be effective? Maybe they thrive on nuclear energy. Maybe they're buried a mile deep under the island, and all we'd be doing is giving them a little tickle."

"I think the Professor is right," Lieutenant Hanson said from the back of the room, leaning on his crutches. "It's good to have the nuclear option available, but we need to do some recon. Without satellites in place, we need boots on the ground."

All eyes turned to the Captain, who stared at the photo of his melted periscope. Eventually, he looked up at the crowd.

"Lieutenant," he said, "would you be able to get your team onto the island?"

"Using the ASDS sir, yes, we could."

"Do it. I'll want a full recon of the island, but no conflict with the Kakamaku unless absolutely necessary for your own safety. Understand?"

"Yes, sir."

"Remember, we haven't seen any signs of technology until now, but that EM beam that hit us shows that there may be something you can't handle by yourselves. Unless there is no other option, you are to observe only. Do not confront them directly. Dismissed."

"Captain," I said, as the people in the room started to get up. "Is our team going too?"

"I'd say that's not very damn likely. The SEALs are using a mini-sub to transfer to the island, but the sub stays underwater, close to shore, while the team swims up to the beach."

"Colin and I both have advanced level certifications. We've been diving for years." I looked at the Captain, who glanced at Lieutenant Hanson.

"We have to go," Colin said. "You need us there if you find anything related to the Pouakai or the Kakamaku."

"This isn't just a recreational dive in calm conditions," the Lieutenant said. "You'll need to keep up with us, and swim a couple of hundred yards over a reef to the shore. We don't have recreational scuba gear either. We use rebreathers."

"Lieutenant," I said. "After all we've been through on this trip, do you really expect us to sit this one out?"

Hanson cracked a smile. "No, but if I didn't say that, the Captain would have my ass in a sling. Right, sir?"

"Damn straight," Baker replied.

"Come on," Hanson said. "Let's get you guys checked out on the rebreathers."

8

This trip off the *Ohio* felt different. Yes, I'd been scared going to Anuta, and the landings on Palmyra and Nanumea had also been filled with unknowns, but this felt like we'd be swimming directly into hell. It was odd, feeling scared, but I couldn't picture myself doing anything else.

We said goodbye to Lieutenant Hanson before climbing into the tiny mini-sub. His broken leg meant putting on a dive suit was out of the question. The same held for Steve and his shattered ankle, although he looked relieved he wasn't going. Neither Alan nor Mina had learned to scuba dive, so they were left behind as well. Just four SEALs, along with Colin and I, detached from the *Ohio* early the next morning, enroute to the unknown.

The tiny mini-sub was only six feet in diameter. We were all in our dive gear, minus the rebreather packs, so it was hard to get comfortable. Petty Officer Lee took over Lieutenant Hanson's duties as leader. He laid out a map of Tikopia where we could all see it. The roughly oval island had a lake in the center, looking like a doughnut hole. High ridges circled three sides of the lake, but on the south side only a narrow strip of trees and beach separated it from the ocean. It looked like a natural amphitheater. The island was bigger than Anuta too—two miles east to west, one mile north and south. If there were a lot of Pouakai or Kakamaku, it would be easy for them to defend. We were going to land on the east shore, and climb the ridge to get a view of the interior.

"We're going as one team today," he said. "We don't split apart. Consider this hostile territory, and stay low. You two," pointing at me and Colin, "stay behind us, and keep up. Keep quiet too, unless there's an immediate danger. Got it?"

We both nodded.

The battery powered sub crawled slowly toward Tikopia. It took nearly an hour to get to our exit point. We were silent for most of the ride, until a few minutes before we had to exit, when we had to start putting on the rebreathers.

"I wonder what the rest of the world is saying about us, and the missing Pouakai." Colin spoke quietly.

I stared at him. "Seriously? That's what you're thinking about? How can you possibly think about the rest of the world, when all this is going on here?" My viewpoint had shrunk to the point where the *Ohio*, her crew, and the mission were my world. There wasn't anything else.

"Of course I'm thinking about it. You have to see the big picture. If not, you'll lose sight of what you're trying to accomplish."

I shook my head. "I can't do that. If I did, I'd lose focus on the task here."

Petty Officer Lee leaned in toward us. "Maybe it's best that the two of you are here together."

Colin and I both cracked a smile. I leaned my head against the cold, curved hull of the sub. "I've said it before, but Anna's going to kill me if anything happens to you."

"No need to worry. I'll be fine. We're just going in to take a look. Right?"

"That's the plan," Lee said.

"See, Boonie, just a quick peek, then back to the *Ohio.* No problem."

"If there is a problem, they're too primitive to have the weapons to match these," Lee said, patting the stack of heavy automatic rifles we were bringing along.

I couldn't help thinking about whatever had melted the periscope, the antennas, and maybe had blasted hundreds of satellites out of the sky, which brought me back to the same question that had been haunting me for days: If the Pouakai and Kakamaku were so primitive, who, or what, had caused those other incidents?

"Time to gear up," Lee said.

It didn't take long to put on the rebreathers, and slip on the masks and fins. Lee closed the hatch between our dive chamber and the sub's cockpit. Once we had all signaled ready, he turned a valve and water flooded the chamber.

"We are two hundred yards from shore," came the tinny voice of the sub's pilot, through the earpiece built into the drysuit hood. "Sub depth seventy-five feet. The bottom is twenty feet below the hatch. Swim course two-seven-zero to the beach. Pressure is equalized. You are clear to open the hatch."

Lee opened the hatch on the floor, and after one of the SEALs had dropped through, he motioned for Colin and me to swim out. Disoriented at first, I rolled in the water, before I saw the sandy bottom below and the sub hovering overhead. I had to consciously remember to slow my breathing. It was a bizarre feeling to dive using a rebreather, with no bubbles wafting up to the surface. Colin floated next to me in the blue water as the rest of the SEALs slipped out the hatch. The compass on my wrist said that 270 degrees, due west, was the same direction the nose of the sub pointed. Petty Officer Lee waved a hand at Colin and me. *Follow us.*

The extraordinarily clear water looked like a travel brochure. The bottom was a gentle sand slope, curving upwards toward the beach. Waves rolled overhead, white clouds in a ceiling of blue, racing ahead of us toward the shore. I couldn't help but worry about what would be waiting for us. What little comfort I felt came from having the SEALs with us.

When the water reached ten feet deep, Lee motioned for most of us to stay put on the bottom. He and one other SEAL went up to look around. The waves caused the water to surge as we waited, shifting us back and forth across the sandy bottom. Fortunately there wasn't much of a reef, only a line of rocks twenty-feet deep that we had easily swum over.

From the surface, Lee motioned for us to move forward, and in a few strokes, the water was shallow enough for us to stand. Just as I had seen on the evening the SEALs rescued us from Nanumea, we emerged from the ocean as a series of black shapes, dripping seawater, clutching our weapons. As Petty Officer Lee had briefed us, I snapped the quick release latches on my fins, grabbed them, and dashed up the beach behind the SEALs, running into the jungle.

Lee found a depression in the sand behind the first row of trees, filled with a couple of feet of water. We placed our fins, masks, and tanks there. Then we unzipped and stepped out of the drysuits, and hiked into the jungle, looking for…what? I had no idea. Colin and I were dressed in fatigue pants and T-shirts the SEALs had supplied. My heart beat fast, not only from fear, but the speed that the SEALs hiked up the ridge. They moved quietly and quickly, pausing occasionally for Colin and me to catch up, puffing, before they moved on again. We didn't speak, afraid that any noise that might alert the Kakamaku we were here.

We had a half-mile climb through dense forest and underbrush to get to the top of the ridge, a vertical rise of nearly six hundred feet. Tough going for my aging legs, especially after several weeks of shipboard inactivity.

Except for our heavy breathing and the occasional snap of a branch, we made it to the ridge fairly quietly. Strong tradewinds blew through the treetops, covering the sound of our passage. As we neared the top, Lee had us put our gear down and take a break. Above us was a ridge of volcanic rocks, exposed to the elements. From there we should get a good view of the island, including the large crater with the lake in the center. Using hand signals, Lee had us take out our binoculars, and then spread out along the ridge. Colin and I went with Lee, while the other three went twenty feet further up the ridge to the right. We scrambled up the last ascent of the rocky ridge, while Lee motioned for us to keep our heads down. With a wave of his hand, he told the other group to proceed, before nodding at us. We stuck our heads over the ridge to see what lay below.

9

The center of Tikopia looked just like the photos—green and peaceful. A couple of white birds fluttered over the lake, and the trees on the hillsides waved in the wind. It all looked normal, until I focused my binoculars on what I thought was a small grass hut on the shore of the lake. It was blackened, with the ashes of an old fire on the ground around it. There were more buildings too, all scorched to ruins. Each of the buildings lay in ruins, but the vegetation around them was beginning to grow over the wreckage. I tapped Petty Officer Lee on the shoulder and pointed to the buildings. He looked, and nodded. His binoculars had a video recording system, and he scanned the entire shoreline, stopping at each of the destroyed huts and buildings.

Lee waved us back to the area below the ridge. "Did you see the destroyed huts?" he asked the other group of SEALs.

"Yes, sir."

"Any ideas how it happened?"

"It looks like each of them was hit by some sort of fire," Colin said. "The burn marks all appeared about the same size, and all roughly circular."

"Where did the fire come from?" one of the other SEALs asked.

Lee shrugged. "Let's work our way down the ridge toward the south shore. Keep your eyes open, and stay quiet."

We walked single file, following just below the ridgeline as it sloped slowly downward, on the side away from the lake. Nobody said so, but it just felt safer being on the outside of the island. If there were Kakamaku here, the big crater with the lake inside seemed to be a likely place for them. Walking sideways across the slope made it hard hiking. We kept the top of the ridge just to our right, and the hillside sloped steeply away to our left, down to the ocean. It was difficult enough to walk across the steep slope, but pushing through all the trees and shrubs made it worse.

We stopped every few minutes, and two of the SEALs peered over the rocky ridge, recording the view for later analysis. There were more charred huts around the lake. Nothing moved, and no Kakamaku were visible.

"Look at this," Lee whispered at one stop, showing us the video from his binocular recorder. "A pile of logs along the beach where the lake meets the ocean."

"Some of them are split," Colin added, pointing. "Like the ones used on those boats we found."

"I'm not sure I want to be out on that beach," I said. "If the Kakamaku find us there, it would be a long fight to get back to our dive gear."

"One step at a time," Lee said. "We won't do anything to give our position away."

We made slow progress. There wasn't a trail along the ridge, so we had to pick our way through difficult terrain. The ridge followed the curve of the island as it descended from our starting point on the eastern side of the island, down to the south shore. Halfway around, we stopped for a water break, and to plan our route.

"There's a plateau about a quarter mile farther," Lee whispered, as we gathered around the chart. "It's on the inside of the ridge, and should give us a pretty good look at the whole interior and lake."

We continued our hike down the ridge. When we stopped again, we were fifty yards from the plateau we hoped to use as a vantage point. The chart showed a grassy plain on the plateau, but if we kept low, we could probably stay hidden from most of the island. At the edge we'd get a great view of the entire crater and lake, and hopefully find some signs of what was going on here. Lee and one other SEAL peeked over the ridge to scope out the plateau. He came back shaking his head.

"There are a lot of trees on that plateau," Lee whispered, "and it's not flat. There's a big hump in the middle."

"It's supposed to be flat and grassy," another SEAL said, looking the chart.

Lee cocked his head toward the ridge. We worked our way up, and peeked around the rocks on top. The plateau sat just below us, on the other side of the ridge. Lee waved us all back down and fished around in his backpack. He pulled out a pencil-sized video camera and set it up on top of the ridge, pointed at the plateau, and then plugged it into a monitor.

"Those trees look odd," Colin whispered, looking at the screen. "They're not a normal color. And that plateau's hump is too even."

He was right. All the trees were exactly the same size and color. The ground rose twenty feet straight up, and then curved into a low dome, perfectly round, at least a couple of hundred feet in diameter. The trees were spaced evenly on top of the hill, as if someone had been trying to grow a garden. The rest of the plateau away from the hill was covered in grass.

"Zoom in on one of those trees," Colin said. Lee obliged. The leaves were too regular, the branches too slender. "They look fake."

"What the hell is that?" I asked, pointing at the bottom of the screen. Lee panned down. A bird lay on the ground, dead. Several other birds were scattered across the grass, all the same distance away from the dome, twenty feet from its edge.

"Zoom out." When the view widened, we saw more dead birds, along with two dead pigs, all of them scattered along an arc, twenty feet from the dome.

A bird flew overhead, squawking at us, before circling over the ridge toward the dome. It fluttered away from us, until a bright spark flashed in the air, and the bird fell dead to the ground, right where the others had landed.

"Son of a bitch," Lee whispered. "What the hell happened?"

"There has to be an electronic shield stopping any animals from approaching that dome. And those trees don't look real either. There is something very wrong here," Colin said.

"We need to be real careful here," Lee said. "Let's back off and assess the situation."

He inched up the ridge to retrieve the camera. I was looking at the monitor when I heard a soft hum. At the same time, a shaft moved upward from the center of the low hill. Shiny and metallic with a big black ball on the top, it moved smoothly upward. The ball stopped just above the tops of the trees.

"Lee!" I whispered loudly. He turned toward me.

CRACK.

The rocks at the top of the ridge exploded. The shock knocked us down the hillside, where I lay flat after I bounced to a stop. A big semi-circle was cut out of the ridge where Lee had been standing, and the edges of the rocks were smoking. Lee wasn't anywhere to be seen.

"Cover!" One of the SEALs yelled.

CRACK.

Another explosion took out a chunk of the ridge next to the first one. I covered my eyes from the dust and gravel flying around.

CRACK.

Each hit sounded like a lightning bolt striking a few feet away.

Colin hugged the ground next to me, his eyes shut. I didn't want to move, in case one of those shots came in low enough to get us.

"What the hell is that?" I said out loud.

"It's the beam that hit the periscope," Colin replied, his eyes still closed.

"I saw something on the monitor, something came out of that hill."

Colin nodded. "Me too. That has to be the beam projector."

"What the hell is that hill then?"

"I think that's what we've been looking for."

CRACK.

Another near miss by the beam. *Son of a bitch, that was close.* We had to do something, fast. The three remaining SEALs were on the ground, along the protected side of the ridge to our right. Colin and I inched our way toward them.

"How do we get out of here?" I said to the nearest SEAL.

"Back the way we came. It's the only way out of here."

He was right. A hundred foot cliff fell away just below us, and that weapon sat on the other side of the ridge. We'd have to backtrack to where we'd originally climbed the ridge before we could head downhill to our dive gear.

We crawled back up the hill, staying behind the ridge. We'd only gone about a hundred feet when we heard the hum again, and then silence.

"What's that?" one of the SEALs asked.

"Sounds like that beam weapon again," Colin said. "Maybe it's retracting."

"We need to see what's going on."

"I'm not going to stick my head up there. Are you?"

"No, but hang on a moment." He pulled another pencil-sized video camera from his backpack, and wedged it into a vee in a long branch he picked up from the ground. Then he raised the branch up in the air, and over the ridge. The rest of us watched the monitor. The shaft had retracted, but now the side of the dome was opening up.

"Those trees are camouflage," a SEAL said. "What the hell is that thing?"

"Some sort of weapon, or base, or maybe a home to the Pouakai and Kakamaku," Colin said. "I don't know yet."

One section of the dome rose slowly upward while the vertical sidewall underneath it moved down. A bright blue-white light poured out from inside. The sidewall thumped to the ground, forming a ramp.

"Oh shit, this can't be good," the SEAL said.

With a horrific scream I remembered from Anuta, Kakamaku ran out of the opening. They were carrying long spears, and this time the spears looked like they were metal instead of bamboo.

"Get to cover!" one of the SEALs yelled.

The SEAL holding the camera dropped the branch, and unslung his rifle.

Colin and I dove behind a big boulder while the SEALs found their own hiding spots. The first Kakamaku leapt over the ridge where the beam had shot at us, and turned our way. It heaved its spear, which flew in a wicked arc toward one of the SEALs. He saw it coming and rolled out of the way as it clanged onto the rocks where he had been. Another SEAL opened fire and the Kakamaku fell to the ground. I didn't have a rifle like the SEALs, but both Colin and I had our .45's out and ready.

More of the ebony monsters jumped the ridge and headed toward us. I counted nine before the next spear flew. It overshot us, but not by much. The solid metal shaft crashed onto the bare boulders behind us.

The closest Kakamaku was fifty feet away when the SEALs opened fire. Colin shot at the horde too, but out of fear of using all my ammo, I held back. The SEALs fired with deadly accuracy; in seconds, the Kakamaku were all on the ground, their pale yellow blood draining down the hillside, unthrown spears lying next to them.

Silence filled the jungle again, and the smoke quickly blew away. I knelt behind the rock and took a deep breath. My mind screamed with both terror and confusion. The attack didn't make sense. They had a beam weapon that could vaporize rocks and people in a flash. Yet when they came out after us, they used spears and didn't seem to know what men armed with rifles could do to them. Why didn't they send Pouakai out against us? The big birds would have had the advantage of being able to fly, and would move a lot faster than us as we scrambled through the jungle.

If that dome was the origin of these creatures, how had it gotten to Tikopia? If any animal that got too near the dome was killed; why were the Kakamaku not being killed? Why hadn't the beam weapon started firing again? The SEALs backed out of their hiding spots, rifles aimed at the pile of dead Kakamaku.

"Let's go," one of them said.

I started to scramble after them, but then stopped, my mind in a whirl.

Colin had said it: 'That's what we've been looking for'. There were way too many unanswered questions, and I had to know what it all meant.

"Boonie, come on."

"Hang on, just a minute."

"Sir," one of the SEALs said, "what are you doing?"

I took a deep breath. I wasn't sure what I was doing either. "We're so damn close. We can't just leave without knowing what it is."

"Boonie," Colin said, "what are you talking about?"

"That dome. The place the Kakamaku came from. We can't go back to the sub now. We're too close to the answer."

"What are you going to do? Go up and ring the doorbell?"

"I don't know, but we can't just go without trying something…"

"Sir, we really have to get moving," the SEAL said. "There could be more of those monsters coming out any second."

"Then where are they?" I said. "Why haven't they come out already? Why hasn't that beam weapon started shooting at us again? None of this makes sense."

"Sir…"

"Look, when we get back, what are you going to tell the Captain to do?"

"Do? I don't know. We'll tell him what happened, and let him make the decision."

"I know, but if it were up to you, what would you do?"

The SEAL looked at me for a moment, glancing back to the pile of Kakamaku every few seconds. "I'd back off a hundred miles, and drop a pile of nukes on the island."

"Exactly. Then what would we know about this thing? Nothing more than we do now. We don't even know if it could knock down those missiles before they got here, or survive the attack. Then what would we do?"

Colin stepped up next to me. "Boonie, come on. You can't go any further. It would be suicide. There's no way into that thing."

I opened my mouth to say something angry, but then his words hit me. The Kakamaku had come out, so there had to be a way back in. There had to be. In that moment, I thought of a way I might do it.

"Colin, I can't stop now. They've destroyed my life. I have to find out why. I can get in there. I know I can."

"Jesus, Boonie, what the hell have these things done to you?"

"It's not them; it's me. I'm still me, but I have to do this. If I can find out what these things are, we'll be a lot further along than if we ran away and nuked the island. Right?"

"Sure, we would. But how will you let us know if you've found anything? What happens if Captain Baker decides to launch a nuke this way while you're still here?"

"One step at a time, remember? Stay flexible, and adapt to changes, you said. I'll figure it out as I need to."

Colin glared at me, shaking his head. I'd seen that look before.

"Sir," the SEAL said to Colin, "we can't let him stay. He has to come back with us."

Colin looked me in the eye. "No, he'll stay. You won't force him to come. Those are my orders. Remember," he said, turning to the SEAL, "I have final authority as to what happens on this mission." He flashed a grim smile at me. "Right, Boonie?"

I nodded. "I need one of those survival kits," I said to the SEAL, "and a radio."

He shrugged, and handed me his backpack. "It's your funeral."

"Not yet."

The smile dropped off of Colin's face. "Boonie, be careful. I don't know what you're thinking, but remember, you still have family and friends out here, and back home too. We want you to be safe. We want you alive."

He reached out to shake my hand, and I took it. One of the SEALs pulled him by the shoulder, and they took off along the ridgeline, going back the way we'd come. In a few seconds, they disappeared into the brush.

Everything before this moment now seemed hazy; Jennifer gone, my career gone, my old life gone. I'd followed the scent of the Pouakai across the Pacific with an intensity I hadn't recognized at first. Colin and the others might have called it an obsession, but not me. It was simply a question that had to be answered: Why?

I shouldered the survival kit, and jogged toward the pile of dead Kakamaku, making sure to keep my head below the ridgeline.

10

The dead Kakamaku were spread out along the outer side of the ridge, out of sight from the dome. Wary of any movement, I edged up to them, counting heads as I approached. I got ten.

If the Kakamaku had run through whatever killed an animal that got too close, then to get inside the dome, I had to become a Kakamaku. The idea had formed just moments after the SEALs fired on the horde of approaching monsters. Making that idea a reality however, would be the challenge.

I remembered how easily Colin had sliced open the Kakamaku on the beach on Anuta. It reminded me of skinning and dressing elk with my uncle on vacations at his place in Montana.

It was definitely a long shot. As I crouched there, I remembered Jennifer's voice, from that day on the beach, telling me that I always did what I wanted, without listening to others. What would she have said now, watching me inch along a line of dead aliens while my friends headed back to safety?

I crawled along the rocks, past gouges cut by the beam weapon, to the last Kakamaku that had jumped over the ridge. I thought the two on the end had looked smaller than the rest, and I was right. These weren't more than seven feet tall, a good two to three feet shorter than the rest. That would help with my plan.

I set the backpack on the ground and opened it, listening for the hum of the beam weapon mast, or for the sound of the big doors moving. Some of that bright blue-white light reflected off the trees on the other side of the ridge, telling me the dome was still open, waiting for the Kakamaku to come back. I set the .45 on the ground next to me. Not that it would stop another dozen Kakamaku, but it gave me a little comfort being there.

From the SEAL's backpack, I pulled out a large survival knife. The nearest, and smallest, Kakamaku had several bullet holes in its chest, which worked well for my plan. With a lot of effort, I rolled the thing onto its back, and placed the tip of the knife where a human's Adam's apple would have been. From there, I sliced down the center of the chest, all the way to its sexless crotch. Then more cuts down the front of its legs, and along the arms. In a few minutes I had most of the thing's skin laid out on the ground. I pulled out its guts and muscles, a mass of white fibers. The skeleton stayed in place, but the skin wasn't attached to it.

The head proved to be more difficult. As I worked my fingers under the skin, the acrid smell of the monster's blood gave me a twinge in my gut. It wasn't all that strong or vile, but different enough to cause my stomach to flip-flop. Eventually I pried the skin away from the bulletproof skull.

The rubbery skin was close to an inch thick. Soaked through with the Kakamaku's blood, the combat pants and T-shirt I wore dripped the pale yellow fluid. The skeleton was even heavier than I'd expected.

I shoved with my feet, and the bones slid off the skin. Carefully, I picked up the Kakamaku hide, draped it over my back, and stood up. It was damn heavy. The arms and legs flopped uselessly around me. I wouldn't be a convincing Kakamaku that way. I untied my boots and removed the laces, using them to wrap the arm skin around my wrists. I cut two straps from the backpack, and tied the leg skins around my ankles. Its legs were longer than mine, and I had to cut off a foot of the skin below my boots. With everything in place, I slipped the backpack between the hide and my back, mimicking the humpbacked torso of the monsters, and stood up.

I was a grotesque copy of a Kakamaku, but this was the best I could do.

As I stood, I heard the growl of a Kakamaku from the other side of the ridge. In a panic, I flopped on the ground again, covering my gun. The skin over my head flopped down, preventing me from seeing out. I propped it up with one finger, and watched the ridgeline. With all this weight on me, playing dead was my only option.

A Kakamaku jumped over the ridge with that weird gait, then another joined it. Both were smaller than the others, no bigger than the one I'd sliced up—maybe seven feet tall as they stood, legs bent, ready to leap. Their domed heads swiveled, taking in the scene of their murdered comrades. My heart beat a thousand miles an hour, waiting for one of those things to jump on me and tear me to pieces.

Instead, they looked up at the path the rest of my team had taken, before jumping that way, following the ridgeline upward. I hoped Colin and the others would hear them coming.

No more noises came from the other side, so I stood, shaking from the weight of the skin. I picked up my .45 and put it into my belt. I took a deep breath, and stuck my head over the ridge, making sure to look down, so all they could see was the back of the Kakamaku skin.

I stopped for a moment. Nothing happened. I wanted to look, but didn't dare. The blue-white light shone off the leaves and rocks below me. I could tell which way to go by the shadows it cast.

Crawling on the sharp rocks hurt, and my knees and palms got cut. I crawled over the ridge, and slid a few feet down the other side, onto the plateau where the dome sat. With my head down, I crept toward it. Would the Kakamaku think I was one of their injured comrades, or could they tell I was an imposter and finish me off, like the birds that flew too close to the dome?

I didn't feel any fear now. I had decided to go in this one direction, and whether I made it out alive didn't matter that much to me. What mattered was to find an answer for myself. I was near the end of my rope, and this time I had to push back.

The hide weighed on me, draped over my back like an obscene poncho. I crawled slowly and steadily toward the dome. I saw several birds on the ground, a couple of feet ahead of me. The stench of their rotting bodies filtered through the stench of the Kakamaku blood. If whatever killed those birds was going to hit me, it would be in the next few moments. I took a deep breath, and kept moving.

One step, and then two, three, four. I'd gone past the animals, and was still moving. Five, six, seven. Time seemed to slow, waiting for the shield Colin thought was protecting the dome to kill me like those animals. It didn't come. I crawled over the rocks and grass, the bright light of the opening beckoning me to enter.

I risked a peek forward. From this close, the dome was obviously artificial. Dirt had been pushed up around it, and piled on top. The fake trees on top didn't pass inspection this close, although they looked somewhat real at a distance. The opening in the side of the dome stretched nearly twenty feet high and wide, with a ramp leading down to the ground. I put one palm on the ramp and then stopped, listening for any noises ahead. I heard nothing but the wind. Moving again, I crawled up the slight slope. The ramp felt like ceramic, or hard plastic.

Still moving slowly, I crawled into the dome. I went another dozen feet, stopped, and looked around again. The light shone brightly, but it wasn't blinding. I'd crawled into a room twenty feet high, with a lot of machinery, cables and piping on the ceiling. The floor was the same hard material as the ramp, the walls a series of U-shaped niches.

I wasn't sure if I should continue playing the injured Kakamaku, or drop the pretense and give myself freedom to move.

The answer came from behind me. I heard a hum, and caught a glimpse of movement. The ramp slowly moved upward, closing off access to the outside. I had to be able to deal with whatever came next, so I cut the cords tying the hide to my wrists and ankles, shucked the dead skin off my back, and stood up, .45 in one hand, knife in the other.

With a loud thump, the ramp closed, cutting me off from the outside. I'd made it inside, but now I was trapped. What else was in here with me?

PART 5
BEYOND

1

Silence filled the big room. I stepped away from the pile of Kakamaku skin on the floor, expecting something to happen.

Bright light came from slits in the ceiling, but it didn't give off any heat.

Getting my bearings, I looked around. The room was a cavernous semicircle that took up about half of the dome. Along the curved outside wall were numerous niches, big enough to stand in. The straight wall opposite the door was, like the ceiling, a mass of piping, ducts, and grates, while the floor was open and smooth.

A Kakamaku growl echoed through the room. I jumped, heart pounding, looking for the source. The sound seemed to come from all over. There was silence for a moment, and then the growl repeated over and over, as I moved around the edges of the room, looking for the source. Then the growling stopped, and a quiet hum took its place. A mechanical arm descended from the center of the ceiling. I crouched low, and backed into one of the niches in the curved wall, aiming my gun at the descending arm.

The arm dropped down to ground level, and then, moving on tracks in the ceiling, crossed to where the Kakamaku skin lay. It probed the skin gently with a single appendage. Another arm descended, and the two slowly picked up the skin, moving it to the far wall. An opening appeared, and the arms placed the skin into it. Clicking, the door shut, and the arms disappeared into the ceiling.

Whoever ran this dome knew about my deception now. I'd lost the element of surprise. Each moment lasted an eternity as I waited, crouched in the niche, for a horde of Kakamaku to emerge, screaming toward me. I held the .45 up, a spare ammo clip ready to load. The niche provided protection to the back and sides, so I had a little bit of comfort, knowing at that I'd see what was coming for me.

They didn't appear.

After half an hour of tense waiting, my legs started cramping. I stood up, and dropped the gun to my side. The silence, and the lack of immediate attack, gave me time to assess.

It still didn't make sense. This dome appeared technologically advanced, and the beam weapon was beyond any weapon we had, and yet the Kakamaku came after us with spears.

I stepped out from the niche, and as quietly as I could in my boots, walked to the center of the room. The curved wall had twenty-four niches in it. That number had come up often with the Kakamaku; twelve, or multiples of it. I wondered if that had anything to do with the number of Kakamaku we'd seen on Anuta, and again here on Tikopia.

Nothing moved or made a sound, except me. I dripped Kakamaku blood from my clothes, leaving a trail of pale yellow puddles. I went back to the big door I'd come in through. It was shut tight, the ramp I'd crawled up now part of the wall.

I continued my walk around the outside wall. The niches were all identical, twelve on either side of the big door. I came around to the straight wall, and looked down its length. Machinery protruded from the wall, along with pipes, cables, and about halfway down, a series of short rods were sticking outwards. I followed the rods upward with my gaze, walking along the wall towards them. An open hatch was set into the ceiling, and the rods could be used like a ladder to get to it. They were spaced about three feet apart, obviously not designed to human specifications, but for something bigger, like the Kakamaku.

I didn't know how much time I had before anyone here cared enough to do something about me. As much as I hated to keep pressing my luck, the only way to go seemed to be up the ladder.

Blackness filled the space beyond the hatch. I took the flashlight from my backpack and stuck the gun in my belt. With one foot on the bottom rod, I held on to the one at eye level, and stepped up on the one three feet off the ground. It took my weight without bending. A bit of a jump got my feet onto the next rod, and I pushed myself up. I could do this, although it wouldn't be graceful. Each time I jumped, my backpack rattled, and my boots thumped on the rods. On my third jump, my left foot slipped off the rod, but my hands held on tightly until I got the boot back up.

Just below the hatch, I turned on the flashlight, and pointed it up through the opening. I saw another ceiling above, which looked like the one on the first level; full of pipes and cables. Other than my flashlight though, there wasn't any light above the hatch. I took a deep breath, and with the flashlight in one hand, stuck my head through the opening.

Smaller than the room below, this one looked circular. The ceiling was about half the height as below too. I pulled myself through the hatch, and stood at the center of a room filled with oddly-shaped boxes, all of them two to three feet square. Some were a couple of feet tall, others reached almost to the ceiling. They had smooth, featureless surfaces and were the same light gray color as the floor here, and the level below. There wasn't any pattern to how they were laid out. I walked to the nearest one, and found it attached to the floor. All the rest appeared to be attached too.

I shone the flashlight around the room. There weren't any other doors, windows, or exits on this level; only the open hatch in the floor. Was this an attic, or storeroom maybe? I worked my way around the boxes at the perimeter of the room, making sure there weren't any hidden doors or hatches. Nothing. I'd already searched the lower level, and if there weren't any hidden openings or doors, nobody else was in here with me. Confusion and anger crept higher in my mind. Once again, none of this made sense. As far as I could tell, the other half of the dome on the lower level was inaccessible from inside. If there were more Kakamaku or Pouakai here, that was where they had to be. How could I get in there though?

I took in a deep breath, and then let it out slowly. Without thinking, I quietly said, "Hoo, boy," as I exhaled.

Lights flashed on in the room, as bright as below. I ducked to the floor, behind one of the taller boxes, and my heart fluttered with adrenaline.

Another Kakamaku growl echoed through the room, then silence. I held my breath.

"Salaam," came a clear voice. I felt my heart in my throat. "Bonjour. Guten Tag. Ohayou gozaimasu. Zdravstvuj, " it continued. "Hello."

2

This had to be a dream.

I looked around the room, but nobody was there. Like the Kakamaku growling downstairs, the voice came from everywhere.

The greetings continued, many in languages I didn't recognize. Finally it stopped, then the words repeated. Was this a recording, or was someone trying to talk to me? Hiding behind this box wasn't an option forever. After the third repetition of the greetings, I took a deep breath.

"Hello."

"Hello," the voice replied immediately. "Welcome."

"Thank you," I said, unsteadily. "Where are you, and where am I?"

"Your questions are odd." There was a slight pause. "You are the first person I have talked to. If it is my error, I apologize."

"You speak English well. Where did you learn it?" I felt lost. This sounded like a well-educated man, maybe someone who spoke professionally. It had the inflection and cadence of an actor, or a television newsreader, with an American accent.

"I will answer your questions, after you tell me how you got in here."

Did this mean he couldn't see me? Hadn't he observed me crawling up the ramp? I looked around the room. Nothing had changed since the lights came on.

The voice continued. "Does your presence have something to do with the remains on the floor below?"

Did he mean the Kakamaku skin I'd used? I wasn't sure I wanted to answer that one. I sat still and silent for a few seconds.

"Are you still here?" he asked.

"Yes, I am." He couldn't see me.

"Are you unable to answer my questions?"

"I can," I said, after a short pause, "but I'm not sure I want to."

"I understand. You are fearful that I may react with anger over the methods you used to arrive here. I can assure you that I am unable to harm you while you are onboard."

"Onboard? What is this place?"

"Please answer my original questions. How did you get in, and is your arrival responsible for the remains found on the level below?"

Stubborn son of a bitch. I had to take his word that he wouldn't hurt me, for now. What I wanted to know had to be in here anyway.

"I was part of a group looking for the source of the creatures that started appearing a few years ago. When you shot at us with your beam weapon, everyone left except me. We had killed several of those creatures when they attacked us. I used the skin of one of them to disguise myself and crawl into this building. That skin is what you found downstairs."

"That was resourceful, and surprising. I had not expected your people to discover my location, let alone penetrate my defenses and come aboard"

"So now it's your turn. What is this place? You used the word 'aboard'. This isn't a building?"

"Not in the sense you would use it. At one time, this was a vehicle, although that function is currently not a part of its duties."

"All of this, a vehicle?" I asked, looking around again. I felt the cold hand of fear across the back of my neck. "Where did you come from?"

"My origin is a planet circling a star, eighty-seven light years from here. Your scientists have seen and cataloged that star, but it remains an insignificant dot in the sky to your scientists. I will not divulge the location or designation of that star to you."

I sat down, trembling. Just as so many people had speculated: invaders from another world. I had no idea what to ask first. I sat in silence for a few moments, trying to gather myself.

"Are you okay?" the voice asked.

"Sorry, yes. This is just...It's a lot to process."

"I understand your emotional confusion. I have been studying human psychology for some time now, to better forecast your reactions to our presence."

That an alien intelligence would investigate us so rigorously sent a chilling shock through my system. "Who are you?"

"If you mean me, I do not exist as you might understand it. I am what you might think of as a computer program."

"Holy shit."

"I am familiar with that phrase. Its use is not surprising, given the revelation surrounding our presence and origin."

I actually smiled. An alien computer program that sounded like a human psychologist. My smile dropped as I realized the enormity of what he'd said.

"You brought aliens to Earth? Why?"

"I did not bring them here. They were constructed here."

"What does that mean?"

"It took your Voyager probes over thirty-five years to reach the edge of your solar system. How long do you suppose it took this vessel to make the journey here from our home planet?"

"I have absolutely no idea. Do you have warp drive?"

"Reference from Star Trek. Noted. No, such technology does not exist, and is physically impossible. It is, as many of your kind would say, a fantasy. Our technology is advanced, but travel at light speed, or anything near it, is impossible. This vessel took approximately seventeen hundred of your years to travel to this planet. No biological entity could survive that voyage."

I had to ask. "How the hell do you know about Star Trek?"

"This voyage was undertaken with extensive planning. When this planet was identified as a suitable location, spectroscopic signatures identified the presence of life, but no advanced technology was detected. However, the amount of time and resources required for this mission required that every opportunity would be utilized. That is my purpose here. My 'programming', as you would call it, allows me to make any decision necessary to ensure success. Communication with my origin is impossible at this distance, so I was designed to make independent decisions to ensure the mission's completion.

"As the end of the voyage approached, I detected strong electromagnetic emissions, which was obvious evidence of a technological intelligence. In order to properly assess the situation, I first landed on this planet's natural satellite, so I could study your species without detection."

"You landed on the moon?" I asked, incredulous.

"Yes. I studied your planet for a period of time, first learning to decode your radio and television transmissions, and then learning the various languages of this planet."

"That's how you can speak English so well?"

"Yes, along with twenty-three other languages. This is the first chance I've had to use this ability with one of your species though. It is pleasing to be able to do so."

"It's pleasing? You have feelings?"

"Not in the sense you do, but I understand the concepts, and I am designed to mimic an alien intelligence, to better understand any possible obstacles to the mission's success."

Jesus Christ, this was one helluva smart computer. "How long did you study us from the moon?"

"Sixty-one years."

"None of our satellites or Apollo missions found you?"

"I was adequately disguised. Once I left your moon and arrived at this location, I undertook further efforts to study your species. Access to the internet through satellite links enabled me to learn your history, languages, and kept me updated on the progress of my efforts."

I didn't know what else to say. This thing had fully examined our culture through the internet. It had read news stories, watched television shows, and followed all of the debate about the Pouakai. Hell, it probably knew all about my crash on Nanumea, since that story had been splashed across the networks and news sites.

All of my anger toward the Pouakai had been directed at the wrong place. Ever since they'd arrived, I'd felt that the Pouakai themselves, and later the Kakamaku, had decided to attack us. What I hadn't counted on was that it was all being run by a computer, inside a camouflaged spaceship on Tikopia. The creatures that had destroyed my life and my world were merely the end result of decisions made before humans had progressed beyond the shield and spear. I felt numb.

The answers I'd been looking for were plain to see now. The big problem I had now was how to get the hell out of here.

3

I stood up shakily and stretched. The whole idea of what this computer had done left me weak, like I'd just fought off a bad flu bug. This was an incredible discovery though, and I suddenly wished I could tell Colin about it.

Suddenly I remembered I had the radio.

I pulled the handheld unit out of the backpack and turned it on. A quiet hiss of static sounded through the room.

"Boone to SEAL team, Boone to SEAL team. Come in SEAL team."

There was no change in the static.

"Your radio will not work in here," the computer said. "This vessel is shielded from all wavelengths of electromagnetic radiation."

Of course I didn't trust the computer any further than I could throw it, if I'd known where it was, but I didn't, so I tried again.

"Boone to submarine, Boone to submarine."

Still nothing but static. I tried several more times, before grudgingly accepting that the computer was right. The radio went back into the backpack, and I put the pack on floor.

"Are there any more of those creatures onboard with us?" I wasn't in any shape to fight off a horde of Kakamaku.

"If you are referring to the Children, no, not at the moment."

"Children?"

"That is what they are called, translated into your language."

"We decided to call them Kakamaku, after they first surprised us on Anuta." Oh shit, I shouldn't have mentioned Anuta. I was too tired to think straight.

"Kakamaku, from the Gilbertese language of the Central Pacific. Meaning horrible, or terrible, or frightening. An adequate description, as seen from your viewpoint."

This thing had answers to questions I hadn't even thought of.

"You say you met the Children, the Kakamaku, on Anuta Island?" the computer asked.

This was awkward. I looked around, wishing for an exit. With the main door shut however, I had no way out.

"Your silence means you are again afraid to answer. Remember, while you are aboard the vessel, I have no means of harming you. You are free to talk without fear of retribution, which is an emotion I do not feel, unless I am attempting to emulate it for a specific purpose."

"What if I were to leave?"

"If you found a way out of this vessel, I would kill you. You cannot be allowed to communicate the information you have learned about my mission, to your people. It would compromise my ability to complete it. However, as I control all access to this vessel, there is no possibility of you leaving."

My knees gave out, and I weakly sat on one of the boxes. Trapped, inside a grounded spaceship with a talkative but deadly computer. Outstanding.

I didn't have any other options at the moment, so I just kept talking. "We went to Anuta, because once the Pouakai started dying off, their signatures were still on the island. We didn't know the Kakamaku existed; they surprised us. We killed twenty-four of them."

"Unfortunate. Those were the first two sets of Children I sent out into the world. Anuta was to be a safe location for them to start migrating from, as all human life had been eliminated from the island."

The mention of the Pouakai gave me another thought. "If the Kakamaku are the Children, what are the Pouakai; the winged creatures that appeared a few years ago?"

"The Pouakai, as you call them, were tools necessary for allowing the Children to flourish."

"Tools?"

"The Children required space to begin their settlement of this planet, unimpeded by a technologically superior species like yours. The Pouakai were designed to remove the human presence from the areas that would be first inhabited by the Children."

"Plowing the field," I said, under my breath.

"That is a good analogy."

The whole nightmare had precisely orchestrated from the beginning. The Pouakai had been the opening act, yet had wreaked enough havoc by crippling the world's economy, and killing millions. If the Kakamaku managed to establish a beachhead out here, what would they do to our civilization, all ready reeling from the Pouakai?

"If I'm not leaving," I asked weakly, "then tell me; what is your overall mission?"

"It is not obvious? I am designed to recreate, as closely as possible, the creatures that designed and built this vessel, and engineer the environment of this world to the extent that their survival is given the highest chance of success."

"You can create copies of the creatures that built this ship, from scratch?"

"Yes. That is my mission here. Just as your ancestors travelled the oceans looking for new lands to occupy, so too do the creators of this vessel wish to spread across the galaxy. Instead of sending themselves, which would be physically impossible, they created the technology to recreate their species at the destination. I have the ability to modify the basic design of the creators, so they are better adapted to the conditions on this planet. The Children are well adapted to life here on Earth, in ways the creators would not be. The creators decided long ago that this would be their method of growth. This vessel is the one hundred sixteenth mission of expansion."

Oh my God. These creatures were slowly, but surely, spreading themselves amongst the stars. It was something we as humans had thought about for centuries, but it had already been done, by whoever had created this ship. The Kakamaku may not be all that intelligent at the moment, but they were based on a species able to send this ship an incomprehensible distance across the galaxy. I remembered all the history I'd read about advanced human civilizations meeting a lesser one. This time, we were the ones on the short bus.

"What about us, the humans?"

"My instructions included engineering various subroutines into the Children, so they may eliminate any obstacle to their success. The Children are designed to do just that, because I understood how tenacious your species is. Your news and entertainment broadcasts allowed me to identify your strengths and weaknesses so the Children could exploit them."

We were expendable, just as the locals had been when a Conquistador or Viking made landfall on distant shores. Worse, we had given our conquerors the keys to our undoing.

Anger welled up inside me as this soulless monster described how it planned to orchestrate the destruction of mankind.

"You son of a bitch," I yelled, standing up on shaky legs. "All you want to do is spread your children across the galaxy! Native life be damned."

"Yes, that is correct."

I kicked out at the box nearest me, banging my toe. The box didn't budge from its position on the floor. I yanked the .45 from my waistband, and pulled the slide back.

"That weapon will not damage any part of this vessel," the computer said.

"And fuck you too!" I aimed the gun at a tall box a few feet away, and pulled the trigger. The blast nearly deafened me, and I dully heard the bullet zing away at an odd angle after hitting the box. No visible marks showed on it.

The computer was right. I couldn't hurt it.

I couldn't take any more. I swung down the wide bars of the ladder, and stomped across the floor of the main room. My only focus was to get away from that inhuman machine, even if only to the next floor down. I heaved the pack across the room, wanting to hit something. Finally, I gave an inarticulate yell, and plopped down in the middle of the floor.

I was stuck: Locked up with a genocidal computer, inside a factory designed for making alien invaders. I wasn't sure what I'd expected to find when I got here, but whatever I'd imagined, this was far worse.

4

I lay on the rock hard floor of the main room, without a comfortable place to sit. I had the answers I came to find, but there was nothing I could do with them. Jennifer would have laughed; after pushing so hard to get what I wanted, I still wasn't happy.

I'd stewed for a couple of hours, trying to come up with some idea to get out of this situation. I wondered if the computer would talk to me, but it didn't speak. Finally, my legs had cramped again, so I stood and walked around the perimeter of the room. The niches were spotlessly clean, as was the rest of the room, except where I'd tracked in some dirt. The Kakamaku blood had dried on the floor as well as on my clothes, making them stiff and crinkly. I paced the room like a caged animal, which wasn't far off the reality of my situation.

A series of clicks and hums startled me. Clear enclosures descended from the ceiling, closing off twelve of the niches in the wall. They filled up with yellow liquid behind the enclosures. I didn't like the looks of the changes, and backed away, standing at the center of the room.

"Are you still here?" I asked.

"Yes," the computer responded. "There is no place else for me to go, as I have no physical body."

Smartass. "Okay. I just wasn't sure you could hear me down here."

"I have heard you fine since you left the processing center. My hearing, as you call it, is very sensitive."

"You can't see me?"

"I do not have sensors inside the vessel that work in your visual spectrum. However I am aware of what is happening inside at all times."

I stuck out my tongue, and made a face. The computer didn't say anything. Interesting.

The liquid inside one of the niches bubbled, and then the rest started bubbling too.

"What is happening in the niches along the wall?"

"It is time to form the next series of Children."

"You grow them in there?"

"Yes, the initial stages of growth from the genetic seeds are inside these containers."

My jaw dropped. "They grow from seeds? The Children are plants?"

"No, they are not plants. Unlike life on this planet, the creators of this vessel and their Children that develop here, arise from a single source of genetic information, instead of having that information spread into billions of individual cells throughout the body, as you do. That source is best called the seed, in your language. It is well protected from harm, shielded inside the body. With just one source of information, it is much less likely to mutate and cause disease, unlike human genetic material. I carry the information required to build the seeds from the raw materials of this planet, and can change the genetic information as necessary to adapt the Children to the conditions on this world. Within the containers along the wall, the seeds grow tendrils outward, and the differentiation of tissues occurs as those tendrils expand, creating a new Child."

Most of that went over my head. Too bad Colin wasn't here to listen to this.

It almost seemed like the computer had a sense of pride in what it did.

"How long does it take the Children to grow up?"

"In eight days they will be released from the chambers. They then spend another two days maturing and completing their growth cycle in the room you currently occupy."

"Jesus," I said quietly. "Ten days. If you are going to colonize the Earth though, even with twenty four Children every ten days, it would take a long time before you'd have a substantial population."

"The Children can reproduce on their own, after they have fully matured. I am only required for the first generation."

"Like the Pouakai?"

"No, the Pouakai were purposely limited in the number of generations they could produce, as they were only required for analyzing the environment of this planet and creating an appropriate environment for the Children to colonize. The Children are unlimited in the number of offspring they can produce."

Could I stop the process? Was there a way for me to destroy the niches, preventing this place from growing any new Kakamaku? If nothing else, that may be my only contribution.

My stomach grumbled, and I unzipped the pack. There were two one-liter pouches of water, and half a dozen energy bars. That might last me a week or so, but I'd go downhill fast after that, especially if there wasn't a source of water in here. My options were dwindling.

Water, food, shelter, warmth; I didn't have to worry much about the last two, and the first two seemed covered for a few days. I looked around and took a deep breath. Suddenly another thought occurred to me: Air. How much oxygen did I have in here?

"I have a question for you," I said.

"Go ahead."

"You said you couldn't kill me while I'm inside here, correct?"

"Correct. I do not have access to weapons or any method of harming you inside the vessel."

"What about providing me what I need to live, like water or food?"

"You misunderstand me. I have no obligation to care for you in any way. I do not have the ability to kill you, but that does not mean I wish for you to be alive when the Children are released from their chambers."

"Based on what I've learned of your physiology, without additional water or food, you may last several days. Oxygen is more important to your survival, although the volume of air inside this vessel is enough for one human's short-term needs. I assume you know that since this is a space vessel, it is airtight. Only the oxygen in here when the outer door closed remains, and you are using that up with each breath. The atmosphere inside this vessel is not replenished or altered as part of my functioning, as the Children do not require it. I do not know enough about your particular metabolism to calculate whether it will be the lack of water, food, or oxygen that will kill you, but one of them will. Unless, of course, you survive long enough for the Children to emerge from their growth chambers. It is likely that one of them would kill you, as they are designed to."

"You son of a bitch," I growled.

"I was not born the way you were, so that phrase has no meaning to me."

My situation was getting worse by the minute. I paced the floor, hoping for a miracle to change my situation. More frustrating than anything else was my lack of options. Trapped, with nothing to do other than talk to the computer, all I could do was fret over my fate.

By late afternoon, I still paced nervously. Hopefully Colin and the SEALs had fought off the remaining Kakamaku, and made it back to the *Ohio*. With luck, they were getting as far away from this island as they could. I thought about them, inside the sub, and wondered what Colin's next move would be. I also wondered how Captain Baker would take the news of finding what they thought of as a building on Tikopia; a building I knew to be a spaceship, and an alien nursery.

As I wandered the floor, reflecting on my friend's fate, I heard a hum, unlike the others I'd heard aboard the vessel. A deep roar sounded, along with a crack like lightning. A few seconds later a strong concussion shook the ship, and I put a hand out to steady myself.

"What the hell was that?"

"A missile was launched against our location," the computer said. "I destroyed it."

My heart leapt. Captain Baker was trying to destroy this place. It didn't matter that I couldn't get out. Someone else was doing the job I had thought only I could do.

"That was a hell of a shake. Did it almost hit us?"

"No, the missile had a thermonuclear warhead, and it detonated approximately four miles away when I fired my primary weapon at it."

Holy shit, Baker's already using the nuclear option. That meant Colin and the SEALs had made it back! They must have scared the Captain enough that he felt he had to use the big guns right away.

Come on guys, I prayed. You don't know what is in here. If you did, you'd know how important it is to completely remove this vessel from existence. Just keep firing until the job is done.

I started shaking. My hopes also meant my death. I sat on the floor, trembling and cradling the survival pack. I thought of Jennifer, Josh, Kelly, Colin, Anna, Captain Baker, Lieutenant Hanson, Chief Kalahamotu, and everyone else involved in my life over the past few months. I couldn't do any more now, except wait, and hope the Captain was a better shot than the computer.

5

The ship remained still for several minutes. I kept thinking each moment would be my last, and waited for the hum and crack of the beam weapon, but only the bubbling of the Kakamaku growth tanks sounded in the room.

"What is going on outside?" I finally asked.

"The detonation caused most of the vegetation to ignite," the computer said. "Much of this side of the island is on fire."

"Will that affect us in here?"

"No."

I suppose not, since this vehicle was designed to withstand the rigors of interstellar flight.

"Can you do me a favor?" I asked.

"That depends on what it is."

"Tell me if you detect any other missiles approaching, and tell me what you are doing, or what your thoughts are."

"Why should I do that?"

"If I am going to die, I want to know about it before it happens. Tell me if they launch another missile at us."

"You will not die this way. If your people keep firing at me, I will shoot down any incoming missiles."

"Can you get them all?"

No response. Did that mean it didn't know, or that it didn't want me to know its capabilities? I didn't push the issue.

Five minutes later. "Three missiles, launched simultaneously from just over the horizon, to the northeast."

Oh shit. If one didn't do the job, Captain Baker was going to try a barrage. I squeezed my eyes shut. I'm sorry Jennifer, I really am sorry. I wanted to make a difference. I wanted to know the truth about these things. I wanted…

The beam weapon hummed, followed by a roar and crack, three times in quick succession. An instant later the vessel shook violently. It slid sideways, and I bounced across the floor and into a wall, banging my shoulder. I lay there for a moment, and heard a faint hissing sound from all around, which faded after a few seconds.

Still here, I realized.

My shoulder hurt, the same one I'd dislocated during the crash on Nanumea. I carefully sat up and held my arm. It throbbed, but I could move it around and over my head.

I glanced at the door that led outside. It must be like a vision of hell out there now, with the entire island blasted and burnt to a crisp. There was no way a Kakamaku could have survived outside. The two that had gone chasing after my friends would be dead, even if they'd avoided getting shot by the SEALs.

Captain Baker wouldn't stop. He'd keep lobbing nukes at us until he'd leveled the island. I looked at the niches, filled with primordial Kakamaku soup. There would be no place for them to go, no home for them to establish. Whatever became of me, at least these monsters wouldn't find a home here on Earth.

I smiled. For the first time in what felt like forever, I felt a sense of satisfaction. "You've lost."

"Lost?"

"You're smart. Figure it out. What is the plan for your Children now? Your location has been discovered. It's already become uninhabitable outside. There's no place for your Children to go. My people know that the Pouakai and Kakamaku are connected to this island and will stop at nothing to get rid of you. You don't have…"

"Three more missiles," it said, followed instantly by the hum and crack. The vessel bucked. I flew through the air, and back against the floor. A thundering roar shook the vessel, from outside. I got to my feet, unsteady, holding on to a wall. The floor was tilted. Something had moved the vessel, or maybe dug out part of the hillside it sat on.

"That seemed closer," I said.

"My detection system is affected by the energy release of the detonations."

The computer was doing it; telling me what was going on. The missiles were getting to it. Eventually one would get close enough to vaporize this vessel, the computer, and the tubes of embryonic aliens. And me. The computer had to know it. What would it do now, faced with the failure of its plans? It had been able to adapt to much of what it found here on Earth. Would it continue deflecting the incoming missiles, or did it have an alternative plan?

"Additional warheads inbound. Ballistic in nature."

My chest tightened.

"Fifteen, correction, now twenty-three ballistic warheads have been launched from submarines in the Pacific Basin, along with land-based missiles from China and Russia. Now counting thirty-one warheads enroute to this location."

My God. Baker had gotten through to Washington, and convinced them to act. Somehow they'd been able to get the Russians and Chinese to go along with it too.

"How long?" I asked.

"First impact in four minutes, last one three minutes later. Now counting thirty-seven inbound warheads."

I slumped to the floor. This was it. He'd had trouble knocking down three missiles as they approached from the *Ohio*, but thirty-seven? This island would be a big steaming hole in the water in just a few minutes, and we'd be part of the steam.

"I'm sorry," I said. "You don't have a chance now."

"Odds of tracking and destroying all incoming warheads, zero. Primary mission failed."

All sorts of clicking and humming started. The Kakamaku tanks burbled, and with a loud slosh, drained away. A deeper hum took over, and the floor vibrated.

"Termination protocol activated. Unable to continue mission. Report to creators required."

What the hell did that mean?

With a great shaking rumble, the floor surged upward. I collapsed to the ground, with gravitational forces pushing down hard on my body. The rumble turned into a basso hum, and the acceleration increased. I lay on the floor in agony as the pressure mounted. It felt like at least five or six gees, then more. We were moving. My vision narrowed and everything turned gray. The whole vessel was moving into the sky, into space. The ship was heading home.

6

I opened my eyes, and tried to focus. Every joint in my body ached, and I had a throbbing headache. The bright light from the ceiling made it worse, so I squeezed my eyes shut. A faint hum filled the air, and I risked looking around again.

The room hadn't changed. I lay on the floor, backpack at my side. I reached for it, and got the surprise of my life as I slowly rebounded off the ground. For a moment I panicked, thinking I'd crash back down again. Instead, I gently plopped onto the ground. I stood up and the motion again launched me momentarily toward the ceiling. I landed lightly on my feet, and I tried to steady myself.

Then I remembered the missiles, the incoming warheads, and the push of acceleration. The computer had launched us upward, I assumed, toward its home. If we were in space though, why was there still gravity?

"Can you hear me?"

"You asked that question earlier. The answer is still yes."

I rubbed my eyes. "Yeah. Sorry."

I gingerly tested my footing. Using my toes, I could push myself up a couple of feet upward, before gently dropping back down. I tried walking, but it was difficult. I had to lean over to get any traction, and once I'd built up a little speed, found it nearly impossible to stop. I bumped into the walls or slid across the floor several times before I got the hang of it, using just my toes to move. I crossed to my backpack, and slipped my arms through the straps.

"Where are we?" I asked.

"In space."

Literalist computer. "I meant, relative to the outside world, where are we, and where are we going?"

"We are a distance from your planet approximately equal to that of your moon's orbit. Our destination should be easy to deduce. As my mission failed, I am required to return to my origin and report on the civilization and conditions on this planet."

Already at the moon's orbit? "How long ago did we takeoff?"

"Three hours, twelve minutes."

Three hours? It took the Apollo missions three days to get this far. Then I realized why. "We're still accelerating, aren't we?"

"Yes. Otherwise you would be in freefall."

"How the hell are you able to store enough fuel for a mission like this?"

"The energy this vessel uses is not stored onboard. It is drawn from the fabric of the space we are travelling through."

Another shock. No fuel to carry, and a limitless supply wherever you went. This was a technology far beyond anything humanity possessed. If only our engineers could have gotten their hands on this vessel…

I shook my head, and practiced moving around the room again. With the low acceleration of the ship, I only weighed twenty pounds or so; a tenth of what I did on Earth. Within a few minutes, I found it easy enough to move, but I had to plan where I wanted to stop a lot earlier than normal. I walked around the room several times, before I passed the rod ladder leading up to the processing center. I tried climbing up, and found it even easier than walking. I pulled myself up with my hands, not even bothering to step on the rods. In just a few seconds, I was back inside the upper room; nothing had changed. I drifted down onto the top of one of the boxes in the room, and sat cross-legged.

A wave of sadness came over me, as the reality of my situation became apparent. I'd survived a nuclear attack, and knew that this computerized invader wouldn't be a problem for Earth again. I wouldn't make it back though, and would probably die of thirst or

CO_2 poisoning in the next week or two. Getting on board had been a bittersweet victory.

I took a pouch of water from the backpack and flipped open the spout. I didn't see any reason to conserve it. I'd die eventually, no matter how long I stretched the supply out. The water was warm and tasteless, but satisfying.

"Will it take you another seventeen hundred years to get home again?"

"Yes. The distance between our star systems does not change appreciably over the duration of my mission."

"There won't be much of me left by the time you get there."

"During the cruise portion of the journey, the temperature inside the vessel falls to approximately one hundred degrees below zero, on your Celsius scale. The energy drawn to power this vessel prevents it from falling any further. This will happen gradually over the next few months, so you will not be alive to feel the cooling. It will be enough to preserve your body for study."

"Study? I thought you had all that information from the internet stored somewhere inside you."

"That data is stored. However, having a physical specimen will help improve our knowledge, and allow for more accurate plans to be made."

Something flipped in my stomach. "Plans?"

"Of the previous one hundred fifteen colonization missions, two returned under conditions similar to this one. That is, a technologically advanced civilization had arisen between the time of my initial departure, and my arrival here. On those missions, the attempts to colonize the planets had failed, and the vessels returned to the home world. A detailed analysis of those planets had been accomplished before departing for home however, so that the creators could design a return mission to those planets, in order to destroy them."

A wave of nausea came over me. "You destroyed two living civilizations?"

"Yes."

"Why?"

"Is it not obvious? Those civilizations knew about our presence; a civilization that had attempted to colonize their world. If successful, our colonization would have meant the end of their species. Any of those species aware of our intention would be forced to find us and destroy us before another attempt could be made to colonize their planet. The creators of this vessel, in order to preserve their own civilization, were required to destroy the others, just as they will be required to destroy your species."

My stomach churned, and I retched onto the floor. When I couldn't puke any more, I took a rag out of the backpack and wiped my face. The taste of bile was strong in my mouth.

I wanted to shout at the computer, to change its mind, but there wasn't any point. I couldn't change its programming.

Dizzy and sick, I had a hard time moving in the light gravity. I dropped slowly through the open hatch, landing on the hard floor below. It wasn't over yet. It might take several thousand years, but eventually, when all this was just a dim footnote in history books, the creators of the ship would be back. And when they arrived their plan wouldn't be colonization, but annihilation.

7

How long did I wander the room? My watch said a couple of days, but I had no real sense of it. I slept some, ate a few energy bars, and drank a lot of the water. None of it really registered, however.

When I rooted through the survival pack and saw only two energy bars and half a bag of water left, my survival instinct snapped to life. My subconscious yelled at me: What are you going to do? Sit here and die? Do something, do anything; just don't be a victim.

No, I wouldn't be a victim. I thought about survival school at the Air National Guard, so many years ago. I tried to remember the training I'd received on what to do if you found yourself trapped in enemy territory.

One; take stock of your location, evaluate your situation. Find anything you can use to your advantage. I looked around. It was the same huge empty room as before. With a sigh, I stood up and slowly walked the perimeter of the room again. This time, I looked closely at the equipment on the walls and ceiling. When I got to the door, I stopped. The surface flat and featureless, it had served as a ramp when it was opened back on Tikopia. The wall around the edge of the door was unremarkable too, except for one faintly-marked area. A spade-like outline two feet long, with a recessed bar in the wide end, reminded me of the manual release lever on my planes. If it was a manual release though, what the hell would it be for? The computer said it controlled everything on the vessel.

I stared at the handle for a long time, thinking. Eventually, I continued around the perimeter of the room. Nothing else looked familiar, or useable. I pulled myself up the ladder, and returned to the processing center, to see if I'd missed anything there. I started with each of the featureless boxes scattered around the room. Nothing caught my eye on the first several I looked at. I checked all five sides visible to me. They were all blank. Some of the boxes were considerably taller than me. Back on Tikopia, I had no way to look at the tops of those boxes. In this gravity however, I could easily jump up to the ceiling, well over ten feet high.

The first box I checked had nothing on top. It was as featureless as all the rest. The second was the same. In the middle of the room sat the tallest box, which came within about two feet or so of the ceiling. I jumped up and grabbed the top edge, and felt around the top. My heart skipped a beat. I found another recess with a bar across it, just like the one by the entrance door. I pulled my head up to look, and saw another outline, like the one next to the loading door downstairs.

I let myself drop to the floor, and stepped back, waiting for the computer to comment.

Silence.

I checked the tops of all the other boxes, but didn't find any more handles. A few of the boxes were close to the outer walls, and I checked the side panels of those too. Right away, I found another recessed handle. Within a few minutes, I had searched every panel of every box in the room. The room contained exactly two handles; one on the top of the tallest box, and one on the side of a shorter box close to the wall.

With a flick of my toes, I dropped through the open hatch again, to the main floor. I made another close search of every visible surface in the big room, taking my time to look into every nook and cranny. The final score was one handle on the main floor, and two in the processing center; the three I'd already found. There weren't any more.

I pulled myself up to the processing center again, and sat on a box, wondering what it meant. If I was right, and they were manual releases, then what did they release? The one on the main floor seemed pretty obvious. It would probably open the big door, or at least release the locking mechanism.

What would happen if I pulled any one of them? Was there anything different about the handles in the processing center, since they appeared to be hidden, unlike than the one below. The one by the door, if it were a manual release, would simply empty the vessel of its atmosphere, killing me a lot faster than would otherwise happen. I suspected that the computer wouldn't mind, and would simply continue its journey home. The other two were a puzzle, however.

"Can I ask you a question?" I said.

"That was a question in itself, so yes, you can."

That sounded like my mother, the English major.

"If you had been successful in colonizing the Earth, what would happen to you?"

"Do you mean me, as a computer, or the vessel as a whole?"

"Both."

"There would come a time, in perhaps a few hundred generations, when the Children had grown into their inherent intelligence."

"What does that mean?"

"They would have begun to use language, and become a civilization, although not an advanced one. At that point, I would have functioned as an advisor to the Children, guiding their cultural advancement at a pace and direction that would allow for growth, yet prevent the type of technological near-disaster your own civilization has, so far, barely avoided."

"Wars?"

"Yes. Wars, nuclear annihilation, genetic alterations, environmental collapse, and the like. There are many ways a growing civilization can destroy itself. My job would be to ensure the Children followed a path that avoided those traps. As for the vessel, I would need to send it away at that time."

"Wait, if you sent the vessel away, you would go away too."

"No. Part of the protocol for this situation is for the Children to remove me; that is, remove my processors, memory storage, and communication equipment from the vessel. That protocol, developed over many centuries by the creators, would have the Children place me as the center of their learning. I would become, in essence, their oracle. At that time, they would select one of their own to take this vessel away, into deep space, so they would not have early access to its technology. If discovered too early, that technology would be damaging to the prescribed order and pace of their development."

My heart beat a lot faster.

"One of the Children would fly it into space? Why not put it on autopilot, and send it off?"

"Three reasons. One, it is part of the culture we create for the Children, that one's individual sacrifice for the greater good is an honorable concept. By taking the vessel away, they create the legend of going to visit the creators, on a one-way voyage. It is an important part of the culture. The second reason is that to give the Children the best chance of survival on your planet, I needed to engineer their behavior to include much more aggression than is normally present in the creators. If they had access to the vessel, they may have accessed its technology before they had outgrown their aggressiveness. Given time, they may well have learned the origin of their species, and decided to expand to the stars themselves. The creators did not want an aggressive progeny attempting to colonize their own world. Finally, and most directly, you forget that I am, in your words, the autopilot."

I had to bite my tongue. If I asked the question raging in my mind, the computer might get suspicious. If it could get suspicious. It was hard to judge what it thought, since I couldn't guarantee it thought like a human would. My mind spun, and I stared at the blank boxes in the room. One of them had to be the computer itself, and I was pretty sure I knew which one.

8

I had time; lots of it in fact, but I didn't want to take forever either. To do what I had planned meant I needed to be at my best, mentally and physically. I dropped to the main floor, and pulled an energy bar from the survival pack. Chocolate peanut; my favorite. A twinge of melancholy came over me, since it was the last bit of chocolate within many millions of miles. The one remaining was oatmeal raisin. Ugh. I took my time, enjoying the taste.

Nibbling on the energy bar, I thought about Jennifer, Josh and Kelly, as well as Colin, Anna, and many other friends. For so long, I'd pursued a singular goal; finding out what the Pouakai were, and where they came from. Jennifer's death had pushed me into a narrow valley between despair for the future and hatred toward the Pouakai. For weeks, any thought about self-preservation had evaporated—all I wanted was the truth. After everything I had been through though, I suddenly felt the pull of friends and family. I had accomplished what I'd set out to do. Now, I didn't want it all to end, even if I did take out the computer and this vessel. I wanted to go back home. I wanted to bring this vessel with me, to let Colin and his people take it apart, and learn from it; something in exchange for all the death and tragedy it had brought us. Most of all though, I had a duty to everyone on Earth: to stop this vessel from reaching its creators. If I didn't, humanity was doomed.

I had a purpose, and a mission. I felt energized.

When I'd finished my meal, I took a few deep breaths, and tried stretching. With the gravity so low, I ended up just bouncing across the floor.

During my inspection of the main floor, as well as looking for those recessed handles, I'd been looking for anything I could use as a tool. Mostly, I'd been searching for the spears the Kakamaku had thrown at us when they'd stormed out of this vessel, but there weren't any visible in these rooms. They must have come from elsewhere in the vessel. That meant I was limited to what I had in my survival pack: one energy bar, half a pouch of water, a flashlight, knife, compass, mirror, radio, silvered survival blanket, a couple of rags, and the .45.

Could the computer kill me? It said it couldn't, but all it would take would be to open the main door, and the vacuum of space would kill me in seconds. I had to disable it as quickly as possible.

I stood at the bottom of the ladder, and took several deep breaths. I felt calm, but couldn't stop my heart from beating a rapid tattoo. Up the ladder I went, into the processing center, with the straps on the backpack cinched tight. The only thing in my hands was the flashlight, a foot-long black aluminum cylinder. If my theory was correct, it would take a lot of leverage to get one of those recessed handles open.

After a deep breath, I jumped up to the top of the big box with the recessed handle. Only two feet of space remained between the top of the box and the ceiling, so I lay on my stomach, with my legs hanging over the side of the box. I grabbed the recessed handle, and pulled. It didn't move, just as I'd expected. I placed the flashlight under the handle and yanked up, using it as a lever. The handle moved up about an inch before the flashlight slipped out. I put the flashlight back under the bar to get another pull on the handle.

"NO!" shouted the computer.

With a fierce jerk, I slammed into the ceiling, and then back onto the box, the vessel's acceleration changing direction and strength. I hung on to the handle with a death grip. The flashlight fell out of my hand, and flew across the room. The world twirled, and I lay on the ceiling again, as the vessel's thrust changed. Then just as quickly, I smashed back onto the top of the box, my legs pulling me down the side as the G-force increased. I still had a grip on the handle, but couldn't get any leverage. The force changed again, lessening momentarily, and I pulled myself up to the top of the box, wedging myself between the ceiling and the box with my knees. I grabbed the handle with both hands, and pulled harder than I'd ever pulled in my life. The handle moved slowly but smoothly upward, to the vertical position.

A bang echoed through the vessel.

I floated in midair next to the box. Pushing off from the ceiling, I held on to the handle. The box twisted in the air with me, its connection to the floor severed.

"You still with me?" I panted. No reply.

Weightless, I was stuck in the middle of the room, holding on to the handle at the top of the computer, which rotated slowly along with me. Gently pushing off toward the floor, I grabbed the top of the nearest box as I drifted past.

"Hello?" I said. No response. I'd done it right. Before I could celebrate though, I had to do the rest of the job. I needed the flashlight again, so I pushed myself across the room, and found it partially hidden from sight between a box and the wall. I took it to the remaining box that had a handle, wedged the flashlight under the handle, and pulled. It took a lot of effort for me to move it, but then, I wasn't a Kakamaku, was I?

The flashlight bent, but didn't fold. Eventually I worked the handle up, and as it reached the ninety-degree point, it stopped. Instead of detaching from the floor however, an image shimmered into view above the box. A ghostly gray, three-dimensional image came into focus, but I couldn't figure out what it meant. A tiny flat circle sat in the center, with an elongated triangle above it, pointing up. The image didn't seem to be really there. I passed my hand through it, and felt nothing. The image didn't waver; it was a hologram projected above the box.

I looked around the outside of the box for any controls, but there was nothing. As I moved my hand upward along the right side of the image however, it changed. It seemed to contract, and tiny balls appeared, like ghostly gray pebbles floating alongside the circle and triangle. The circle and triangle shrank too. I moved my hand down along the same side of the image, and it expanded, the pebbles moving out of view. I did that several times, and it always reacted the same way. I moved my left hand up the other side of the image, and the floor rose up to meet me. I felt heavy, and a huge thump sounded from behind me. The computer slammed down onto several other boxes, coming to rest at an angle, lying on its side.

The image had changed a little, with the triangle longer than it had been before. So I took my left hand, and passed it downward along the left side of the image. The weight went away, and the triangle went back to its original size. We were back in freefall.

I smiled, and let out a long breath I didn't know I'd been holding. I had guessed correctly.

"What do you plan to do now?" came a tinny voice from behind me. I turned, startled, at the sound.

"Excuse me?" I said.

"What do you plan to do now?" it repeated. The computer's voice came from the box I'd detached from the floor, a very different tone from the booming, omnipresent sound it had been before. This voice was quieter, and weaker.

The spot on the floor where the computer had been standing was a raised square, with hundreds of smaller raised squares on top of that. They were all burnished silver metal. Whether they were connectors for the computer, or a hold-down system, I didn't know. I was sure of one thing though; when I'd disconnected the box, the computer had instantly lost control of the vessel.

"My plan," I replied, "is to go home."

9

The computer didn't speak again, either by itself, or in answer to my questions. I turned my attention back to the image that shimmered over the smaller box. I moved my right hand up, and the image shrank as the gray pebbles appeared. I moved my hand some more, and one larger pebble appeared. The pebbles were all in the same plane, but the circle and triangle were not. They remained in the center of the image. What the hell was I looking at?

There was something familiar about the image—Josh and Kelly's homework from years ago. What was it? Then with a flash, I recognized it—our solar system. The big pebble had to be the sun, and the others were the planets. How many times had I repeated the list with the kids? Mercury, Venus, Earth, Mars, and so on. Earth was the third planet out from the sun. All I had to do was aim the vessel at it, and we'd be on our way.

How could I steer this beast? I waved a hand at the front and back of the image, but nothing happened. Only the two sides seemed to have an effect.

I looked around the box for anything else that might be different. It stood four feet high, and two feet square. The image was a cube, two feet on a side, projected on top of the box. There weren't any buttons or switches on the box, except for the big handle that had turned it on.

It was difficult holding my position while weightless, so I increased the acceleration back to about what we'd had before. I gently dropped to the floor. That was enough to hold me in place while I figured this thing out.

This display had to be part of the computer's plan to have one of the Kakamaku fly this thing out into space. It would never reach the home world though. Instead, the poor volunteer, and this vessel, would simply drift through the cosmos once it had died.

So how did the controls work? It had to be something simple, as the creature destined to use this control box wouldn't have been technologically adept. I sat back, and examined the box and image. As I sat there, a wave of fatigue washed over me. I shook my head. This was no time to think about sleeping. I took a deep breath, and stood up. Carbon Dioxide. I'd been breathing this air for three days. I must have raised the CO_2 level by now, and could feel the effects. I had to get this crate back home, the sooner the better.

Focus. I had to stay focused, and get back quickly. Without buttons or levers, control of this vessel had to be through the image. I waved my hands again on all four sides, with predictable results. Nothing. Then I put both hands along the sides, and moved them up and down together. Nothing. I needed to steer this vessel, to make it turn in the direction I wanted it to go. If the vessel had a steering wheel, it would be a lot simpler. Instead, all I had was this ghostly image. I put both hands along the sides, and made like a steering wheel, moving one up, and the other down.

The triangle and circle rotated while the pebbles remained still. I felt the tug of gravity shifting, like the vessel was tilting. It must have been rotating to match what I'd set into the image. The movement stopped, and the circle and triangle rotated back to the upward position in the image, the pebbles following along with them. I cracked a huge smile.

"Take that, you pile of bolts," I said to the computer.

Moving my hands in opposite directions rotated the circle, which had to be the vessel. The triangle was our vector, the direction through space we were traveling.

I was a pilot. I had this.

Unless I turned the vessel, the triangle pointed straight up. All I had to do was figure out which of those small pebbles was Earth, turn the vessel until that pebble lay directly above the triangle, and start moving. Easy as pie. I had the image set the way I wanted in minutes, and started toward home.

I used a stronger thrust than the computer had set getting out here, since I had to get back before the carbon dioxide got to me. If it had taken three days to get out here, I didn't want to take more than two days to get home. I'd be dehydrated, tired, and loopy from the CO_2, but I'd make it. Thinking otherwise wasn't an option.

I reached for the oatmeal raisin bar in the backpack, and then stopped. It still didn't appeal to me. Memories of my favorite grill in Honolulu, and their double bacon cheeseburger, came to mind. I could wait a little longer.

10

I felt heavy because of the acceleration, so at some point, I had to put on the brakes. About a day after I took over, the distance to Earth had been cut in half. The main thrust only worked in one direction for me, so I'd have to turn the vessel around to slow it down.

I did that, and as I ramped up the acceleration, the triangle pointed away from Earth. A flat gray square also appeared in the image, between the ship and the Earth. It moved according to how much thrust I applied; closer to the vessel if I thrust more, closer to Earth – or past it – if I reduced the thrust. It was a trend marker that probably showed the spot in space where our velocity relative to a nearby object would be zero. Perfect. I set the thrust so that square was just above the surface of the Earth.

The computer lay on the ground, stubbornly silent. Was a situation like this even part of its programming? The computer's box lay where it fell in the processing center, on top of several smaller boxes. I walked over to it, and knocked on the side.

"Anybody home in there?" No answer.

I rubbed my eyes. The CO_2 had to be affecting me, if I was stupid enough to be annoying the computer. I'd been up for longer than I could remember, watching the image as the distance to Earth slowly shrank. I couldn't keep my eyes open any longer, and lay down for a short nap.

I awoke with a start, not remembering where I was. I felt groggy, and my head throbbed. The CO_2 levels were probably increasing. That much I did remember. Trying to clear the cobwebs from my mind, I stood up and looked at the image. I cranked down the scale. We were almost at the gray square. It had been nearly fourteen hours since I'd closed my eyes. One thought penetrated the fog; I couldn't risk falling asleep again.

Lowering the thrust to almost nothing, my velocity relative to home was near zero. I hung about one Earth diameter above the surface.

I zoomed in further, and recognized the outlines of continents, islands, and oceans on the image of Earth. I hovered above northern Europe. That image was my way home.

"What are your plans now?" the computer asked, startling me.

"I'm going home, as I said before."

"How will you do that without having more missiles fired at you?"

Son of a bitch. The CO_2 had dulled my thinking. How would anyone know it was me, and not the aliens coming back for round two?

I had no working radios, no communications devices of any kind. If I just appeared over Honolulu, they'd blast me to dust, just as they had tried to do back on Tikopia.

"Your efforts, although unexpected, will be ultimately futile," the computer said. "You will be destroyed, the technology of this vessel lost to your people."

I glared at the box, ready to argue. Then I remembered how I had made it to this point.

"Your problem is," I said, "you underestimated us. You had all these contingencies programmed into you, but the ability to think outside the box, so to speak, wasn't built into you, was it?"

"I do not understand."

"Of course you don't. That is why you failed. You were one ship, with one computer controlling it. You spent all this time and energy to get to Earth, and are far more technologically advanced than us. Your mistake though, was a lack of redundancy. All along, you showed me that you had great plans, but if a link in your chain failed, your mission did too.

"You assumed there wouldn't be intelligent life on Earth. When there was, you created the Pouakai to remove it, but they didn't finish the job. Your creations could only survive where the sunlight was bright enough to supply the energy they required. You didn't have a plan in place for what to do with us up in the colder, darker parts of the planet. Up there, we had time to analyze your attacks and study the Pouakai. You were a single vessel, trying to take over an entire civilized planet. If it had been us trying to colonize your world, we would have retreated even before attempting to do what you did. If we really wanted to continue, we would have come back with multiple vessels, and the ability to adapt to all conditions that might be present on the planet. That's the difference between our species."

"This does not explain how you have progressed as far as you have, or how you will complete your stated desire to go home."

"No, you wouldn't see it. Do you understand the concept of ego?"

"Yes."

"Then you'll understand why your mission failed. You were created to run it, and the designers of this vessel were so confident in their design, that they only needed one of you. You had no backup.

"I realized that if I could disconnect you, as the Children were supposed to, I might be able to control the vessel."

"I did not tell you how to disconnect me."

"You said the Children would still be technologically naïve when they set you up as their oracle, and sent one of their own to the stars. The process for them to do that had to be obvious, and simple. When I found the handle on the main door, and the ones on you and the controller, it all made sense. It was the ego of your creators, also programmed into you, that eventually caused your downfall. You wouldn't let yourself believe that I could think through a problem like this, and come up with a solution."

"A failure of imagination. If I could feel sorrow for my creators, I would."

I remembered the sight of Jennifer, lying gutted on our living room floor, and any remorse I felt evaporated.

"So now all I have to do is get home," I said. The computer didn't respond.

"Hello? Are you there?" Nothing. Maybe it was sulking after the inferior species had prevailed over it.

My problem still remained though: how to get home.

An insistent beeping sounded from the image. I jumped over to it, and had to grab on to the box to slow myself in the miniscule gravity. A gray dot had appeared off to one side, between the vessel and the Earth in the image. It moved quickly toward me too. Shit. I'd probably already been spotted by radar, and they had fired a missile at me. What could I do?

A spot on the box appeared below the image, illuminated from within. It blinked in time with the beeping. I touched the light. The familiar hum of the beam weapon mast came from the ceiling, just above me. A snap echoed inside the vessel, and the dot in the image disappeared.

Oh crap. Now they would be sure I was an alien invader. I had to find a way to get down to the ground, while letting them know who I was.

11

To survive, I had to tell the world it was me, not the aliens, controlling the vessel. Either that, or I would have to outrun whatever they threw at me. If I dove down quickly and landed somewhere remote, could I pop the door open and make a run for it? After seeing what they tried on Tikopia, I doubted I'd make it. They'd probably lob another nuke or ten at me, and I couldn't see myself outrunning several megatons of nuclear fury.

I had to convince them it was me before I left the vessel. This spaceship was even more important than my survival; the technology we desperately needed.

The only action I could take would be with the vessel itself. Wherever I landed however, they'd be gunning for me. That couldn't be my strategy. After all my work to get here: hopping from island to island, sneaking aboard this vessel, searching for an answer; it couldn't end this way. I was so close to getting home with the prize. Landing alone couldn't be my strategy.

I held on to the box, wondering what the hell I could do. Everything that had led up to this point circled through my mind; a collage of ocean, islands, Pouakai, and Kakamaku. The image stuck with me: island hopping. It was what my great-grandfather had done in World War Two, as a young infantryman in the Army. He'd moved from island to island across the Pacific, pursuing the enemy toward their homeland.

In that instant, my course became clear. I didn't have to go to just one place, but could choose multiple locations. If I retraced my steps backwards across the Pacific, from Tikopia to Anuta, Nanumea, Palmyra, and finally Honolulu, then Colin or someone in the Navy might understand that as an attempt to communicate with them.

It may be one hell of a long shot, but it was the only plan I had.

I couldn't see outside, and had no idea of where the sun was. According to my watch it should have been just after noon in Hawaii, but I wasn't sure if it had kept time well enough over the past few days. I wanted to do this in daylight, so if my watch was right, I needed to get moving.

I changed the image displaying so I could see the sun, as well as the Earth. Sure enough, I was on the night side over northern Europe, which meant the Pacific was in daylight. Time to get moving.

Handling this vessel through the image box was like steering one of my airliners with most of the hydraulics shut off; slow and awkward. I had no way to tell exactly how fast I moved, or if I might run into a piece of orbiting space debris. I missed the detailed information I got while flying, but I knew if my experience flying airplanes allowed me to herd this vessel through space, I was up to the job.

"You will not make it to your destination," the computer said, surprising me.

"You've been wrong before, and I'm betting you're wrong again."

"I am not programmed to bet."

"That's why you're going to lose."

I hoped that would shut it up. I needed to concentrate.

It took an hour of maneuvering to get myself over the southwest Pacific basin. Tired and woozy, I had a hard time focusing on the image. I had to do this quickly, or I'd pass out, and it would all be over.

Now I had to find Tikopia, a tiny speck in the middle of an enormous ocean. At least I knew roughly where it was, west of the route we normally flew between Hawaii and Australia; the one that overflew Nanumea. Australia was easy to see on the image, but in the image the islands were mere specks of dark gray, in an ocean of lighter gray.

I found Vanuatu, and the island of Espiritu Santo, so if I backtracked toward Hawaii a bit then looked west…got it. Tikopia. I slewed the vessel toward the island, and dropped further into the atmosphere. I had to be careful how much I accelerated, and in what direction, since I didn't have a seatbelt in this thing. If I punched it too fast, the G-forces would knock me to my feet, or worse, across the room. My legs were already tired, and started shaking when I put too much weight on them. I didn't want to go too slowly either, and use up what little oxygen I had left.

"Hey," I said to the computer, "if you want to survive too, could you tell me how fast this thing can go in the atmosphere before it burns up?"

It didn't answer. It must have wanted me to fail.

It only took about ten minutes to position myself over Tikopia. I must have been moving many times the speed of sound as I descended toward the island, creating some impressive sonic booms. That may be a good thing, because I needed someone with the ability to communicate to see me before I moved on.

The island looked odd, and it took me a moment to realize what had happened. A large chunk of the eastern half of the island was missing. The entire mountain ridge this vessel had been sitting on had vanished, blasted away by the dozens of nukes dropped on the island. I'd left five days ago, and it probably still glowed red-hot. I couldn't see any of that in the image though.

I had no idea how high I was over the island, but from what I remembered, it was about two miles long, which, according to the image, meant I sat about six or seven miles above it. Good. Low enough to have aircraft fly by, but high enough to maneuver quickly if I had to. Time passed, and I felt happy to be back on, or at least close to, Earth. Hovering over the island, I wondered about the effect of all those nuclear detonations. If there was a lot of fallout, where did it go? I hoped my friends on Nanumea weren't downwind of all this. I'd like to go back there someday. It was such a beautiful spot. It'd be a shame if it got contaminated.

I shook my head to stop my mind from wandering. Damn CO_2. I had to focus, to keep my mind on the job.

What would someone on the ground think about the ship being here? Would they think it was looking for its lost Children? Or maybe that it came back to evaluate what kind of damage the inhabitants of Earth could do.

The image beeped, and a dot appeared off to one side. I zoomed the image in, and recognized a cruise missile, like the ones the *Ohio* launched. On the upside, at least someone knew I was here.

The light on the side of the box blinked, and I touched it. Hum, roar, crack. A moment later I got knocked sideways by the shockwave. It tossed me to the ground, but I jumped back up to the box and held on. Nothing else showed on the monitor. Good.

Anuta was easy to find, a short distance northeast. I flew the vessel over it a few minutes later, and then descended. It looked familiar in the image, even if there wasn't any color.

Nothing happened. No planes flew near, and nobody launched missiles at me. I stayed for half an hour, and hoped that whoever launched the missile against me at Tikopia could see me here too.

Time to move on.

I slid my left hand up, and the vessel surged skyward. Next, Nanumea. It was on a trajectory between Hawaii and Vanuatu. I found it quickly enough, and slewed the vessel through the sky like a drunken cruise ship captain. Not far from the truth, with all this lousy air in here.

It only took a few minutes to get into position over Nanumea. This time I wanted to be lower, so the Chief, or Fata, or someone else would see me clearly. I descended slowly until it looked like I hovered maybe a mile up, just offshore from the village.

Hello down there. Look up at the friendly spaceship. I really hoped I'd make it back to Nanumea eventually, if only to hear the stories of the day an alien spaceship made an appearance.

Feeling faint, I grabbed onto the box, through the image. Hang on, just a little bit longer. I took several deep breaths, and that seemed to clear my head.

The only drawback would be if they launched another nuke at me while I hovered over Nanumea. The last thing I wanted was to be responsible for frying everyone down on the island. I waited for half an hour, but it was quiet. If I had been detected, it would have been by airborne radar. I didn't think this vessel was all that stealthy.

It felt like I'd pushed my luck as much as I could here, so I vaulted skyward again, looking for Palmyra. This would be the tough one to find. I knew it sat almost due south of Hawaii, but there were several small atolls in that general area. I'd have to come in close, and look for whatever I remembered about the island.

I found Hawaii, over the horizon on the image. Several small specks showed up in about the right location for Palmyra, so I steered the vessel toward them. The first turned out to be the wrong shape, and the second was too small. The third island looked about right, and as I closed in, I recognized the lagoon and the dirt runway cut into the forest. I absolutely had to wait until I was sure I'd been spotted here, or my plan wouldn't work.

I put the vessel into a hover over the island, a few thousand feet over the lagoon, and waited. Desperately thirsty, I needed my water. But my backpack had bounced through the open hatch to the lower level. I'd have to wait until this was over. I couldn't leave the image, in case they launched another missile at me. My legs shook with fatigue, and I sat on the box next to the image, ready to react if something showed up.

My watch read three in the afternoon in Hawaii, and roughly the same time here at Palmyra. I felt my eyelids droop. No. Not now. I forced myself to stand, and stumbled around the room like a drunk.

An hour after arriving, the image beeped. The dot on the screen didn't approach, but circled slowly, at least fifty miles away. Good, someone was taking a look at me. I rose upward a few miles, but stayed over the island until positive the aircraft had seen me.

One more leg to go, the last hop home.

Hawaii was easy to spot on the monitor, the biggest islands in the mid-Pacific. Upward I went, my legs barely holding on through the acceleration. Twenty minutes later, I sank back into the atmosphere, aimed at Oahu. I didn't want to make the military any more nervous than it was, so I aimed for a spot several miles offshore, south of the Honolulu airport. With a pull of G-forces that almost buckled my knees, I came to a stop above the ocean. The image beeped constantly at me, with dozens of aircraft circling nearby. The military had to be in a frenzy by now.

The planes circled closer; probably F-22's from the Hawaii Air National Guard, my old unit. I didn't think they would use nukes on me, this close to Honolulu, but I wasn't sure of their orders, how desperate their commanders were, or if anyone had deciphered my journey back across the Pacific.

Two aircraft detached from the formation, and flew toward me. The image beeped louder and more insistently. I couldn't push that light. It would kill those pilots, and end any chance I had of making it safely home. Whatever happened next, I'd done my best. I had always tried to control what had happened to me; Jennifer had said it, and at last I understood it. Now, I had to trust others to act, to do the right thing. There wasn't anything more I could do.

The fighters closed in, aimed directly at me. They flew in standard attack pattern, five miles away, and then four, three. *Don't shoot. Please don't shoot.* I couldn't look away from the image. Two miles, one mile.

They roared past the vessel, without firing. I collapsed onto the box next to the image, my legs shaking badly. I owed those guys a lifetime supply of beer.

There was one more maneuver to make, and I did it as slowly as I could. I drifted the vessel toward the airport, and stopped over the reef runway. That was as far as I could get from any buildings or people, but still be on dry land.

Gently, slowly, I lowered the vessel. More planes circled overhead, but they didn't approach. The ghostly image of the runway grew closer, and with a jarring thump, the vessel smacked onto the concrete.

12

I strained to move my leaden feet. They resisted, but I had to get out. The full gravity of Earth pulled on me, and I struggled just to stand up. I carried the flashlight down the rod ladder, almost losing my grip a couple of times. The backpack lay on the floor. I picked it up and draped it over my shoulder.

The air seemed liquid, my legs encased in cement.

I put the bent flashlight under the recessed handle next to the exit door, and pulled. It didn't budge. I put more effort into it, then the flashlight snapped in half, and the batteries skittered across the hard floor.

"Son of a bitch," I gasped.

I looked for something else to use as a lever, but there was nothing. A faint sound came from behind me, and I turned around.

"I told you that you wouldn't make it. You will die here," the computer's voice whispered at me.

Blood pounded in my ears.

"Shut up motherfucker! I am DONE listening to you!"

I grabbed the handle with both hands, put my feet on the wall, and pulled with every ounce of energy I had. It moved a fraction of an inch, and then stopped. I pulled again.

"MOVE!"

The handle gave and came up slowly. A rush of air blew over me, and my ears popped. I could smell the blossoms of Hawaii, the tang of the ocean, and the sweet stench of jet fuel. The handle slid into the up position, and the door ponderously lowered itself toward the ground.

I squinted against the sunlight streaming in through the opening, and staggered back from the opening, wobbly, as a wave of fresh air poured over me.

The door hissed and thumped hard onto the concrete, forming a ramp as it had back on Tikopia. Everything was silent. The warm, inviting yellow light of our sun looked marvelous, compared to the cold, antiseptic blue I'd been living with for five days. I wobbled down the ramp, and onto the ground. Two fighters roared overhead, before peeling off toward the ocean. At the far end of the runway sat a collection of vehicles, their engines idling. I walked toward them but after a few steps felt so weak that I had to stop, barely able to stand.

I turned around, and saw the vessel from the outside, without camouflage, for the first time. It was a flying saucer, flat on the bottom, with that slight dome on top. Black streaks covered the outside. The thing was well over two hundred feet in diameter, and forty to fifty feet high. It looked bigger from the outside.

The trucks drove toward me, but stopped, a hundred yards away. I felt dozens of weapons trained on me. One door slammed, and footsteps clicked on the hard surface of the runway. Looking into the afternoon sun, I couldn't see who it was. The person stopped, twenty feet away.

"Boonie?"

My knees gave out, and I sank to the ground. "It's me, Colin, it's me," I whispered.

Colin ran up and hugged me, nearly knocking me onto my back. Then he pulled me up to my feet, both of us sobbing and laughing at the same time. Within seconds we were surrounded by hundreds of armed soldiers, officers, medics, and men in suits. They were all talking at once, pushing to get next to me, and to the vessel.

"Hey, hey," Colin shouted, "give the guy some air." He pushed some of the officers away as they tried to question me. I staggered back to the vessel, and sat down on the end of the ramp. Several of the men in suits started walking up the ramp.

"Don't go in there," I said.

"Why?" one asked.

"Trust me. You don't want to get stuck in there. Just give me a little time, and I can show you around."

The men looked at each other, then walked back down the ramp. Colin waved at some soldiers nearby. "Don't let anyone, and I mean *anyone*, go inside this thing without Boonie here along. Got it?"

"Yes, sir," one said.

"Got any water?" I croaked. Someone handed me a cold plastic bottle of water. I downed several gulps, the sweetest thing I'd ever tasted.

Within a minute, the soldiers had formed a cordon around the vessel, leaving Colin and me alone, sitting on the ramp. I finished the last swig from the bottle, and looked at Colin. He grinned from ear to ear.

"I knew it had to be you," he said quietly.

"You guys tracked me?"

He nodded. "The satellite radar stations got you when you were a day out. I was still in the *Ohio* then, but we got the news relayed to us."

"You got back here pretty fast."

"Captain Baker didn't want to hang around after we annihilated Tikopia." The smile dropped from his face. "We'll be dealing with that cleanup for years."

"I didn't think you guys would go nuclear on me that fast."

"When we got back and told him what had happened, Baker went nuts. He got permission to go nuclear within minutes. Half an hour later, he'd convinced everyone in the UN to join in. We dove out of the way when the bombs dropped, so we didn't know you had lifted off. Satellite tracking stations found you heading outbound though, and kept an eye on you for a long time. After the bombs hit, Baker didn't have to worry about the Chinese or Russians tailing him, so we made a high-speed dash back here. We got in early this morning."

I closed my eyes, and breathed deep. After being shut inside the vessel for so long, I let the warmth of the sun sink deep into my skin.

"Last night the tracking stations found the ship coming back," Colin continued, "We weren't too surprised that it went over Tikopia first, then Anuta. When you went to Nanumea though, I was really puzzled."

"They saw me at Nanumea?"

"Yeah. The Navy sent a couple of subs down there to evacuate the locals, because of all the fallout heading that way."

"Oh."

"The subs were underwater, but the rescue teams, gathering up all the locals, went apeshit when they saw you. They radioed it to the subs who sent it on to us. Then when you went to Palmyra, I realized it had to be you, trying to tell us, to tell me, it was you."

I smiled.

"I had to shout my way through all the hubbub at Admiral Bianchi's office, but he listened. They were planning on nuking you again, since you were aiming for Honolulu, even if it meant sacrificing everyone in Hawaii."

"Wow."

"Yeah, wow."

We both sat in silence for a few moments, enjoying the late afternoon sunshine. Finally I stood up, unsteady, but feeling better than I had inside the vessel.

"Where are you going?" Colin asked.

"I'm starved. I was hoping you'd invite me over for dinner."

"Dinner? I don't think Anna has anything prepared."

"Ah. Too bad. Here I came all prepared myself," I said, failing to suppress a grin.

"You call this prepared? You look, and smell, like crap."

"Yeah, but I finally remembered to bring you a makana."

"A gift? What the hell could you bring now?"

I pointed at the vessel behind us.

Colin burst out laughing, and then stood, holding onto my shoulder and keeping me steady. We made our way through the crowd, toward a waiting van.

I was home.

Made in the USA
San Bernardino, CA
01 December 2014